The Only True Genius in the Family

"Very well-written, fast-paced . . . the characters are multi-faceted and believable; they were people to think about. A very good read."   —*Story Circle Book Reviews*

"A five-star most enjoyable read . . . perfect for book clubs."
—*Armchair Interviews*

"A true page-turning delight."   —*Book Club Classics!*

The Last Beach Bungalow

"Jennie Nash's first novel is a wonder—searching and true, seared with light and love, wholly honest and good."

—Beth Kephart,
author of National Book Award Finalist *A Slant of Sun*

"A wonderful story, woven with threads of a life interrupted and jolted to a new awareness by a bout with breast cancer . . . This book allows us to see what our yearning for home is really about."
—Sarah Susanka, author of *The Not So Big House*

"Nash writes with gentle certainty of the fact that life is full of uncertainty." —*Booklist*

"[A] winning debut . . . This grown-up fable replaces the erotics of sex with the erotics of floor plans, but April's midlife crisis and difficult adjustments ring true, as do the plot's surprising turns."
—*Publishers Weekly*

"A lyrical first novel from Nash about a breast-cancer survivor searching for a home . . . A sensitive novel that will appeal to many women and resonate with cancer survivors."
—*Kirkus Reviews*

"A fascinating character study of a woman who has physically defeated cancer, but mentally is still fighting windmills . . . a strong family drama." —*Midwest Book Review*

"Nicholas Sparks, move over, as Nash writes a touching tale of a cancer survivor trying to secure her dream beach house."
—*Lazy Readers' Book Club*

"Debut author Nash shines with a mesmerizing story of one woman's triumph, not only over the demons of her past but also over the obstacles threatening her future happiness. The characters are captivating, and the plotline will hook readers from the first page." —*Romantic Times*

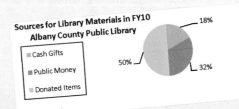

THE
threadbare
HEART

Jennie Nash

BERKLEY BOOKS, NEW YORK

THE BERKLEY PUBLISHING GROUP
Published by the Penguin Group
Penguin Group (USA) Inc.
375 Hudson Street, New York, New York 10014, USA
Penguin Group (Canada), 90 Eglinton Avenue East, Suite 700, Toronto, Ontario
M4P 2Y3, Canada (a division of Pearson Penguin Canada Inc.)
Penguin Books Ltd., 80 Strand, London WC2R 0RL, England
Penguin Group Ireland, 25 St. Stephen's Green, Dublin 2, Ireland
(a division of Penguin Books Ltd.)
Penguin Group (Australia), 250 Camberwell Road, Camberwell, Victoria 3124,
Australia (a division of Pearson Australia Group Pty. Ltd.)
Penguin Books India Pvt. Ltd., 11 Community Centre, Panchsheel Park,
New Delhi—110 017, India
Penguin Group (NZ), 67 Apollo Drive, Rosedale, North Shore, 0632, New Zealand
(a division of Pearson New Zealand Ltd.)
Penguin Books (South Africa) (Pty.) Ltd., 24 Sturdee Avenue, Rosebank,
Johannesburg 2196, South Africa

Penguin Books Ltd., Registered Offices: 80 Strand, London WC2R 0RL, England

This is a work of fiction. Names, characters, places, and incidents either are the
product of the author's imagination or are used fictitiously, and any resemblance to
actual persons, living or dead, business establishments, events, or locales, is entirely
coincidental. The publisher does not have any control over and does not assume any
responsibility for author or third-party websites or their content.

PRINTING HISTORY
Berkley trade paperback edition / May 2010

Library of Congress Cataloging-in-Publication Data

Nash, Jennie, 1964–
    The threadbare heart / Jennie Nash.—Berkley trade pbk. ed.
      p. cm.
    ISBN 978-0-425-23410-5
    1. Disaster victims—Fiction.   2. Loss (Psychology)—Fiction.   3. Psychological
fiction.   I. Title.
PS3614.A73T47 2010
813'.6—dc22

                                                              2009037950

PRINTED IN THE UNITED STATES OF AMERICA

10   9   8   7   6   5   4   3   2   1

For my sweet sister Laura

ACKNOWLEDGMENTS

Thanks to Jackie for her enduring support, her clarity of thought, and for sharing her passion for fabric; to Faye, of course, for everything; to the whole team at Berkley for doing what you do so well; to Kitty Felde, whose stories about sewing were so inspiring, and who helped me design Lily's dress; to my dad for that key week in Colorado, and to Bonnie Inouye, weaver, whose looms got me into this story; to Jane Broket, Jennifer Balis, and Elaine Murakami for talking about their fabric collecting habits; to Chuck Marso at F&S Fabric in Los Angeles for helping me pick real fabric for my fictional dress; to Stacy Lantagne, for insight into Red Sox Nation; to Lynn Solaro for walking and talking about these characters as if they were real; to Annie Webster, ceramic teacher at Chadwick School, for helping me get the clay right, and to Shelley Frost for showing me how it's done. (The pots with arms and legs that I describe were designed by Erica Reiss in her senior year at Chadwick School; I saw them at a school art show in 2008, and couldn't get them out of my head.) Thanks to all the members of the Wellesley College Club of Houston's BookClub (Georgina Armstrong, Jesse Berger, Anna Grassini, Suzanne Jester, Jackie Kacen, Lydia Luz, Maneesha Patil, Rebecca Saltzer, Martita Schmuck, Sandy Simmoms) who read and critiqued an early draft of this story, and helped me get it right. Thanks to Laura for helping me with the timeline, the details of academia, the record of the Harvard baseball team and a hundred other facts; to Carlyn and Emily for helping me with the beginning and for challenging me to write a character with two sons; to my mom and Doug for being willing to let me take their story and run; to Hannah for insisting that the dog had to live; and finally, to Rob, for teaching me so much about love.

Lily

LOVE was the one thing Lily always thought she did better than her mother. She believed that she knew exactly what love took, what it cost, and what it meant, and she thought of her long marriage to Tom as proof of it. But in the short period of time between Christmas and the start of fire season, everything she understood about love unraveled, the way jeans do at the hem, the way tweed does so that it reveals the intricate relationship of the warp and the weft, and she realized how very little she knew about the way love worked. People naturally assumed, after everything that happened, that it was a bitter revelation, but they were wrong.

"Would you do it all again, knowing what you know now?" her mother, Eleanor, asked. Eleanor was, at that moment, seventy-five years old, about to be married again herself, and hoping that this time she might get it right.

"In a heartbeat," Lily said—not only because she believed

it, but because she knew it was what her mother needed to hear.

It had started, simply enough, in December of 2007 in a bookstore in Burlington, Vermont. She and Tom still had a few weeks of classes left to teach before the end of the semester—he in biology, she in math—and they had come into town to meet some old friends for dinner. Church Street was at its most charming—lights in the trees, snow dusted on the ground, the shops warm and welcoming. Even though they were wearing gloves, they held hands as they walked home.

"I didn't get you a Christmas gift," Tom said. "Again."

Lily smiled. After twenty-six years of marriage, what was there to get each other? She had recently brought home Tom's favorite cinnamon bread from the bakery because she knew how much he liked to toast it for breakfast, and he had replaced the broken birdfeeder that hung from the big elm tree outside the kitchen window because he knew how much it delighted Lily when the jays came, and the woodpeckers, and the cardinals. These small gestures gave them as much surprise and indulgence as they needed. "Then we're even," she said.

"And we'll have less to haul out to California."

"I don't have anything yet to give to Brooke," Lily said. "It's as if I never had a two-year-old. I can't remember what two-year-olds like."

"Cardboard boxes," Tom said. "Don't you remember the way

Luke used to pile all his pillows in boxes, and sleep in there? And how Ryan made that castle in the basement?"

She laughed. "I'd forgotten that."

"We could get her a book," Tom said. They were coming up on the Burlington Bookshop. There were pine boughs encircling the window and the sound of jingle bells as someone came out the door.

"A book would be good," Lily said. She stopped in front of the shop, Tom held the door for her, and they went in. They each meandered through the tables and the stacks, drawn in by titles and covers as if by a magnetic field. Lily got pulled toward a table where the cookbooks were displayed. She loved the idea of cooking—and the fact that there could be an entire cookbook featuring nothing but tacos or mushrooms or cupcakes—but she wasn't much of a cook herself. She made soups and stews, salads and sandwiches. When the boys were home, she would roast a chicken with herbs from Tom's garden, but she didn't need a recipe for that. She wandered over to a section of art books, and picked up one on master quilters. She sat in a chair, and lost herself in the photos of intricately made quilts that looked like pointillist paintings, and abstract murals, and in the words of the artists who spoke about layering fabric and layering time.

The owner of the shop came quietly up to her. "Can I bring you a cup of hot chocolate?" he asked.

Lily looked up, surprised to find herself in a bookstore and not in an art gallery.

"It's Lake Champlain," the man said, referring to the brand of artisanal chocolate. "Aztec spice."

"Sure," Lily said. "Thank you. That would be nice."

But chocolate was, in fact, a dangerous thing. She had been struck with debilitating headaches when she got pregnant with Ryan, at age twenty-six, and they had never gone away. Over the years, in an effort at self-preservation, she had figured out exactly what triggered them: the glare of lights from oncoming traffic, chocolate, strawberries, bananas, aspartame, sleeplessness, and red wine. She learned the combinations that would cause the most damage, the inherent risks of every offending food or situation, and then she set out systematically to avoid them. She politely declined strawberry daiquiris and walnut brownies, late-night parties and late-start movies, night driving, and Diet Coke. Far from feeling deprived, she felt that she had become master of her migraines, and she had a strange affection for the strict logic of it, and the power she wielded.

That night, however, she'd already had two glasses of sauvignon blanc at dinner. She felt happy—so much a part of the holiday, and the warmth of the store, and the charm of the town where she and Tom had lived for so long—that she couldn't imagine anything going wrong. She couldn't imagine a headache. What harm could a bit of chocolate do? She accepted the mug gratefully, and took a sip.

A few minutes later, Tom caught sight of Lily across the store—his wife, curled up in a soft chair like a child, a book in her lap, her brow knit together in concentration—and he was overcome with a rush of love. He had picked out some books for their granddaughter, and he approached Lily to show her his discoveries. When he got up closer, he smelled the chocolate and the hot spice of the drink Lily held in her hand. He bent down next to her chair.

"What are you doing?" he whispered—his voice a quiet demand.

"Reading about quilts," she said, turning the book so that he could see what she was seeing. "Look at these colors."

"But you're drinking hot chocolate." He knew what would happen if Lily got a migraine: she would turn inward toward the pain, hold her head in her hands, lie down in the dark, and hope that if she lay perfectly still, she could keep the pain at bay. An hour later, or three, or maybe in the middle of the night, she would be crouched on the bathroom floor, crying out in pain, begging for mercy, begging for him to help. And he would help, because that's what Tom did. He would hold her. He would get her ice. He would remind her to breathe.

"I'll be okay," she said.

"You don't know that, Lily."

"Tom," she whispered. "Please. I'll be okay."

"I think you're making a mistake."

"Then I'll deal with the consequences."

"No," he said, standing up and speaking too loud now for a bookstore. "I'll deal with the consequences. *I* will. Your headache will be *my* problem."

She stared up at him. He had never spoken to her like

this before. "Can we talk about this later?" she whispered. "Outside?"

"I'm not going to stand here and watch you drink that," he said.

She clenched her teeth and took a deep breath through her nose. It smelled of dark chocolate and chili, but in that breath she also sensed vulnerability—her body's vulnerability in its fifty-first year, and the vulnerability that came from loving another human being. She was bound to Tom, beholden to him, and there were good things that came from that, and compromises, too. She wordlessly set the hot chocolate down on the table.

"I found something for Brooke," Tom said. "A collection of Richard Scarry books. Isn't that perfect?"

"Well," Lily said, "it was perfect for the boys, but for a girl? I don't know." She remembered how Ryan and Luke would pore over the pages of their Richard Scarry books, naming each truck and airplane, each job undertaken by one of the enterprising townsfolk, but she wasn't sure whether the books would have the same appeal to a little girl. Ryan and Olivia had moved to California when Brooke was just three months old. Lily had missed Brooke's first steps, her first teeth, her first words, and because she had missed those milestones, she wanted to give a gift that Brooke would adore.

"Everyone loves Mr. Fixit and Sergeant Murphy," Tom said.

It was true; they did. But the whole thing made her suddenly tired—the whole business of being a wife, a grandmother, a daughter about to go home for the holidays. She wanted to get out of the shop and go home. "Okay," she said. "Fine." She figured that she would have enough time to sew something for Brooke, maybe a little flannel blanket for her bear. She'd pieced together a quilt when Brooke was born—nine log cabin blocks in a riot of colors and patterns sewn in a square. Perhaps she would make a dress or a pillow from some of the floral prints she had in her stash.

"You're right," she said. "Let's get the Richard Scarry books. And I'm going to get this quilt book. It can be my Christmas present."

He smiled. "I'm going to get this gardening book," he said. "It can be mine."

WHEN they were back out in the cold, Tom began to talk about the book he had just purchased. It was a treatise on the importance of preserving heirloom seeds. The author was arguing for the beauty and integrity of food grown without intervention. Lily listened, and agreed that it was a timely and necessary argument, but she was waiting for a pause in the story, a chance to make a different point. When Tom seemed finished talking, she said, "What did you mean when you said, 'Your headache will be my problem'?"

"Just what it sounds like," Tom said. "You can be cavalier about chocolate or wine or whatever, but I'm the one who has to deal with it."

"I'm the one who'll have the headache."

Tom shifted his feet on the snowy ground. He looked off into the dark night. "You think it's been easy for me all these years?" he asked. "To stand by watching?"

"Well, no," she said. "Of course not." None of it was easy—watching someone have doubt or have the flu, watching them lose their nerve or lose their parents. Even just watching Tom's hair turn gray, or watching his skin become more susceptible to the cold, dry air, or watching his knee become stiffer by degrees. It was all hard. All of it.

"You think I *enjoy* hearing you beg for the pain to stop, hearing you moan about wanting to die?" Tom said.

She stopped. She could see her breath forming in the cold air in front of her face. She had had only a few migraines a year these past several years. She had begun to think, in fact, that maybe she was becoming immune to headaches, that maybe this was something that got better as she got older. She had begun to think that she could risk a mug of hot chocolate. Tom's display of doubt rubbed up against her hard-won hope and caught her off guard. "I didn't know how much it was bothering you," she said.

Tom laughed—a kind of snort that meant, *How on earth could you* not *know?*

"I don't get this sudden concern, Tom," she said. "Is something wrong?"

He shrugged. They were older now. Their boys were grown and gone now. Things that used to flit past Tom like clouds or birds bothered him now. Things he used to handle without much thought now seemed insurmountable. Lily's headaches were something he had handled for years without complaint. But the last few times, they had grabbed hold of him in a way that frightened him. He had imagined Lily spiraling farther down into pain than she had ever gone before, spiraling so far away that she was out of reach. It made him think about her dying and his being alone. That wasn't something he felt like he could endure.

"It's nothing," he said. "I'm sorry I said anything. Let's get out of the cold."

BUT Lily knew that it wasn't nothing. She had lived with Tom for a long time. As they moved through December, through their classes and departmental parties, through final exams and holiday cheer, she had a feeling of unease. She thought, for a while, that it was the fact that they were going through their first holiday season with no children in the house. Things were so quiet, and so strange without the boys, and she noticed that Tom was taking extra long treks in the snow by himself, and coming back to the house pensive instead of exhilarated. Perhaps he missed the kids more than she knew. Later, she thought that the unease was due to the fact that when she and Tom came back from vacation neither of them would be teaching a full course load. She had won a grant to update her textbook and he had been tapped to help the university write a plan for transitioning to an integrated science curriculum. Maybe they were both just feeling a little untethered.

When she looked back at it all, however, and tried to figure out when everything began to unravel, she would go back to that moment in the bookstore when her sense of contentedness was so quickly replaced by a feeling of unease. One minute she was sipping hot chocolate like any holiday reveler, reading about fabric and design, knowing that her husband was happily wandering the bookstore aisles, and the next moment, she felt the full weight of the ordinary dangers of the world—chocolate, a holiday in her mother's house, marriage itself.

2

Tom

THEY all gathered at Eleanor's house in Santa Barbara for the holidays. It was a three-story red-tiled town house with five bedrooms, a dining room that looked out at the mountains, and a living room that looked past the landmark courthouse down to the sea. Luke, Lily and Tom's younger boy, lived only a half hour away from Eleanor now; Ryan, Olivia, and Brooke were two hours to the north in San Luis Obispo; and there was nothing Eleanor liked better than organizing meals and outings, especially during the holidays. Each day, she had a full lineup of events, from a trip to the zoo, to wine tasting in Santa Ynez Valley, to a seating at Seagrass, the new seafood restaurant that had opened around the corner. Eleanor had a seven-foot noble fir erected in her living room, and another one on the rooftop deck, both of which she had hired a florist to decorate. Under the tree in the living room was a pile of gifts, all expertly wrapped by the department stores where they had been purchased. There could never be enough revelry for Eleanor, or enough people in the house, or enough gifts. She adored a party.

Four days before Christmas, after Brooke had been put to bed, Eleanor announced that she was thinking of ordering a girl-sized dress to match the one on the doll she had already purchased for Brooke's gift. The doll came with storybooks, satin slippers, and a wardrobe that included a plaid pinafore, white nightgown, and red velvet party dress. Her eyes and hair were the same color as Brooke's—green eyes, curly dark hair. "The girl-sized party dress is darling," Eleanor said, "and there's still time to have it FedExed if I call right away. What do you think?"

Ryan, who was twenty-five years old and didn't know enough about his daughter and dresses to comment, turned toward his wife for help.

Olivia smiled. "You were so generous to get the doll," she said. "Please don't feel that you need to do anything more."

All Lily and Tom had for Brooke were the Richard Scarry books—and Lily felt suddenly that this wasn't enough. She hadn't sewn anything, hadn't picked out anything memorable, anything girlish and sweet. The fact that her mother had hit upon such a fantastic gift—a beautiful doll, with a matching girl-sized dress—made jealousy rise in Lily like a fever. Eleanor had always had such an easy way with people, such a natural way of charming them. She always knew just what to bring to a party, what to wear, what to say, and Lily, more often than not, would spend the entire time just wishing she could go home. "I could make a red velvet dress," she blurted out.

"You sew?" Olivia asked.

Lily smiled wryly, and nodded. How odd that there was someone in her life who didn't know that she sewed. "I sewed all my own clothes in high school and college," she said. "I used to love it. It was the perfect hobby for a mathematical mind—all those angles and shapes."

"The point of this dress," Eleanor said, "is that it's exactly the same as the doll's."

"I'd actually like to do it, Mom," Lily said with a casualness she did not feel. "I can go to Beverly Fabrics tomorrow morning."

Eleanor sipped her wine. "We were invited to the Hailwoods' for brunch tomorrow morning," she said, and turned toward Tom to explain that the Hailwoods lived on an avocado ranch in the foothills, with a sweeping view of the Channel Islands. "And besides," she added," I don't own a sewing machine. I never have."

"You own a factory full of high-speed looms in Italy, but you don't own a sewing machine?" Luke asked. The boys loved to poke fun at their grandmother. She looked like a woman whose silver hair was never out of place, but Ryan and Luke knew better. Eleanor would fly across the country to take them to a baseball game, swim in frigid water on a dare, and beat the pants off any of them in a hand of bridge.

"I run a multinational company," Eleanor said with a theatrical flourish. "I don't do manual labor." Ryan laughed at Eleanor's perfect description of herself, and Luke said, "Touché."

"I can buy a sewing machine," Lily said. "I've been thinking about getting one of the programmable ones they use now for quilting."

Tom glanced up, curious at what his wife was saying—she wanted a new sewing machine? Something besides her grandmother's clunky cast-iron Singer that swung up from a wooden cabinet? Lily was devoted to that machine, and always said that adding bells and whistles to a sewing machine didn't equal progress.

Lily caught Tom's eye and silently implored him to be quiet while she made her argument. "I can just ship it home when I'm done with the dress," she said.

Tom got the hint and said nothing.

Olivia said, "That sounds wonderful."

Eleanor stood up, waved her hand dismissively through the air, and said, "Fine. Whatever you like. I'm going to bed."

By the time Tom had finished breakfast the next morning, Lily was dressed and ready to head to the fabric store.

"You don't mind if I go to the brunch, do you?" Tom asked. "I'd like to see that avocado ranch."

"No," Lily said. "You should definitely go."

"You sure you don't want to join us? You could buy your fabric this afternoon."

She shook her head. "I want to get started on the dress while Brooke is out of the house."

Tom had grown up walking in the green woods of New England, and he and Lily had raised their boys there among the evergreens and the birch. The silver sage colors and Mediterranean climate of Lily's hometown had at first seemed alien to him, but over the years, over many visits, he had come to find their spare beauty captivating.

As they drove to the Hailwoods', Tom drank in the scenery. Behind them was the whole glittering ocean. In front of them were sandstone peaks, chaparral-choked canyons, and stands of towering eucalyptus trees. The road wound gently upward toward a neat grid of avocado trees, which spread over the hills in stately procession, their leaves flat and shiny, their fruit black and gnarled.

At the party, kids ran around eating fistfuls of tortilla chips. Adults gathered around the bartender, drinking margaritas made with fresh limes, even though it wasn't yet noon, and even though back in Vermont a lime would cost at least a dollar. Ryan and Luke slipped into the crowd, and discussed how Marian Jones's drug scandal would impact track sponsorships. Olivia followed Brooke around like a shepherd, making sure she didn't fall off the deck, keeping her fingers out of the salsa bowls, which sat on low tables, as tempting as candy.

Eleanor introduced Tom to their hosts, Gail and Ted Hailwood, and Tom immediately started asking questions about
the trees.

"The ranch is twenty-seven acres," Ted said. "Three hundred mature trees. We're contract growers, so all our fruit goes
straight to the Calavo warehouse down in Carpinteria."

"Has your yield been impacted by the diminishing bee
population?" Tom asked.

"Everything impacts the yield," Ted said, "the bees, the
drought, and now you have to think about the market demand
for organic on top of it."

"You're running conventional, then?"

"For now," Ted said. "Times are changing, though, they're
definitely changing. But you should taste these beauties." He
stepped over to a table nearby, and Tom followed. A woman in
an apron was scooping the green flesh of an avocado from the
black skin, mixing in minced garlic and onion, and mashing it
in a stone bowl to make guacamole.

Tom took a chip; his forehead was creased in thought. "You
harvest in winter?" he asked.

"Harvest year-round," Ted said. "There's a variety called
Fuerte. It's got a thicker skin that can withstand just about any
frost. We've got half Fuerte, half Haas."

Tom's eyes opened wide. "I'd like to see the difference
between the trees, if you don't mind."

They slipped off the deck and into the orchard, and by the
time Tom emerged, he was thinking about mashed avocados

and running a small ranch in a place where fog was the worst weather you would ever expect and no one cared a whit about an integrated science curriculum or the role that freshman biology played in weeding out students who couldn't handle the premed curriculum.

WHEN they got back to Eleanor's house, Lily had hidden away her purchases and her project. She asked everyone how the party had been. Tom smiled. "Ted Hailwood gave me a tour of the property," he said. "There's a variety of avocado that thrives in the winter, and they've got those trees planted on the southern sector to take advantage of the winter light. The roots actually like to be dry, which is why the hillside location is ideal. It was fascinating."

Eleanor put down her purse and, with the air of someone telling a secret she knew wasn't hers to tell, said, "The ranch is for sale. Ted told us on our way out. They're moving to a retirement community as soon as they can find a buyer."

For a heartbeat, no one said anything. Tom and Lily both turned to look at Eleanor—Tom shocked that Ted's offhand parting comment had registered with Eleanor, and Lily shocked at what she felt certain her mother was gearing up to say. And then Eleanor looked at Lily and said it: "Maybe you and Tom should snatch it up."

"Snatch it up?" Lily said. To Eleanor, a cross-country move, a new occupation, a radical change in lifestyle, required as much thought as buying a new lipstick, but to Lily it was as if her mother had proposed a trip to the moon.

Ryan, who had grown up working in his dad's summer garden, picking tomatoes and stringing peas, said, "You'd be the perfect gentleman farmer, Dad, with your straw hat and your tools, tramping through the trees."

"Yeah," Luke added, "and it would give you an excuse to buy as many trowels as you'd ever want."

Tom laughed. "I do like trowels," he said, "and tramping through trees. Maybe someday I'll get my hands in the dirt of an orchard of my own."

Lily gaped at her husband. He taught biology, and grew tomatoes and peas and sunflowers in the backyard. She couldn't recall a single time he had talked about farming. He wanted to travel when they retired. And walk in the woods. And he often mentioned getting involved with the board at Burlington's Intervale Community Farms so that he could help raise funds for their school garden programs—but wanting an *actual* farm? Wanting a new occupation? This was completely new. She spoke to him quietly, as if no one else were in the room. "Tom?" she said. "You want to be a farmer?"

Tom shrugged and looked at his wife with such affection and longing that Eleanor and Olivia and the boys all looked away; the moment seemed too intimate to watch. "It was a spectacularly beautiful spot," he said. "I could just picture us there—walking through the trees in the morning, taking stock of the birds and the bees, the sun and the rain."

"Wow," Lily said breathlessly, as if the air had suddenly been sucked from the room and she was struggling to get enough. "I had no idea that's something you wanted."

Tom got up and went over to Lily and took her head in his hands and kissed her. "I'm a man of many surprises," he said, and Ryan and Luke both burst out laughing, because their dad was so clearly not.

"Well, listen, Tom," Eleanor said. "If you're serious about wanting to buy that farm, I'll help foot the bill. I don't need to die with all my money in the bank."

"You can give it to me," Luke said, and they all laughed again, because Luke had just graduated from college, and five months ago had moved from Vermont to take a job at Bertasi Linen, his grandmother's textile company. He was still in shock about how taxes eviscerated his paycheck, about how hard it was to pay the rent on his tiny apartment. Everyone laughed, that is, except Lily.

"What are you all *talking* about?" she asked. She and Tom owned their house in Burlington outright. They were each five years away from earning their full pensions at the University of Vermont. They were not planning a move, and certainly not a move back to the hometown she had once left for good. Just because Tom had been inspired by an avocado farm didn't mean they were going to buy it.

"I'm talking about investing in real estate," Eleanor said.

"That's obvious," Lily said, "but are you *serious*? Did you happen to forget that your moving from place to place on a whim was one of the central realities of my childhood? Tom and I have worked hard to build our life in Burlington, and it's a good life and a stable life and we're not just going to up and move because you can write a check."

"Having the money to do the things you want isn't a crime, Lily."

Lily turned, fuming, and then spun back toward her mother, but Tom spoke before Lily could open her mouth. "Stop," he said, raising his hand like a traffic cop. "Both of you. Please. I was just musing about a beautiful spot on the map."

At the end of the day, when they were alone in the guest room on the third floor, Lily turned to Tom. "Thank you for calling my mom off this morning," she said.

"You take her too seriously," Tom said. "She doesn't mean any harm."

Lily laughed. "I think my mother would like nothing better than to cause a little harm. She causes harm for sport. I hope Luke knows what he got himself into, signing on to work for her."

"It's a good opportunity for him," Tom said, "and I wouldn't worry about Luke. He can hold his own."

She sat down on the bed. "I miss him," she said. "I didn't realize how lucky we were to have him so close to home for college."

"Yes you did," Tom said, smiling. "You talked about it every time he brought friends home for dinner. You talked about it every time he brought you a duffel bag full of laundry."

"I guess," she said. "It just went so fast. And now here he is—my baby, out in the world." She slipped off her shoes, and thought again about the conversation from the morning. "Tom?" she asked. "You *were* a little serious about that avocado farm, weren't you?"

He shrugged, shy like a little boy who had been caught red-handed. "You should have seen those trees," he said, "that view."

3

Ryan

Ryan and Olivia were encamped in the guest room on the first floor. They had a portable crib for Brooke set up against the wall. By the time Ryan had finished playing cards with his grandmother that night, Olivia and Brooke were fast asleep. He brushed his teeth, pulled off his clothes, and slipped into bed beside his wife.

Being with his parents was more difficult than he had anticipated. They were a constant reminder to him about what a poor job he was doing as a husband and father. His parents just seemed to get it right; they always had. When he was a teenager and other kids' parents argued about money, went on separate vacations, and took other lovers, his parents seemed to be as devoted to each other as they always had been. No matter what was happening, they were good to each other—kind and caring. They respected each other. And they had plenty of affection left over for him and his brother. Ryan had lately been thinking that maybe he just wasn't cut out for marriage.

Some days he came home from running a late workout at the pool and Olivia and Brooke would be giggling and playing some private game, and he would just stare, wondering who the little girl in pink was and what she was doing there in his house. Other days, when he hugged his wife and cupped her breasts in his hands, she recoiled the way she had sometimes done when she was still breast-feeding Brooke. Some nights when he came home late, Olivia didn't even look up from the book she was reading. He often wondered if she even *liked* him anymore.

He squeezed his eyes shut, and then opened them and turned to look at Olivia. She was so sound asleep that she was hardly moving. Her breathing was deep and even. He fit his hand over her hip bone and lay against her and listened to her sleep. He tried to imagine what it would be like if she was just suddenly gone, and his throat constricted and he pressed harder against her because he wasn't sure he could bear it. She was his wife, the mother of his child. He slid his hand over her pelvis to the soft hair between her legs, and he entwined his fingers there and felt her breath move in and out of her body. She shifted, and he felt her body press against his hand—a small show of desire. He groaned, and pressed against her and moved his fingers farther down. Now she moaned, and shifted her weight so that she could receive his hand. Then she woke up. She lifted her head. She pulled up her knees. "What are you doing?" she said—groggy, confused, displeased.

"Making love to my sexy wife," Ryan said.

Olivia pulled herself up on the pillows, pulled up the sheet to cover herself. "Brooke's right there," she said—and it was true: Brooke was asleep in a portable crib against the far wall.

"She's asleep," Ryan said.

"She could wake up any second."

"We have sheets," he said. "Blankets." He reached his hand to her hip again, an invitation.

"I can't," she said, turning away from him. "I'm sorry."

He flung the covers off. "I'm tired of all your excuses, Olivia."

"Shhh," she said. "You'll wake her."

"I'm tired of that, too—turning our lives upside down for a two-year-old."

"That's what parents do," Olivia said. "That's the job definition."

"I'm pretty sure the job definition involves having sex more than once in a blue moon. You used to like it, you know. You used to want it."

"Ryan," she said. "There'll be time for that later. She's so little."

"I think it's bullshit," he said, and stood up. "I know plenty of guys whose wives still put out after they have a baby."

"*Put out?*" she scoffed. "Are you kidding me? You dare to talk to me like that? I'm the mother of your child."

"I'm just calling a spade a spade."

"Fine. Then if you want it so badly, go out and get it some-where else, Ryan. Go out and find some sweet thing who'll *put out* for you."

He stood up, picked up his pillow. "I've come that close," he said, holding his thumb and forefinger a quarter inch apart. "That close."

The air in the room got thin then, as if they were in a plane that had suddenly lost pressure. She had to concentrate on breathing. "Don't bother holding back on my account," she finally said. "Brooke and I will be just fine without you."

"Is that what you want?"

"Apparently it's what *you* want."

"I didn't do it yet, Olivia. I just said I had come close."

"Congratulations," she said. "Your mom and dad would be so proud."

Just then, Brooke lifted her head, and then she lifted her-self up and stood at the side of the crib. Olivia flung back the covers on her side of the bed, scooped Brooke up in her arms, and kissed her hot and sweaty cheeks.

"I'm going to sleep on the couch," Ryan said, and walked out the door.

4

Lily

On the day she picked out the velvet for Brooke's dress, Lily walked up and down the aisles of the fabric store in a state of rapture. Surrounded by meaty wools, diaphanous silks, and row after row of vibrant cotton prints made her pulse quicken, and her mind spin. *I could make a quilt*, she thought, *I could make a coat, I could make a dress, a tablecloth, pillows.* She had once heard an interviewer ask Willie Nelson where he got his ideas for songs, and Nelson had said, "The air is full of tunes; I just reach up and pick one." Lily felt that same sense of possibility here in the store. All she had to do was choose the yardage, and the project would suggest itself. She had stopped sewing regularly when the boys were small, when the demands of teaching and raising children had overwhelmed her. She stopped buying fabric, too, convincing herself that she had enough for a lifetime, that the basement could hold nothing more. Standing in the store, on a mission to buy red velvet, she realized that she was wrong; she could never have enough fabric.

She reluctantly left behind the riotous cotton prints from Anna Maria Horner's latest collection, the block print silk from Japan, and the improbably thin merino wool from Milan, and bought three yards of ruby red velvet and three yards of muslin. She picked out an electronic Singer sewing machine that seemed more akin to a rocket ship than it did to her grandmother's cast-iron workhorse, and grabbed an eight-inch zipper, a pair of Gingher scissors, a box of pins, a spool of thread, and a package of needles.

"No pattern?" the saleswoman asked.

Lily smiled. *You sew? No pattern?* She used to sit in her grandmother's sewing room rearranging the wooden spools of threads as if they were soldiers, and listening to the sounds of the sewing machine as if it were a choir, singing them off to battle. She loved everything about Hattie's room—the color, the sound, the smell, the feel of the fabric, and the way that her grandmother could unfold a bolt of muslin, make a few cuts, and suddenly have the pattern for a princess's dress, a witch's cape, or a thick red wool peacoat that would keep her warm all winter. When she was eight, her grandmother taught her this magic trick. She guided Lily to cut a pattern from newspaper, to hold it up to her waist, to leave an allowance for the seam. "It's all a matter of getting the vision right," Hattie said. Lily pinned her pattern to a piece of red-checked cotton with long, thick straight pins. Hattie showed her how to use pinking shears to cut out the shapes, and then how to thread the sewing machine—over, under, around, and through. When Lily began to sew, her whole body became involved as she pressed the pedal to make the machine hum and leaned forward to guide the fabric underneath the needle: her hands, her feet, her arms, and her mind were all working together to make something that she could use that very night. That was what she loved most about sewing—the wholeness of it.

In high school, during the summers when her mother traveled the world to visit mills and factories and to secure the business of new hotels, Lily traveled to Boston to stay with her grandmother, and to sew. At the end of each summer, Eleanor would have a whole new wardrobe, custom-made by tailors in London and Milan, and Lily would have a whole new wardrobe made by hand on her grandmother's black Singer sewing machine. Each year, she tackled more and more complicated designs—from simple dresses and A-line skirts to lined jackets and collared shirts. The year she turned sixteen, Lily made a knockoff of a Pucci dress, a miniskirt, and a caftan, whose neckline she embellished with beads. Hattie, appalled at the loose designs, suggested that Lily learn how to make a formal, fitted dress suitable for a dance.

"I don't go to dances, Grandma," she said.

"They don't dance in California?"

Lily thought about the funky dances everyone was doing now—the Twist, the Boogaloo. "They dance," Lily said, "but not the way you're thinking. And I don't go to the dances anyway."

"Why on earth not?"

She shrugged, thinking of the loud music, the frantic couplings, the hemlines that were up and then down, the whole hazy frenzy of it all. It reminded her so much of her mother. "I guess I'm too shy," she said.

"A pretty dress will fix that," Hattie said. She got up, opened a cedar chest under the window, spent several minutes moving cloth around, and finally took out a parcel of brown butcher paper. There was lace inside. It was silvery white, with wide, open flowers, whose petals formed the scalloped edges of the cloth. Around the flowers, delicate ribbons curved and spun like tiny shimmering roads, and in the center of each flower was a burst of seed pearls.

Lily reached out to feel the embroidered petals, and trace the ribbon with her fingers, "What is it?"

"Hand-embroidered, hand-beaded French lace. My father brought it back for my mother when he was in the war, but she didn't live to see it."

"It's gorgeous."

"I was going to make a dress," Hattie said, "to wear to a dance, but after Mother died, things started going badly with my father's business and then there were no more dances."

"Why didn't you make something else?" Lily asked.

Hattie shrugged. "When Grandpa asked me to marry him, I designed five different wedding dresses, and dozens of veils, but I could never bear to cut the lace. I ended up using machine-made lace from Stein's. I almost used this to make a gown for a charity ball during the years when Grandpa and I went to those sorts of things, but you can see that I never did."

"So you just kept it?"

"I liked imagining the possibilities more than I would have liked making it into any single thing. Maybe you'll be braver than me." She held the lace out toward Lily.

"Oh no," Lily said, backing away as if the fabric had sharp edges. "No way; I'm not touching that fabric."

"It would be lovely over a petal pink shift. That's how the flapper dresses were made—lace over silk."

"I can't," Lily said, thinking how preposterous pink silk and hand-embroidered lace would be at a time when girls were wearing go-go boots, cutoff jeans, and wooden beads. Still, she let her grandmother take her down to a fabric store in Lynn, not far from the original family mill. They selected five yards of a soft pink satin, and three yards of tulle, and Lily made a party dress that looked like something from the fifties, like some kind of costume. She tried hard to sew her seams as straight as her grandmother's, to press her darts as sharply, to finish her hems as neatly. She did not use a pattern and she did not use the lace.

She never wore the dress.

When Hattie died in the spring of Lily's junior year in college, Lily went and sat on her floor and carefully went through the fabric in the cedar chest. Eleanor didn't want any of it; she called it dusty, old, useless junk. There was a length of beautiful black cashmere. A yard of rich Harris tweed. At the bottom of the chest, still wrapped in butcher paper, was the lace. Lily stuffed a suitcase full of fabric and wrestled the sewing machine into the trunk of a borrowed car.

She had her grandmother's blood in her veins and her grandmother's fabric in her stash; she did not need a pattern to sew her own granddaughter a Christmas dress. She turned to the fabric saleswoman in Santa Barbara. "No thanks," she said. "I don't need a pattern."

WHILE the rest of her family went to the party at the Hailwoods' ranch, she learned how her new sewing machine worked, and sketched out patterns on the newspaper. In the afternoon, while her mother, Olivia, and Brooke went to the zoo and the boys went sea kayaking, she measured and cut, basted and stitched. On Christmas Eve, she stayed up by herself to hem the velvet dress. The fabric was soft and substantial. It was a deep crimson red, the kind of color that had once been reserved for nobility. Brooke would feel like a princess when she put it on, and Lily felt a secret thrill that the gift she made with her hands would equal the gift her mother had bought with her money. When she was done with the dress, she wrapped it up and put it under the tree. She poured out the milk Brooke had set out, and ate the sprinkled sugar cookies they'd brought home from the bakery, and hoped that having sugar so late at night wouldn't keep her up or give her a migraine.

In the morning, Eleanor and Ryan got up at dawn to go down to the beach for their annual Polar Bear swim. They were back sipping coffee by the time the rest of the family was awakened by Brooke's cries of glee.

"Santa came," Brooke called. "Santa came!"

They made their way downstairs, and even though no one but Eleanor knew that Ryan had slept on the couch, Lily noticed that while Olivia crouched down with Brooke to examine the cookie crumbs and the empty glass of milk, Ryan sat on the couch, his hair still wet, looking as if he'd rather be anywhere else. It was a split-second observation of a tiny moment of discord, but it lodged in Lily's brain, and would stay wedged there, like a thorn.

Brooke turned her attention to the gifts under the tree, to the big red box wrapped in a white satin bow. She ripped the paper off the doll. Her mouth formed a perfect "O" when she held the beautiful doll in her hands.

"It's from Nana," Olivia said, and Brooke threw herself at her great-grandmother, squeezing the doll between them. Lily stared at her mother's sun-spotted hand stroking her grandchild's gleaming hair, and felt a wave of jealousy. Brooke returned to opening her other gifts, including the red velvet dress, but as soon as everything was opened, she retreated to a corner of the living room, where she laid out the doll's clothes and shoes and storybooks, and fell into a world of her own making. The red velvet dress, *The Busy Town of Richard Scarry*, and the other toys and gifts were left untouched.

"Brooke," Olivia said, "your grandma Lily made this beautiful dress so you could match your doll. Why don't you try it on?"

Brooke ignored her mother. She was talking softly to the doll, stroking its hair.

"Brooke," Olivia said sharply, but still the girl did not turn around.

Olivia stood up and walked over to her daughter. She crouched down.

"I'd like to help you try on Grandma Lily's dress."

Brooke shook her head. "No," she said.

Olivia took the doll, set it up high on a bookshelf, and Brooke began to scream. She flung herself on the ground, wailing.

Ryan brought his hands to his face as if he could block out the scene, and Olivia simply picked up Brooke and marched downstairs to the room where they were staying.

Lily quickly got up and went to the kitchen to make pancakes.

Tom followed her. "The dress is pretty, sweetheart," he said. "You did a nice job."

Lily waved her hand, dismissing his comment. "It was silly of me to make it," she said. "A two-year-old doesn't care about clothes."

"Don't be so hard on yourself. A few years from now she'll be able to appreciate your skill."

Lily raised herself up on her toes and kissed him on the cheek.

"That's nice of you to say," she said, but she still felt the sting of the rejection, and the shame of how she had been so jealous of her own mother.

Tom reached down and wrapped his arms around her. Just then, Ryan walked in.

"Whoa, sorry to interrupt," Ryan said, skidding to a halt as he rounded the corner. Lily and Tom smiled at their son.

"I just wanted to make sure you were okay, Mom, about the dress and everything."

"Don't worry about me, Ryan. You just take care of your sweet family."

He shrugged, and a shadow crossed his face. "I'm trying," he said.

Lily got out the flour and the eggs, the butter and the syrup. Tom pulled bacon from the refrigerator.

"You and Dad have set the bar pretty high for family happiness," Ryan said.

"The secret to a good marriage," Tom said, "is breakfast."

Lily and Ryan both raised their eyebrows in question.

"It's the small things," Tom said. "The daily things that make life a little easier because you're sharing it."

"Is that from *Old Tom's Almanac*?" Ryan teased.

Lily laughed.

"Very good," Tom said, and laughed, too. "*Old Tom's Almanac*."

THAT night, Tom got into bed, took off the round glasses that made him look like a caricature of a professor, and did not pick up the book he had been reading on the horrors of modern food production. He just lay there, staring at the ceiling. Lily washed her face and brushed her teeth as if it were any other day, but her mind was spinning. She slipped in beside Tom and then turned out the light.

She thought about her headaches, her mother, her son, the avocado farm, the red velvet dress. She thought about how infrequently she and Tom made love anymore, and how, when they did, it was like a chore—grade the papers, attend the meeting, stroke the thigh, kiss the lips. After a while, she spoke into the darkness. "Are you happy?"

"It was great to be with all the kids," he said. "I get such a kick out of seeing Ryan with Olivia and Brooke, and Luke with a job now. God, it seems like just yesterday when they were making snow forts in the front yard."

Lily smiled wryly in the dark. "I meant on a more cosmic scale."

"Oh," he said. "Am I happy? I don't know. I keep thinking about a short story I once read about Gregor Mendel."

"The Andrea Barrett story? The one about how Mendel was duped."

He turned to face her, thrilled that she knew what he was talking about. It was proof of how connected they were, how interdependent they were. Who else would know all his obscure references? Who else would agree when he lamented the changing face of biology? "Exactly," he said. "There was some very good science in that story. But it also depicted a very old man, a man who had lost his mind. People kept having to convince him of who he was, and what he had contributed to the world. Sometimes I feel like that man."

"You haven't lost your mind, Tom," she said, and reached out and stroked his hair, which was still quite thick. "Far from it."

"I know that," he said, "but sometimes I can't remember what the point of it all is."

"You've educated generations of students. You've been a pillar of our community. You're a wonderful father and husband. Grandfather, too. And you grow the best tomatoes in the state of Vermont. That's point enough, I would think."

He leaned over and kissed her. "Thank you," he said, and then, "Good night."

She lay there in the dark while Tom slept.

Is something wrong? she had asked that night in front of the bookshop.

You want to be a farmer? she had asked yesterday.

And just now, *Are you happy?*

The truth was that Lily wasn't sure of so many of the things she had once been sure of. She had always thought that the longer you were married, the closer you would get to the other person—that the gap between you would close over time. But it didn't. There was, even now, a part of Tom she could never reach. She accepted that, but at the same time, she wanted to make sure that the gap didn't widen. Even though it had been her mother's idea, even though it was such a radical departure from the road map they had made for their lives, she found herself playing with the idea of buying the avocado ranch the way a child works a loose tooth. She would present the ranch to Tom as if it were a gift tied up with a bow. She would make an impassioned speech about following one's heart. And while Tom tramped through the trees in the California sunshine, she would sit by the window and sort through her fabric and imagine the possibilities, and at night, they would talk about the things they were making, the problems they were solving, and how lucky they were to still be together after so many years.

5

Eleanor

AFTER everyone in her family had come and gone for the holidays, Eleanor felt bereft. The problem with being the life of the party, she thought, is that every time the party comes to an end, you die a small death. On December 28, she sat in her empty kitchen, looking at the Tupperware containers filled with leftover chili and slices of roast beef, and at the Christmas tree, whose needles were now yellow and dry, and she realized that what she had to look forward to in the New Year, for the most part, were other deaths and dissolutions.

The death part was a given. She was nearly seventy-five years old, and everyone around her was dying. They moved with increasing frequency out of their houses into assisted living facilities, or they moved in and out of the hospital, until one day, there was a phone call, or an e-mail, or a short paragraph on the obituary page of the newspaper, and they were gone.

It was starting to really get to her. This year, she expected to have to say good-bye to two more people from the group of six who she always thought would live forever. There was her old college roommate, Gracie, whose cancer had migrated to her brain and taken up permanent residence there. And there was Judy Vreeland, who kept falling and breaking bones, and each time it took her longer and longer to recover. These were the people who most remembered the noise and the pop and the chaos of the prime of her life, and over the years, Eleanor had always joked that when they were gone, she might as well go, too. Now that it was actually here, however, she didn't feel sorry for herself so much as she felt angry at all of them for leaving.

She had counted on her friends far more than she had counted on her husbands or her family—counted on them to understand her, to entertain her, to always be there for her—and for years and years, it had been a smart choice. Her husbands were all gone, her daughter had taken off to live a quiet, academic life in the northern woods, but her friends remained. With one phone call, she could have a place to go for the holidays, get counsel on a business matter, find a companion to travel to the ends of the earth, or just enlist someone who would stay up late to play a hand of bridge. Eleanor thought that friendship was the most enduring relationship of all, until the calls started coming in—cancer, stroke, heart attack—and she began to see that she would be left alone in the end anyway, cursed by long-lasting genes and short-lived marriages.

The dissolution part of her premonition for the New Year was just a suspicion—something she could smell in the air like the sea. She had lived a long time, and it was her experience that marriage didn't last. She married Billy Edwards because he had gone to Harvard and because his future looked bright, and although they had a child and gave dinner parties and traveled to the Cape in the summer, she never really loved him, not the way Judy loved Gordon, not the way she imagined love to be. When he fell to the floor of the airport in Buenos Aires, dead of a heart attack at the age of thirty-five, it was a liberation. Her relationship with her second husband, Elliot Taft, had been based wholly on desire, and before long, their marriage burned itself out. There was another husband after that, an art dealer who considered Eleanor a beautiful investment, and she used him to increase the reach of her business the same way he used her. After just four years into their marriage, the art dealer had doubled his list of exclusive contracts and Eleanor was selling high-thread-count sheets and towels to hotels on five continents, instead of just two. They agreed to divorce when there was no advantage left for either of them.

It was one thing for Eleanor to have handled marriage so recklessly, but now she smelled trouble with her grandson, Ryan, and she didn't like it. She didn't want to leave a legacy of botched love. Lily had proved capable, somehow, of a good, long marriage—a relationship that Eleanor both envied and cherished. Envied because she'd never had it herself, and cherished because her daughter's success at marriage vindicated

Eleanor's many failures. But now she could see Ryan standing apart from his wife and his daughter, as though he lived in the same territory but not the same tribe. He had married too young, and for the wrong reason. It wasn't going to last. And she felt a desperation about it that surprised her.

ON Christmas morning Eleanor and Ryan got up in the dark, at dawn, and drove down to Miramar Beach for the annual Polar Bear swim. Eleanor had been a record-holding backstroker in college, and still swam three mornings a week with a Masters Group. Ryan had been an age group sprinter in Vermont, and when he was in high school, there was some talk of his being able to make an Olympic qualifying time. He never did and never succeeded to recover, completely, from the disappointment. He was now the assistant swim coach at Cal Poly, where he put young athletes through their paces and recalled, daily, what it was like to be that strong, and that free. Swimming was a language grandmother and grandson both understood—the way the body slipped through the water, the way the sensory assault of the world stopped when you were underwater—and there was no reason for them to speak as they drove.

When they got to the beach, they walked out on the sand and joined the other early-morning risers, who slapped shoulders and called out, "Merry Christmas," in voices too loud for morning. The sky was clear and cool, and out in the channel, perched in front of the islands, the oil rigs looked like giant, brooding black birds. When the swimmers ran into the waves, the cold of the water was a shock. People whooped and hollered as they made their way out to the buoy, around it, and back to the beach. Eleanor was the oldest female swimmer who'd come out that day. The skin on the undersides of her arms sagged and her legs were crisscrossed with purple veins, but she was trim, and her lungs were strong, and she didn't mind the cold. She was, still, the kind of woman that men called a good sport, the kind of woman that men adored because she was both small and beautiful, and game for a good time. She swam just behind Ryan, making her way through the choppy sea, thinking how good it was to move her arms and her legs, to take air into her lungs, to swim in the same water as the dolphins.

On the way back in, they waited at the break line for a good wave to ride, and chose to kick out on the same smooth-breaking swell. They let the water carry them along, feeling the pull on their feet, the froth in their face. Ryan stood up quickly when he got to shallow water, and was right beside Eleanor to give her a hand and help her get her legs underneath her. Bob Shafer, who came in on the wave behind them, said, "Good idea to bring your grandson again." Bob lived on a yacht in the harbor, and swam every morning in the sea. Sometimes, when Eleanor needed an escort to a party, Bob would put on his tuxedo and accompany her. Every so often, he invited Eleanor to come back with him to his boat, but she would toss her thick silver hair, flash her blue eyes, and say, "Oh, Bob, you don't really mean that," even though she knew he did.

John O'Hara, who swam three mornings a week at the club with Eleanor, was already standing on the beach. He looked at Ryan and said, "Chip off the old block, is he?"

"God, I hope not," Eleanor said, and they all laughed, because everyone knew how many times she had been married, and how many hearts she had broken in between.

But later, in the car, Ryan said, "Turns out I *am* a chip off the old block, Nana."

"How so?" Eleanor asked. She had come upon Ryan sleeping on the couch only a few hours before, with nothing more than a pillow. She knew exactly what that meant.

"Things aren't going so well with me and Olivia," he said.

"You have a toddler," Eleanor said. "Sleep deprivation magnifies every chink in the armor. You have to just wait it out."

Ryan kept his hands on the wheel of his grandmother's white Lexus, and looked straight ahead at the road. "There are more than chinks," he said.

"What's wrong?" Eleanor asked.

"I don't know," Ryan said. "It's hard to say." And then after a while, he said, "There are other women."

"Other women?" Eleanor repeated, and felt the dread she had been fearing settle on her shoulders.

"Just friends I see sometimes after work."

"Failing to keep your pants on is what got you into this

situation," Eleanor said. "Don't make the same mistake twice. You have no idea what it costs to walk away."

"You're talking about money?" Ryan asked. "We don't have any money so that's not really an issue."

"Money?" she repeated. "Dear God, no, I'm not talking about money." She was talking about the shock of being old and alone, the slow dawning of understanding about the ways in which your actions and decisions reverberate through your family. "Money comes and money goes," she said.

She turned and looked out the window. She was talking about seeing the repercussions of your actions played out in the next generation, and the next. She hadn't paid much attention to Lily, and maybe Lily had paid too *much* attention to Ryan and Luke. Everyone expected a mother to be perfect, to give the child exactly what that child needed, and no mother could ever live up to it. Then the children grow up and go out and try to make up for what was missing—by living a carefully structured life the way Lily had done, free of risk, free of fun. Or by giving up on having as good a marriage as your parents when you were only twenty-five, the way Ryan was doing now.

Ryan snorted. "That's what Mom always said you believed about men."

Eleanor laughed bitterly. "I'm sure it looked that way to her, but I . . ."

"Nana," Ryan said, "you've said it a hundred times—*love is just an illusion, you can't count on love.*"

THAT phrase rang in Eleanor's head throughout the holidays. *You can't count on love.* She wondered if it was really true, and tried to think through all the couples she knew who had proven her wrong. She came up with just two. Her old friends Judy and Gordon. And Tom and Lily, her only child. But then, on the day before Christmas when the family came back from a party at the Hailwoods', there was the tense exchange about an avocado ranch, and Eleanor began to wonder even about them.

AFTER everyone went home, Eleanor called Gracie in New York. "What will we resolve this year?" she asked.

"I'm going to resolve not to die," Gracie said. "It works, since I never was very good at keeping my resolutions."

Eleanor was tempted to say, "You're not going to die, Gracie," just as she had said in college, "You're not going to fail." But it was too late for all that now. Gracie was dying, and they both knew it. "Just be sure you make it till Opening Day," Eleanor said.

"As long as you can wheel me to a skybox, honey, I'm going to Opening Day," Gracie said.

They had been making a party of the Red Sox Opening Day since the spring of 1952. That was eight months after they arrived at Wellesley College, with their wool kilts, their cardigan sets, their pearl necklaces. Gracie knew a baseball player from her hometown who was starting that fall at Harvard, and on the weekend of the Harvard-Yale football game, he brought two friends with him—a shortstop and a first baseman—so that Eleanor, Judy, and Gracie could each have a date. The six of them piled into a two-tone four-door Studebaker Commander with flasks of hot buttered rum, and drove out from Wellesley to the game. The couples were paired off by height, because that seemed the easiest thing to do, and because Eleanor took an instant liking to Billy Edwards, the shortest of the three boys. He was strong and athletic and wore his blue blazer and penny loafers as if they were his birthright.

"Do you know much about football?" Billy asked.

"Not a thing," Eleanor said coyly, "except that the men look ridiculous in those helmets. I far prefer baseball."

The boys hooted and whistled. "Do you now?" Gordon Vreeland asked. He was driving, and spoke without taking his eyes from the road.

"That's my girl," Billy said to the other boys—already claiming Eleanor, already staking his turf.

"Her daddy owns one of the big mills in Lynn and he has box seats at Fenway," Gracie blurted out, and the boys cheered again. The war was over, and life was good for all of them.

"And she swims, too," Judy said, just so she would have something to add to the conversation. "She swims fast! Isn't that right, Eleanor?" Gracie and Eleanor had been paired as roommates, and Judy lived down the hall from them, with a girl whose glasses were thick as Coke bottles and who preferred to spend her evenings in the library.

"But she doesn't know a thing about football," Gordon said to Billy. "She said so herself. So that means you've got some coaching to do today, sport."

The boys took the girls to three other football games that fall, and to a winter dance at Winthrop House, and when baseball season started in the spring, they invited them to their first game against Dartmouth—a game they lost quite badly, as they would so many games that season and the next. In exchange for all their kindnesses, Eleanor invited all six of the group to watch Ted Williams in the Red Sox Opening Day game, and they sat behind home plate on the first base foul line and ate hot dogs and felt like royalty. When Williams was called up to the Korean War a few weeks later, they were shocked and sobered, and their sense of having experienced something special was solidified.

"We should make this a tradition," Gracie said during the seventh inning stretch. "We should come back every year to Opening Day at Fenway, no matter where we are in our lives."

"It's a deal," Billy said, grabbing Eleanor's hand and squeezing.

Eleanor married Billy in June of the year they graduated. Judy married Gordon later that summer, but Gracie would choose a Yale man over Bucky Harrington. Still, they kept their promise as often as they could, returning to Fenway, as jobs, children, wars, and the vagaries of life allowed. Other friends from college joined them, now and again, and sometimes friends they made at work, or in their communities. Eleanor was accustomed to eating at fine restaurants all over the world, but there was little she liked better than a hot dog and a cold beer at Fenway Park.

Now, some sixty years later, Gracie asked her old friend, "Are you resolving anything this year?"

"I'm swearing off men," Eleanor said.

Gracie laughed, and it sounded as though it made every bone in her body hurt. "That's a new one."

"I'm serious," Eleanor said. "It used to be fun; now it's just pathetic. Now they just want someone to keep them company or to nurse them in their old age."

"I'm not seeing you in that role," Gracie said.

"No," Eleanor agreed. "And I think I'm going to resolve to invest in a new family venture."

"So you're too old for men, but not too old for business?"

"I didn't say I was too old for men," Eleanor said. "I said they were too old for me. And family businesses have paid off quite handsomely for me, in case that's slipped your mind." She had helped run her father's textile company after Billy died, and took it over completely after her second husband died, too. In four years, she turned a regional operation into a multinational one.

"It hasn't slipped my mind," Gracie said, "believe you me. So what's the business this time? Anything to do with baseball? Fine art? Four-hundred-thread-count sheets?"

"No," she said. It was about making sure that Lily and Tom had reason to thank her, to include her, to be near her. It was about making sure that she would have someone in her life after her last best friend of was dead and gone. "Avocados."

•6•

Lily

Back in Burlington, it was cold and wet. There was no ice on Lake Champlain, but each night, the tree branches would become encased with ice and they would creak and moan under the added weight. The students weren't due back until January fourteenth and it was unnaturally quiet on campus. Lily walked through the cold to her office. She flicked on the lights and turned up the heat.

Marilyn, one of her colleagues, poked her head inside the door. "Hey," she said. "Welcome back to winter. How was Santa Barbara?" Lily considered telling Marilyn about Tom and the avocado ranch and what happened with Brooke and the red velvet dress—but she decided against it. Maybe Marilyn used to be the kind of friend she would confide in, but she wasn't anymore. No one was. All the friends Lily had when the boys were young—other mothers who went to swim meets and Little League games and who baked birthday cakes and nursed kids with the chicken pox—had drifted out of her life as her boys had grown up and moved away. Sometimes she would run into one of the women in the grocery store, and they would ask each other about their children and share the headlines of their lives, but then they had nothing left to say to each other, and they would smile and say good-bye. She often went on walks with Marilyn, and in the winter sometimes swam laps with a woman who worked in admissions, but they never really talked about anything more than the weather, the goings-on in the department, the new crop of freshman.

"Good," Lily said. "Fine. And did you survive the twins?"

"One of them bit me," she said, and held out her hand for proof.

Lily laughed, relieved that there were other people besides herself who didn't automatically get along with their grand-children, who weren't automatically adored.

"And Jerry and I decided to separate," Marilyn said, but her voice was no longer light.

"Separate?" Lily said, more loudly perhaps than she needed to, because she was surprised to hear this sudden pronounce-ment. Hadn't she just seen Jerry holding a coat for Marilyn as they left a party a week before Christmas? Hadn't Marilyn just bought Jerry a new set of cross-country skis? "I didn't know you were having trouble."

Marilyn shrugged. "It's my own damn fault," she said matter-of-factly. "We got tangled up with another couple, and Jerry would rather be with her than with me."

"Oh," Lily said. Her mind raced for the next appropriate thing to say. Didn't Marilyn *mind* that everyone would know this private business about her life? Wasn't she the least bit *embarrassed* by what she was saying? "Are you . . ." Lily asked. "I mean, are you and this other man . . ."

"God, no," Marilyn said. "The whole thing was just a diversion for me, something I agreed to in order to keep Jerry happy. I had no idea it would end like this."

Lily just stared at her, stumped now.

"I was an idiot," Marilyn said. "I should have just done whatever the hell I wanted to please myself. The result would have been the same anyway."

Lily nodded. "I'm sorry," she said. She felt like she had so many times in her childhood—naïve, clueless, embarrassed at how much she hadn't seen or even guessed. Just a few weeks after Lily's father died, she had walked in on her mother, naked in bed with another man. Lily was ten years old—which was old enough to have some understanding of what she was seeing, but too young to fully comprehend. "This is Elliot Taft," her mother had said. "Elliot, this is my daughter, Lily," as if it were the most normal introduction in the world. Two years later, when her mother told her that Elliot was going back to Houston and they would be staying in Santa Barbara, Lily was stunned again. She hadn't seen it coming. She had grown to like Elliot Taft. He helped her with her homework, kept her mother somewhat grounded. She thought she might never understand the world of adults—a belief she felt again now that she was decidedly a part of it.

Marilyn shrugged again. "Life goes on," she said. "You starting work on that textbook website yet?"

"Today's the day," Lily said, relieved to be moving on to another topic. "What about you? What brings you into the office during winter break?"

"I'm on the search committee for a new assistant professor," Marilyn said. "We've got candidates coming in from Florida and Texas for the start of classes and I'm trying to make sure all the logistics are set."

"It's supposed to snow," Lily said.

"Well," Marilyn said, "it's not like we're pretending to be a tropical island."

Marilyn left, and again Lily's office was quiet. She turned her mind to *Discoveries in Geometry*. She needed to hire a web designer because her publisher wanted everything to be interactive, but she kept circling back to what Marilyn had said: *I should have just done whatever the hell I wanted to please myself.* That could have been Lily's mother talking. And it was, Lily thought with a certain amount of smugness, precisely the thing Lily had resolved not to do in her marriage, and precisely why she was still married to this day.

At noon, she gave up searching for a web guru who understood geometry and went home for lunch. She ate a turkey sandwich while reading about a quilt artist who worked exclusively with vintage fabrics, and when she was done, she went down into the basement. She had piles of fabric sealed in Rubbermaid boxes, impervious to mice and moths and sunlight. She had collected fabric everywhere her mother dragged her, and when she traveled by herself. One bin contained nothing but tablecloths—pristine white damask, hand-embroidered linen, woven cloth from India, and the brightly colored cotton cloth she and Tom had bought in Lyon. It was threadbare at the edges now, and at the creases, consigned to the Rubbermaid containers in the garage after a long life of service. She took it out, unfurled it like a flag. They had purchased it when they were in their midtwenties, in the days before they decided to marry. Tom had finished his graduate studies, and gone to Ethiopia with the Peace Corps to teach beekeeping. Lily had stayed on at the University of Denver, where she had done her graduate work, and was now teaching and working with an older mathematician on the textbook project she would ultimately inherit. She met Tom in Paris and they took the train to Lyon.

In the previous six months, they had written each other letters every week, talking about their work. They were worlds apart, and they had each begun to forget the spark of connection they had felt when they met in the mountains of Colorado the previous summer. Tom would write about pollen counts in African tribal hives and she would write about the difficulties of using English to describe math and they would each read the other's letters and think, *He is so far away; she is so far away.* In Lyon, however, they wandered through the street markets, took long walks along the river, and remembered how easy it was to be together, how easy it was to talk about everything, from what kind of cheese to buy for lunch to the probability of whether or not there was a God to what would become of their friends who had gone to work on Wall Street. They began to talk about looking for jobs at the same university, starting a family. One day, in a stall on a shady street, they saw a table-cloth printed in a bright cacophony of red and cream paisley swirls. Lily stopped to look, and Tom stood beside her, trying to see what she was seeing.

"It's printed cotton," Lily explained, "similar to the kind of cloth Matisse draped on the table of his still lifes. He was a huge collector of textiles. He painted them again and again, and called them his 'noble rags.'"

"Let's buy it," Tom said.

She laughed. "You want to buy a tablecloth?" she asked. They were young, just starting out in the world. They didn't have a house, a table, a set of silverware.

"First the tablecloth, then the table, then the house," Tom said, "and then a garden, of course."

While the woman at the stall rang up their purchase, she chatted with Lily about Bohain-en-Vermandois, the town where

Matisse was born, several hundred miles to the north. "An ugly, industrial town," the woman said, "but they say that the river used to shimmer with a rainbow of impossible colors from all the dyes from the weavers' shops. Can you imagine it? A bright magenta river?"

Lily and Tom always repeated that part of the story, when they told it, time after time—*Can you imagine it? A bright magenta river?* Their friends would comment on the tablecloth, and Lily and Tom would talk about finding it in Lyon, which was really a story about how they found each other, how they committed to each other, and how they shared a love that sustained them.

SHE closed up her tubs, brought the tablecloth up from the basement, got out her ironing board, and set it up in the kitchen. She used to bring out the Lyon tablecloth for special occasions—birthdays and when they got their tenure appointments and promotions. The boys always liked it, and the stories that would follow about Tom and the bees and Lily trekking to France.

When Tom walked in, he said, "Hey, I haven't seen that in a while."

"It's been in the basement," she said, "but it's funny because I can't remember putting it down there."

"I find things down in the basement that I haven't seen in twenty years," Tom said.

Lily laughed. "That could come in handy if you ever wanted to find a *National Geographic* from the bicentennial."

"I remember that issue, actually," he said.

"Tom! I was kidding!"

"No, I do. There was an article by Isaac Asimov about life on a space colony fifty years in the future. It was fantastic, and people actually believed that's what the future would bring. I remember that there were these illustrations accompanying that article, and there was this girl in a minidress on a moving staircase. She kind of looked like you."

"You remember that?"

"Sure," Tom said.

Lily began to press the iron to the old tablecloth. "You're amazing," she said, "and a little frightening."

Tom got out a plate, made himself a sandwich, sat down at the table. "What were you doing down in the basement anyway?" he asked. "Have you been here all morning?"

"No," she said, "I went to the office to try to start my research for the website."

"I take it that didn't go well."

Lily set the iron down. "Nothing's changed in geometry," she said, "but I still have to find a way to modernize it. As if Euclid alone isn't enough."

"What would happen if you told them you weren't going to do it?"

"My book would become even more obsolete. I'd have to

teach from a book written by someone who drank the 'make math whiz-bang' Kool-Aid."

Tom got up from the table. "You and I," he said, "are old school. We are definitely old school."

"Oh," she said, "speaking of that. Marilyn Mason came by my office this morning. Did you know she and Jerry are separating?"

"No," he said, "I hadn't heard that."

She decided not to tell him the rest of the story just now, and he didn't ask. She was still thinking about what Marilyn had said: *I should have just done whatever the hell I wanted to please myself.*

LILY did not go to the office the next day. She went instead to visit Elizabeth Stewart, her neighbor down the street. Elizabeth was a potter, a tea drinker, a dog lover, a mother, a widow, a third-generation New Englander. Although they mostly only waved at each other as they passed on the street, or knocked on each other's door when there was an emergency with the electricity or a deer trapped by a fence at the end of the street, Lily considered Elizabeth to be one of the only people with whom she could still have a meaningful conversation. Elizabeth was practical, grounded, kind.

"You're just in time," Elizabeth said when she let Lily in. "I'm glazing today. You can keep me company."

The older woman led Lily through her house to the studio

out back. On the workbench, there were fifteen pots made out of a gritty clay the color of wet sand. Some were small creamers and pitchers, others traditional urn-shaped vessels. Each pot looked like a little pear-shaped human, with either legs and feet, or arms and hands. Some of the smaller bowls stood upon little feet, or sat upon outstretched legs. One pitcher had two arms that wrapped around itself in a hug; the elbows were the handles. The bowls and vases looked like they might come to life at any moment and walk away, or start clapping. Lily laughed.

"Strange, aren't they?" Elizabeth asked.

"Strangely wonderful," Lily said.

"A gallery over on Church Street asked me to do a series for them, and this is what came to me. I love the color of the clay, so I'm giving them a clear glaze."

"They're really great," Lily said. She perched on a stool near the window, and got right to the reason she had come. "I'm supposed to be working on a website for my textbook today, but you can see that I'm not doing that."

"Creativity is not a linear process," Elizabeth said. "Maybe you're solving a problem you're not even aware you're solving."

Lily shrugged. "It's not that," she said, not bothering to explain how little creativity had to do with a digitized version of a geometry textbook. "There's an avocado ranch for sale in Santa Barbara."

Elizabeth was stirring a barrel of glaze on the floor with a wooden stick. She lifted her face and raised her eyebrows. "Don't go," Elizabeth said.

Lily laughed at her neighbor's directness. "Why not?"

"New Englanders don't do well out there. I can't tell you the number of people I know who moved to California, and came back within a year. They keep waiting for the fall, and it never comes."

"Luke's there now. And Ryan. They love it."

"Luke is twenty-two years old, Lily. Ryan has a young family. They're in a different phase of life."

"Tom asked me the other day what would happen if I gave up my textbook project, and I keep thinking about it. About what I would do instead."

"You'd farm avocados?"

Lily shook her head. "No, that's Tom's thing," she said. "I would sew. And I might make an art quilt. God knows I have enough fabric."

"You don't have to move to Santa Barbara to make a quilt."

"I was also thinking about getting a dog," Lily said, although the idea has just occurred to her. When their last shepherd died during Luke's junior year of college, they didn't get a new dog, the way they had done so many times before. By mutual, silent consent she and Tom decided to be without a pet, now that they were so decidedly without kids in the house. It was easy enough to make the decision; they simply didn't visit any kennels where they would be swayed by the big brown eyes of a pup; they didn't respond to any DOGS FOR SALE signs that would lead them to a sweet, loving dog in need of a home; and they didn't go out of their way to notice dogs with distinguished dispositions around town who might have sisters or puppies. When Ryan or Luke came to visit, the boys would comment on how silent and still the house was, and they would ask about a dog, and Tom would mumble something about being too busy and Lily would change the subject because she didn't want to look too closely at what it all meant—a life with no kids, no dogs, a life that would grow increasingly quiet. A dog, all of a sudden, seemed emblematic of what they had lost, and what they might gain.

"And there are no dogs in Vermont?" Elizabeth asked.

"I know it sounds crazy," Lily said, "but I think everything would come together on the avocado farm." Having said it out loud, now, it suddenly didn't seem so crazy at all.

THE wind was howling as she walked home from Elizabeth's house. She remembered how cold she had been when they first moved to Vermont. They were living in a third-floor apartment of an old house on Brattle Street, and the cold came through the windows as if it, too, were paying rent. She was cold at night, cold in the morning. She was happy the winter she was pregnant with Ryan, because she felt better insulated, and after Luke was born, they left the apartment with the thin windows and moved to a small, well-built house. The cold, however, was always a threat, and being well organized was Lily's best defense. She had a basket for hats, gloves, and scarves just inside the door. She always had chili or stew in the refrigerator for a fast, warm dinner. In just a few winters, she became as resilient as a native New Englander. Her home was worlds away from mild and easy California, and she liked it like that; each passing season proved to her how far she had come from her mother's world—a place where fabric was just a means to an end and marriage was something that didn't last.

In the middle of night, the wind blew hard off the lake. There was a thundering crash in the backyard, which sounded like an explosion and shook the house like an earthquake. "What was that?" Lily gasped. Tom leapt out of bed and they raced down from the bedroom to see what had happened. They turned on the outdoor lights, peered out the window, and lurched back. The big elm tree had fallen, crashing through the branches of two other trees, crushing the fence around Tom's garden, and coming to rest just feet from the kitchen door. The leaves knocked against the windows, whipped by the wind, scratching and scrabbling as if they were alive.

They stood at the window for a moment, transfixed by how close they had come to a disaster. Had the wind been blowing at a slightly different tack, the tree would have fallen on them where they slept. "Jesus," Tom said.

They went to the closet to get boots and coats, and Tom fished a flashlight from the drawer in the kitchen. They walked out the front door, leaned into the wind, and made their way around to the back. The wind was bitter and cold, and the rain drove down into their faces. They surveyed the damage, and determined there was nothing they could do until morning.

They got back in bed, but they did not sleep. They sat up and talked about who they could call to come with a chainsaw in the morning, and who could haul away the debris. They talked about what would have happened if the tree had fallen through the kitchen, and what would have happened if it had fallen on the roof over their bedroom. They talked about other times they had narrowly escaped tragedy—the time the ice cracked when they were skating on the lake, the time Ryan's car skidded out on black ice the night of his junior prom, the time they were supposed to be on the Metrolink train that ended up in a twisted mass of steel.

"I guess we're just lucky," Lily said.

Tom nodded and wrapped her tightly in his arms, and they fell into a fitful sleep.

THE next day, while chainsaws buzzed in the backyard, Lily slipped away, picked up the phone, and called her mother. She took a deep breath while she waited for the call to go through. When Eleanor answered, Lily said hello and told her about the tree, and then she said, "Were you serious about buying that avocado ranch?" She spoke quickly, before there was time to change her mind.

"Funny you should ask," Eleanor said. "I spoke to Ted Hailwood at the Farmer's Market the other day."

"About the avocado ranch?" Lily asked, as if there might be something else in question.

"Well, no one was interested in a lemon ranch that I knew of," Eleanor said.

"Oh my God," Lily said, and she flopped down on the couch. She couldn't believe her mother's presumptuousness, her mother's ability to trump her every move, her mother's knack for having an answer to everything. "You're going to *buy* it, aren't you? I should've known you would do this. I should've known."

"It's a good investment," Eleanor said. "And I was inspired. That's a combination that can't be beat."

"And you think Tom and I will just say, '*Great! Let's pack up and move to Santa Barbara?*' like it's nothing?" Even saying the words out loud made Lily's throat go dry; suddenly the thing she had been dreaming about was a real possibility, and she was going to have to face it.

"I think it's a good bet. Otherwise I wouldn't have made an offer."

Lily shook her head. "Before I picked up this phone," she said, "buying that ranch was just a vague idea. I mean, I've thought about it," she said, refusing to betray that she had, in fact, been turning it over and over in her mind. "But it's not like it's something I'm convinced I want to do."

"That's poppycock," Eleanor said.

Lily laughed. "Poppycock, Mom? No one says *poppycock* anymore."

"I do," Eleanor said, "and it *is* poppycock. You know why you called. You know what you want."

"Well, maybe I've thought about the ranch," Lily said, "but most people don't act on whims like that. There have been a thousand times when I've dreamed of something, or wanted something, and didn't do anything about it. I remember falling in love with this bolt of merino wool in Como. It was the most exquisite fabric, printed in an exaggerated paisley pattern. I can still picture the exact colors—browns and golds and a beautiful rust. Every cell in my body screamed out for me to buy that fabric, but we had spent all our money just getting there. I couldn't have it. But I had the experience of seeing it, and of wanting it, and in some ways they amount to the same thing."

"When you get to be my age," Eleanor said, "there's no time for regret like that. There's only time for action. "

"I'm not your age."

"No, but you can learn something from your own mother, can't you? Tom loves that ranch. You didn't see his face when he was out there that day, but my guess is that you wouldn't have to see his face to know what he's thinking."

"What's that supposed to mean?"

"That you know what makes your husband happy."

"Why would you say that?"

"Because it's true," Eleanor said.

"Wait, Mom," Lily said, suddenly wondering if her mother was sick, if she was going to die. "Why are you doing this?" Lily had been trying for years to talk seriously about what steps they would take when Eleanor could no longer live by herself. Eleanor would mention friends who had brought in caregivers when they could no longer drive, and people she knew who had sold everything and moved into beautiful apartments that came with twenty-four-hour nursing care, but she would never talk about her own plans or her own wishes. "I'm healthy as an ox," she insisted whenever Lily brought it up, "so why waste time thinking about it?" *Because*, Lily thought, *I don't like surprises. I can't stand uncertainty.*

"Everyone I know is dying," Eleanor said, "all my old friends. Mostly, I just go to funerals these days. I need a better reason to throw a party."

Lily laughed. "You're crazy, Mom."

"So I've heard."

"Fine," she said. "Fine. I'll talk to Tom."

7

Ryan

RYAN stayed late at the pool to meet with the team trainer and a sophomore butterflyer whose shoulders were giving him problems. He had helped recruit the swimmer from Texas, and suspected he was making up his ailment because he didn't like the weight training the coaching staff had added onto the workouts. Going into the last phase of the season, the kid was swimming fast and complaining hard. The head coach was not pleased. The trainer worked with the kid's shoulder and cleared him to keep training. When the meeting was over, Ryan lingered in his office. He read the headlines on ESPN. Cleaned out his personal e-mail. He knew that once he got home, there would be no time for any of that—no time to rest, to breathe, to recharge for the next day.

When he got back to the apartment, Brooke was dressed in pink footie pajamas. She was sitting on the floor with her new doll. When she heard him, she dropped the doll, ran to him, and threw her arms around his legs. "Daddy!" she yelled.

Ryan eyed Olivia. She was sitting on the couch paging through *Newsweek* magazine, and she barely looked his way.

"Your dinner's on the table," she said. "You probably want to heat it up."

Ryan stepped over the doll, gave Olivia a kiss. He could feel the anger coming off her in waves.

"Sorry I didn't call to say I would be late," he said.

She shrugged.

"Remember that kid Tad I was telling you about? He claimed he had sore shoulders again. I had to talk with the trainer."

Brooke had padded off to her room and come back with *Harold and the Purple Crayon*, which she held up toward Ryan. "Read to me," she said.

He was starving. The last thing he'd eaten was a handful of almonds around three o'clock. It was eight o'clock now. "After I eat the dinner Mommy made," he said.

Brooke turned on her heel and faced Olivia. "Read to me," she said.

Olivia glared at Ryan. She stood up. She slapped the magazine on the coffee table. "Come on, pumpkin," she said, scooped up Brooke, and walked out of the room.

She had said only three words—*Come on, pumpkin*—but they contained a whole argument. Ryan could hear the whole thing as if it had been spoken word for word: *I've been with*

her all day, entertaining her all day, and I let her stay up past
her bedtime so that she could at least see you today, and the least
you could do is take ten minutes to read her a bedtime story.

He closed his eyes. He wondered how anyone survived
having a toddler. He wondered what his life would be like,
now, if Olivia had never come to him, trembling, and whispered, "I'm pregnant." He couldn't believe that he was twenty-
five years old, and responsible for not only himself, but two
other people besides. He thought about how his own father
had read him endless books when he was a boy—Richard
Scarry and Robert McCloskey and then Twain, Kipling, London. How had Tom had such energy at the end of the day?
How had he had the time? He heard Olivia's soft voice falling
into the rhythm of the story, and he wanted to go to his wife
and child, he wanted to cross the divide that separated him
from them, but he was hungry, he was tired, and he felt as
though he wouldn't be entirely welcome.

He cracked open a beer, and then heated up the bowl of
pasta left for him, and sat alone at the table. There was a pile
of mail there—a bill from the water company, a reminder that
he needed to get his teeth cleaned. In the pile was a letter from
his grandmother. Ryan recognized her cream-colored Crane
stationery and knew how heavy it would be when he picked
it up, and how the texture of her address, embossed on the
back of the envelope, would feel against his fingers. Eleanor
was always sending him clippings about swimmers who had
performed amazing feats, or about trips she thought he should

consider taking, or about an interesting wine she had tried on a trip to Seville or the Seychelles. Sometimes she just wrote little notes of encouragement—quotes from John Wooden, or from Coco Chanel. They always made him smile.

He opened the envelope and pulled out the card.

Dear Ryan,

I would like to give you and Olivia a gift for the New Year. It's a little late, I realize, but sometimes it takes me a while to hit on the right thing. I would like to buy you the services of a chef. I will leave it to you to select one that is appropriate, as I know that Olivia is very careful about what she eats. A check is enclosed.

Love,
Nana

Olivia came out of Brooke's room while he was still eating. He got up, went in to kiss Brooke good night, and then came back to his place at the table.

"So she saw you for, what? Three minutes today?"

"I said I was sorry," Ryan said.

"And you're leaving for a meet on Thursday, right? For three days."

"Yes," he said, and because he knew he was in trouble, he added, "Will you be okay?"

"It's actually easier when you're gone," Olivia said, and he felt as though a knife had been slipped in under his ribs, but he also recognized the truth in what she was saying. It was easier for him when he was gone, too. It was easier not to come home. Last week, he had actually stopped at a bar on the way home. There was a Patriots' game on, and he stopped in for one quick beer, but he found that the room was full of guys his age who hadn't yet married and women who didn't yet have pink children at home, and he stayed for a few hours, enjoying the relief, awash in the guilt.

"You're saying you'd rather I didn't come home?" he asked.

"No, I'm just stating a fact. It's easier when you're gone. Then we're not expecting you, we're not waiting up for you. I don't make a real dinner."

"Speaking of that," he said, and held out the card to her.

She read it without smiling. "So she's going to bail you out?"

"Bail me out?" Ryan asked. "She's trying to do something nice for us, Olivia. What the hell's wrong with that?"

"Sure, it's nice, but it lets you off the hook, doesn't it? You don't have to worry about coming home, you don't have to choke down the dinner I made with a screaming kid on my hip."

"Olivia," he said, "you're a great cook. This isn't a statement about your cooking."

"No, but I'm supposed to interview chefs? After I spend four hours transcribing tapes, take Brooke to the pediatrician, do the laundry, pick up all the toys in the house, and find a plumber?"

"You think I'm doing nothing all day?"

"I don't know what you do all day."

"You know what?" Ryan said as he went to the refrigerator for another beer. "I don't get you. You wanted a baby, you wanted to stay home with her," he said. "We're bending over backwards so you can do that. And here my grandmother has offered us this gift and you're pissy about it? What's the matter with you?"

"I didn't think I'd be a single mom," she said.

"A single mom doesn't have someone going out every day earning a living for her," he said.

"You think that's all I want from you? Money?"

"Seems pretty spot on to me."

She started to cry then, and went into the bedroom and shut the door.

Ryan had another beer, and turned on ESPN. He figured he wasn't welcome in bed with his wife, so he stayed on the couch, under a thin blanket, and in the morning, he took a shower and left for work without waking her up to say good-bye.

8

Eleanor

THE second week of January, the carcass of a blue whale washed ashore on Miramar Beach. Eleanor heard the news at swim practice at the Harbor Pool, and when Bob Shafer said he was going to drive down to the beach after their workout to see it, Eleanor went along.

She felt that the death of the whale was somehow personal. She first moved to Santa Barbara in 1966 when Union Oil began erecting the oil platforms in the channel. Her new husband, Elliot Taft, was in charge of communications for the company, and they wanted him on hand during the development phase. He sent out press releases about the technological advances being put to use and spoke to reporters about the numbers of barrels of oil being pumped every day. In 1969, there was a massive oil spill. There was a buildup of pressure on a Union Oil platform, and a rupture on the ocean floor. For eleven days, thick crude oil bubbled to the surface, creating an eight-hundred-mile slick, and a death trap for marine animals. The community rallied together to try to save the thousands of shore birds, whose feathers were matted with crude oil, who floundered in the black waves and on the contaminated beaches. College students, businessmen, hippies, society women, and surfers flocked to the beaches to lift the helpless birds into their cars and drive them to emergency treatment centers. The rest of the country watched, transfixed by the sight of the thick oil lapping on the beach and the army of people who refused to stand by and let the birds die.

Elliot was in charge of the heated public relations effort. He was part of the team that held press conferences and tried to minimize the damage being done by such a photogenic disaster. While Elliot was holed up in conference rooms and television studios, Eleanor and Lily, who was thirteen years old, went down to the beach to watch the rescue effort. Lily cried at the sight of seals and shorebirds covered in oil. She begged to join the swarm of people trying to help. Eleanor said no, but they kept returning to the beach to stand and stare—and finally, four days later, Eleanor relented; she put on a pair of blue jeans and a clean white pair of Tretorn tennis shoes, and took Lily down to Miramar Beach. They spent the afternoon lifting oil-covered seagulls and cormorants into the company car so that they could take them to the zoo for rescue. Eleanor and Lily were a very attractive pair—a petite girl with a thick black ponytail and tear-stained cheeks, and her slim, animated mother with a chic bob—and their picture was snapped by the *Santa Barbara News-Press*. It went out on the national wires—an emblem of the emblematic disaster—and Elliot was fired by the end of the week. When he packed to leave town, Eleanor refused to go with him.

"How can you just walk away from this disaster?" she asked.

"I was fired," he said. "I have no business here."

"I want to stay," she said.

"If you stay, our marriage is over," Elliot said.

Eleanor shrugged. Her marriage was already over. Elliot had divorced his first wife in order to marry Eleanor, but he had never actually given her up. All the upheavals happening in the world—the marches and the protests, the movements and the demand for equality—proved to Eleanor that she didn't need a husband, particularly not one like Elliot Taft. She owned a majority stake in Bertasi Linen. She still had money from Billy's life insurance policy. "Then so be it," she said.

THREE weeks later, before any papers had been filed or any actions taken, Elliot dropped dead of a heart attack in the driveway of his first wife's house. Eleanor flew back to Houston, baked the rum cake her mother always made when someone died, served it to well-wishers, and pretended that she was bereft. She wasn't, but neither was she completely relieved. Behind her back, Eleanor's friends chattered on about the bizarre circumstances of her husbands' deaths—two husbands, two bad hearts? Was there something more to it than mere coincidence? Secretly she wondered the same thing. Perhaps she wasn't meant to be loved.

ELEANOR sold the Houston house, and purchased a modern home in Santa Barbara—all white stucco and windows. She announced to the board of Bertasi Linen that she would be taking control of the business, moved the headquarters to State Street, and began a mission to woo more clients all over the world. She traveled everywhere, with samples of sheets tucked into her suitcase, and charmed hoteliers wherever she went. A year later, on the anniversary of the oil spill and on a day that would later come to be known as the first Earth Day, Eleanor took Lily on a whale watching boat in the Santa Barbara Channel. They cruised out to Santa Rosa Island, and on the way back, when they were in the middle of the shipping lane, a mother humpback whale and her calf approached the boat. The captain announced that he had to cut the engine because the whales had ventured so close. The boat floated free in the sea and the two whales came up to the boat, dove under, circled back, and then repeated their circuit again and again. For half an hour, the mother and baby swirled around them, and all the passengers on the boat scrambled to the railing to get a better view.

"Come on, Lily," Eleanor said, grabbing her daughter by the hand.

Lily refused to leave her seat. "I'm going to throw up," she said.

Eleanor led her to the small bathroom, and then dashed to the rail so she could see the whales. She felt the spray from the whale's blowholes, counted the barnacles on their rubbery skin, looked the mother directly in the eye when it poked its head out of the water. She was dazzled by their size and their grace and their presence in the ocean. For years, she and Lily would argue about the trip—with Lily saying how Eleanor had dragged her to a new city, away from her friends and her school, and dragged her away from a chance at having a normal family after her own dad had dropped dead; and then abandoned her in the middle of the ocean during her time of need. Eleanor would say how she had left her for only a moment, and that the experience of seeing the whales had been so precious to her that she would do the same thing again.

She was telling the truth: she would do the same thing again. But that didn't mean that she was proud of her behavior. She found being a mother agonizingly difficult. Other women seemed content to dote on their children, to spend hours in the kitchen making noodle casseroles and sewing pinafores and witch costumes. Eleanor couldn't sit still long enough for any of that. She could take Lily to the boulevards of Paris and to the small mill towns in Italy, and she could take her to museums and shops and parties—anything as long as she was moving—but sitting alone in a room, where the air stayed still and the hours ticked slowly by, made her feel trapped, and being trapped was something she couldn't bear.

She felt safest at work. She felt relieved when Lily went back East to college, and when she married Tom. She felt absolved, somehow, of responsibility for any life but her own.

THE road out to Miramar Beach was jammed. Eleanor and her swimming friends had to park nearly a quarter mile to the south. They could see the whale before they could smell it—a creature so big, it defied comprehension. It lay heavily in the sand. A group of people stood by its side, talking and gesturing to a woman who sat atop its back. This woman, who seemed to be the scientist in charge, was clad in a white tank top and yellow rubber overalls. It was a warm day, and her skin glistened with sweat. From time to time, she bent over and seemed to be whispering to the whale, as if she was coaxing it, and Eleanor had the sense that the whale might lift its head, turn over, and slip back into the sea.

She stopped on the road above the beach, and held her breath, and when she finally inhaled again, the smell hit her— salt and sand and the sweet, gut-twisting odor of decay. She looked out at the vast blue ocean and tried to imagine other whales out there, swimming and mourning. She scanned the crowd, who were dressed in bikinis and cover-ups, board shorts and flip-flops. Despite the fact that they were dressed for a day at the beach, she felt their collective grief and awe. No one was rushing toward the whale, hoping to touch the barnacles on its snout or look into its antediluvian eyes. No one was standing at the yellow tape, peppering the scientists with questions. Even the young children, who clung to their parents' hands or stood solemnly by their sides, had an aura of reverence about them.

Eleanor couldn't help it; she began to cry. Tears poured from her eyes, and she stood there silently thinking about her friends Gracie and Judy, and how death would be coming for them one day soon, too.

Bob, her friend from swimming, came up to her, and put his arm across her shoulders. "It's a hell of a thing," he said.

She reached up and squeezed his hand, and nodded.

"Would you like to go for lunch at the Nugget? Nothing like a great burger to soothe the soul."

"No, thank you, Bob," she said. "I need to be getting to the office."

"You ever going to stop working so hard?" Bob said.

"Why should I?" she said. "I love my business, and I have good people. Even my grandson works for me now, did you know?"

"You're something else, Eleanor," Bob said, and he shook his head and walked away.

THE next day after breakfast, Eleanor headed down the hill to the beach. This time she had to park even farther away. They were performing the autopsy of the whale right on the beach, as if the sand were a stage and the cars on the highway an audience. There were more people inside the yellow caution tape, and several trucks parked on the sand. There were bystanders near the rocks, people lining the road, and a slow stream of cars making their way along the highway, where the shimmer of heat rose in distorted waves. The scientists were stripping the skin on the whale's flank, revealing a wall of pure white blubber. Blood pooled in the sand. She guessed that they were looking for bruises and contusions, and that they would soon learn what the whale had eaten, how old it was, where it had traveled, and how, exactly, it had died. She felt a wave of affection for these men and women, and deep grief for the whale.

ON the way home, Eleanor stopped off at Vons to get the ingredients to make rum cake. It was the perfect cake to set out for guests, to take to a church reception hall, to leave off on a porch, but Eleanor wasn't going to do any of those things this time. After years and years of eating it and baking it, the cake defined comfort for Eleanor and she just wanted to smell it baking. It was an old-fashioned yellow cake, made from a boxed mix, baked in a Bundt pan, and soaked in butter, pecans, and Mount Gay Barbados Rum, which she had first tasted on the actual island of Barbados. She didn't cook much anymore. She never had, really. So she had to buy a bottle of vegetable oil, a bag of nuts, and a dozen eggs. She felt as though she were preparing for a siege.

While she was standing at the checkout line, she heard someone call her name. She turned around to see Gail and Ted Hailwood.

"I was going to call you tomorrow," Ted said as he fell into line behind her. "I've got another offer on the ranch. A movie producer. Seems pretty eager. You still want to move forward with the deal?"

WHILE the cake was in the oven, Eleanor called Lily back in Vermont. This was something Eleanor almost never did—called just to say hello. She usually called if there was a decision to make, some legal matter, a discussion about plane flights. Lily was immediately on guard.

"Do you remember the whale watching trip we went on when you were twelve?" she asked.

"Every minute of it," Lily said.

"A blue whale died in the channel yesterday. It washed up on a beach. I went down there to see it, and it got me thinking."

"About throwing up?"

"Lily, don't start . . ." Eleanor said.

Lily could hear the wounded tone in her mother's voice—a kind of neediness that was new, and that worried her. "Sorry," she said. "What did it get you thinking about?"

"It got me thinking about all the contrivances of being human," Eleanor said, because it was the closest she could come to saying what she was feeling about death and longing, and wanting her family nearby. "Whales don't worry about real estate and they don't plan funerals and they don't sit up at night fretting about the price of cotton. They just swim, you know? They just swim and then they die. I was envious."

Lily didn't know what to make of this phone call. It was so unlike her mother. It felt like some kind of confession, but Lily wasn't sure of what. "The whales are probably envious of you, too, Mom," she said, but then she replayed the conversation in her head and stuck on one of the phrases her mother had used: *worry about real estate.*

"Is something happening with the ranch, Mom? Because I haven't found the right time to bring it up with Tom. Things have been a little crazy here. They canceled Tom's only class this semester due to low enrollment and gave him more responsibility on the curriculum integration committee instead."

"I saw Ted Hailwood yesterday," Eleanor said. "He has another offer on the ranch. He needs an answer."

On the third day after the whale's death, Eleanor read in the morning paper that the scientists had concluded that the whale had been struck by a ship. Its bones had been crushed, its body bruised. It had probably been dragged for some time through the channel. The experts decided that the best course of action was to bury the carcass of the whale right on the beach, where bacteria and natural forces would break it down over time. Eleanor felt a sense of outrage as she imagined the whale, the biggest creature in the ocean, overcome by a thing that was a hundred times bigger, a thing that would only rust and never die. She thought about calling Gracie to tell her that the largest creature on earth was suffering from broken bones, too, but she decided against it. She decided to go back to the beach again instead.

When she pulled up alongside the rocks on the road, she saw a gangly bulldozer bent over a massive hole at the surf line. It reached out its long neck, grabbed a mouthful of sand, and spit it out into the hole. The carcass of the whale was no longer visible, although you could still sense its shape under the sand. Eleanor parked and got out and sat down on the rocks to watch the end of the hot day and the end of the drama. She sat there until the last rays of sunlight had disappeared, and when she stood to go, she paused to let her knees adjust, and then drove silently home.

SHE cut a slice of rum cake and called Gracie, even though it was late in New York. The home nurse answered, and it took some time for Gracie to come to the phone.

"I was just thinking about you," Eleanor said.

"Is this a deathwatch?" Gracie asked. "You're calling to see if I'm still here?"

"I'm calling to make plans for Opening Day," Eleanor said. "Did you hear where the game is going to be played?"

"Detroit?"

"Japan!"

"What in hell are they thinking?"

"Something about being ambassadors for the sport and letting Matsuzaka and Okajima play in their home country. It's looking like we'll be having the first ever Opening Day *breakfast*."

"You're talking about flying to Japan?" Gracie asked, and Eleanor could hear the resignation in her voice; Gracie could make the trip from New York to Boston, even if it killed her, but a trip to Japan was out of the question.

"I'm talking about having breakfast in Boston and watching the game. A six a.m. start, they say."

"Good lord."

"So do you think pancakes or hot dogs?"

"Hot dogs," Gracie said. "It has to be hot dogs. By the way, how's the new business venture going? The avocados."

"Slipping away," Eleanor said. "Due to inaction by certain parties."

"Ah. So you have no control over the family?"

Eleanor laughed bitterly. "No," she said. "I don't."

9

Lily

AFTER dinner, Lily asked Tom if he wanted to go for a walk in the snow. They put on their boots and their coats and gloves and walked out into the dark, cold night. They walked, as if by agreement, to the center of the central green. The wrought iron lamps along the pathways glowed in the cold air, and yellow light shone from isolated windows in the stately old buildings that lined the square. Someone had built a snow sculpture, with turrets and tunnels. Tom began to explore it, walking around to see where the entrances and the exits were. Lily just stood at the place where the paths crossed the green, and closed her eyes and felt the cold creep into her fingers and her toes.

She watched Tom poking around the snow tunnels. She loved him. She loved his constancy, his loyalty. She loved his green eyes, his methodical brain.

"Tom?" she called.

He came around a snowbank, and stood beside her, his breath visible in the air.

"Were you serious about wanting to own that avocado ranch in Santa Barbara?"

He laughed, and she could see his teeth—the gold crown on the back molar. "Is this a hypothetical question?"

"No, actually," she said. "It's not. My mother made an offer on it."

He shoved his hands deeper in his pockets, kicked his boot into the snow. "She did what?"

"She ran into Ted Hailwood, though I'm not entirely sure that it wasn't by design. She made an offer."

"Sounds like your mom."

"I know," she said, "but it also sounded tempting. To be near the boys again. To forget about curriculum integration and interactive textbooks and just . . . walk away and start something new. I was thinking it could be good for us."

"You're serious?"

"I was thinking about maybe getting a dog," she said, and hoped that the comment conveyed everything she felt about their marriage and their home and who they had become.

"A dog?" he said, peering at her. "Why a dog?"

"I miss the noise of a family," she said, "the energy. I miss the way we were with each other when we had all that. I guess I thought that the ranch and the dog would bring some of that back."

"If you want a dog, we could get a dog," he said.

"Tom, come on. That's not what I meant. What I want is something completely new, something that we can do together."

"It was a beautiful ranch," he said.

"So you'll think about it?"

He shrugged. "I will."

WHEN they got back to their house, Tom ripped off his jacket, and his sweater, and scratched at his forearms, which had bloomed with a scaly eczema as the temperature plummeted. Sometimes Lily would wake up at night because there was a movement, and a sound, and it would be Tom, sound asleep, scratching.

He asked Lily if she would like tea.

"Tea would be nice," she said.

He got the new teapot and filled it with water. While it was heating, he got out two of the stoneware mugs they had bought from a potter in Maine—two left out of a dozen—and unwrapped two tea bags. She didn't really know what was in Tom's heart. She knew that he liked chamomile tea with honey and oatmeal cookies with walnuts, and that he loved the first day of classes, when the students came in, so eager and young. She knew that skin rashes plagued him and that he got blisters in the summer when he gardened and that he pressed flowers and leaves between the pages of books and put them in envelopes and sent them to his granddaughter. But she knew, too, that even after twenty-six years of marriage, one person couldn't really know another.

Tom set the mugs on the table, then looked up at his wife. "You would really take your mother's money?"

"After an entire lifetime of turning it down?" Lily asked. "Of letting her stew in it and telling her I didn't need it, and didn't want it? I'm thinking I would."

"Why now?"

"Because I care more about making sure we're okay than I do about the power she might have over me."

"You would really just—go? It's so not like you."

"I know," she said. "But I think it could be good for us—for you and me."

Tom took her in his arms and pulled her into his warmth. "We're okay," he said.

"I know," she said, "but okay is never what I was after."

THE next day, she came home for dinner and found Tom sitting in the living room reading a book on tree grafting. Another on organic composting lay nearby, and she saw that he had printed out articles on the nutritional makeup of the avocado and the origin of guacamole.

He looked up. "Okay was never what I was after either," he said.

One call later, it was a done deal.

THEY listed their house with a woman who lived around the corner and told their department heads that they were resigning their duties. Tom's only class had already been canceled, so covering for him was a matter of finding someone else to head the curriculum integration committee—a physicist or a chemist. Lily had no classes that semester, and had the distinct feeling that the math department was secretly happy they were getting rid of a senior professor, whose salary was so costly. When Lily told her textbook editor that she was ceasing work on the interactive project, there was a flurry of phone calls to try to talk her out of it, but she was resolute. She just kept saying, "No," until there were no more questions, and no more calls.

Lily began to sort through their belongings. She started making piles in the basement—things to throw away, things to give away, and things to take with them. She kept calling Olivia out in San Luis Obispo.

"I found a ski jacket Ryan used to wear," she would say. "Can you use it for Brooke?" "I found a trophy Ryan won in college; do you have room for it?" "There's no reason to send out a sled, is there?"

Olivia could hear the excitement in her mother-in-law's voice, and she tried to stay upbeat as she said, "No, thank you," "I'll ask Ryan," and "I don't think so."

Tom was more difficult. He wanted to keep everything—towering stacks of *National Geographic*s, a trekking pole that no longer had a mate, and all his gardening tools, whether their handles were splintered, their tines were rusted, or their blades as dull as a piece of wood.

"It doesn't hurt anything to throw the stuff in the moving van," Tom said.

Lily disagreed. "Yes it does," she said. "We'll just have to sort it all out when we get to Santa Barbara. And besides, it's good to cast off old junk."

"To make room for new junk?"

She pointed to a floor mat that had mildewed during the last big storm. She'd washed it, bleached it, but the dark splotches remained. "You'd rather hold on to things like that?"

He shrugged. She had a point. "Okay," he said. "But this doesn't give you free rein to get rid of everything you always wanted me to get rid of. No secretly giving away my *National Geographics*."

She smiled. "As long as I get to take all my fabric."

THE second week in March, their colleagues threw Tom and Lily a party, and didn't bother to conceal their jealousy at their spontaneous departure.

"A gentleman farmer, eh?" Pat Cordoba said as he slapped Tom on the back.

"So you'll really have a view of the ocean?" Janet Barnes asked three separate times.

Marilyn came up to Lily, lowered her voice, and said, "What are you going to do, now that you've let the textbook go?"

"You make it sound like a crime, Marilyn."

"Not at all," Marilyn said. "I envy you. But I know you; you're not going to sit on your hands while Tom picks avocados."

She shrugged. "I've been thinking about making a quilt," she said.

"A quilt? I envy you," she said again, and Lily knew that her friend was not just talking about a creative undertaking. Lily and Tom were setting off on an adventure together. They had made a new plan together. They were, still, together.

"Take care of yourself, Marilyn," Lily said. "Don't let the faculty right out of grad school get you down."

Marilyn laughed, took Lily's hands in her own, and kissed her friend good-bye.

ONCE the house was completely empty, they walked through the rooms one last time, saying farewell to the views they had looked at for so many years, and following the paths their boys had followed as they learned how to walk, and standing on the raw dirt patch where the roots of the big elm tree had once grown.

Out of habit, Tom noticed all the things that needed

repairing—the water stain on the downstairs bathroom ceiling, the faded paint in the family room, the light in the basement that flickered when you turned it on. Lily looked one last time at the view from the living room window and at the backyard where Ryan had broken both his arms when he leapt off the swing from the top of its arc, where Luke had tried to plant dinosaurs, and where Tom had grown his peas and tomatoes.

"This was a good house," Lily said.

"Very good indeed," Tom agreed.

THEY spent their last few nights at the Sheraton, with a room that had a view of the lake. They had thrown out truckloads of things they no longer needed, given away bags of clothes. The furniture they were keeping—their dining table and chairs, the brass bed, the entry table with its inlaid wood edging, Hattie's old Singer sewing machine—was on a truck to California, along with seventeen plastic tubs of Lily's fabric and twenty-three boxes of books. Lily had the unsettling feeling that something was going to go wrong with the truck carrying all their possessions. She kept imagining that it wouldn't make it, somehow, to California, and that without all the furniture and fabric she had spent her whole life collecting and caring for, without her steadfast coats and shoes, without her well-aged sheets and wool blankets, she would feel adrift. She tucked a few things into her suitcase that she couldn't bear to lose—a tin sugar scoop Luke made in shop class, the small stone Ryan has presented to her after he and Tom and Luke finished their mountain climbing challenge, the Matisse tablecloth, and her grandmother's six yards of hand-embroidered French lace.

Before they went to sleep, Lily went over to where Tom was sitting in a green leather wingback chair, reading the town newspaper that had been neatly folded on the coffee table. She took the newspaper from his hands and laid it back down on the table. She sat on his lap, and leaned in to kiss him. He kissed her back more deeply. He lifted her up, and laid her down on the bed. He lifted her nightgown over her head, and she raised her hands to allow it. He ran his hands over her small breasts and her narrow hips, kissed her collarbone, then removed his own clothes and lay on top of her.

"You excited?" she said.

"About this," he said, "or about the move?"

"Both," she said.

He kissed her again, on the ears, the nose. "Yes," he said.

10

Eleanor

JUDY Vreeland died the first week of March. Gracie called to tell Eleanor the news, and to report that the funeral would be on Saturday and that Gordon was expecting them both. Within a few hours, Eleanor had a plane ticket, a room reserved at the Pierre, and her suitcase opened on her bed.

Eleanor was an expert at funerals. She had buried both her parents, all three of her husbands, a younger sister, and friends from every phase of her life. She knew that the worst possible thing a guest could do was to show up in a somber black outfit, sip chardonnay, and say in a whispered voice how sorry they were for the person's loss. For the funeral of Judy Vreeland, Eleanor packed a claret-colored, formfitting knit dress, patent leather slingbacks, and a pair of chandelier diamond earrings. She sat in St. Thomas Church on Fifth Avenue and listened to the soaring hymns and the raspy readings of

Corinthians 12 and to the old relatives cough and wheeze, and then afterward, she went straight to the bar at the Pierre and ordered a scotch. She delivered it to Gordon discreetly while he stood in a receiving line listening to a blue-haired lady wax on about losing her husband in the war. Gordon winked, mouthed *thank you*, and then Eleanor went to find Bucky Harrington and Gracie Dooley to talk about the Red Sox's abysmal performance in the play-offs.

Gracie found her first. "You owe me five bucks," she said.

"Whatever for?"

"On the day Gordon married Judy in 1956, you bet me that it wouldn't last."

Eleanor took a sip of scotch. "Why on earth did you take such a sucker bet?"

Gracie shrugged. "I always like a long shot."

"And why would you still remember it fifty-two years later?"

"I never forget a bet," Gracie said.

Eleanor opened her beaded evening bag and pulled out a five-dollar bill. "Well, you certainly earned it," she said, handing over the cash. "Gordon never so much as looked at another woman in all these years."

"Poor thing," Gracie said. "He looks horrible. He looks downright bereft."

"I guess that's the price you pay for love," Eleanor said, and Gracie looked at her and shook her head and laughed.

Bucky Harrington walked up then, and kissed each woman

on the cheek. "Evening, ladies," he said. "How nice of you to come to mourn the Red Sox." Bucky had been the pitcher for the Harvard baseball team, a member of the original Great Date, and he was now a congressman from Massachusetts.

"We're in Yankee territory," Gracie said.

"Ah, but the failures of the Sox are so colossal they cannot be contained," Bucky said.

"Quite true," Eleanor said, "quite true. Were you at Game 7 last year?"

"I'm at every game," Bucky said. "It's part of my job description. Mingle with the constituents, you know."

"I should run for Congress," Eleanor said. "It's the cushiest job in America."

"No one in Congress is as beautiful as you, my dear. You'd be out of your league. And the pay cut would kill you."

Eleanor laughed. "You flatter me, Bucky," she said. "Which is why I adore you."

THE after-memorial party went on into the night. There were crab cakes, buttermilk rolls, and chocolate cake, and toasts and speeches by the family. Everyone talked about how sweet Judy had been, how loyal, how generous. Eleanor sat listening and thought that Judy probably deserved such praise. Judy was the perfect housewife, a Betty Crocker mom. She organized bridge games, ran the charity ball at the hospital, deferred to her husband when asked her opinion on everything from finance to what color to paint the walls. Judy had been all the things girls in their generation were raised to be, all the things Eleanor could never bear. When the crowd thinned, Eleanor got up from the table where her old friends still sat.

"Brunch at eight a.m. tomorrow," Gracie said. "And then the Cézanne show at the Met."

"I'm looking forward to it," Eleanor said, and went to find Gordon.

HE was standing near the bar, trapped by a plump woman in a pantsuit. He was much taller than she was—he was taller than most everyone—and he had to stoop and turn slightly to hear her with his good ear. His shirt was clean and crisp and his wingtips were polished enough to pass inspection, but his eyes were sad and drawn, and the skin of his face seemed as if it had been drained of color. He looked like a general who had carefully dressed to sign the treaty of his own defeat. He pulled himself away from the woman by saying, "Excuse me, Gwen," and stepping toward Eleanor.

He held out his big hands, palms up, and she placed her small hands in his. He pulled her toward him, and when they embraced, she could smell Ivory soap and starch, and she had the thought that Gordon smelled like a whole era—that his scent defined the whole generation of people who had gone to college before anyone had even dreamed of the sixties and who were growing old in the age of YouTube.

"Thank you for the scotch," he said, "and for coming all this way. It means the world to me."

She pulled back and looked up at him. "It was a lovely service," she said, "and believe me, I've been to a lot of funerals, so I would know."

Gordon laughed, a tired laugh that belied his exhaustion. "I guess you would," he said. He fidgeted with the change in his pockets, and with his keys. "I dread it being over, actually."

"Today?" she asked.

He nodded, and swallowed, and tried to hold back the tears.

"You don't have to be brave," Eleanor said.

He looked away. "I've had to be brave all my life."

"And you've been good at it, Gordon. But you're almost seveny-five years old. Your wife just died. You can stop."

He laughed. "You make it sound so easy."

"It can be," she said. "When everyone goes home, we'll go on a walk. We'll walk down to the Oak Room and have a drink. And we'll see if they can conjure up a rum cake. It works wonders."

"That would be nice," he said.

She smiled. She remembered seeing Gordon for the first time standing under the porte cochere at Tower Hall in the fall of 1951. He was the tallest of the group of boys, with arms that looked like crooked wings, and a shy smile. Her eyes passed over him that day and settled on Billy, a boy who had grown more quickly into his skin and whose feet seemed like less of a liability. She considered herself fully mature at age eighteen and wasn't interested in a boy like Gordon who was a work-in-progress. But now such distinctions were irrelevant. Gordon was one of the last of her oldest best friends.

At eleven o'clock, they stepped out of the Pierre and headed south down Fifth Avenue. They hadn't gone half a block when Gordon stopped, and gasped. He buried his face in his hands, and slumped against the limestone wall. "How will I live without her?" he sobbed.

Eleanor didn't answer the question. She was a good nine inches shorter than Gordon, even in her heels. She stepped toward him, and embraced him, and then she pressed her hand on his back to guide him back to the Pierre, where she asked the doorman to hail them a cab.

They sat on either side of the backseat as the cab slipped through the streets of Manhattan. Gordon looked out the window on his side, and Eleanor looked straight ahead at the stoplights and the buildings and the people. When they got to Seventy-third Street, the driver opened the door for Eleanor, and Gordon fished in his pocket for a tip while the doorman waited without a trace of curiosity on his face.

"Evening, sir," he said. "Evening, ma'am."

"Evening, Marvin," Gordon said.

"Everything okay, Mr. Vreeland? With the evening and all?"

Gordon turned to the man who had served him and his wife steadfastly for the past seven years. He reached out and put his hand on the doorman's shoulder, and his face screwed up in pain.

"It was a fine funeral," Eleanor said. "Judy would have approved."

When they got to his apartment, Gordon opened the door and went to the couch and folded himself forward, his elbows resting on his knees, and his head resting in his hands.

"Do you still keep the liquor in the dining room?" Eleanor asked crisply, as if she were about to dress a wound—an actual tear in the flesh, an insistent flow of blood.

He nodded.

Eleanor clipped across the walnut floors in her heels. She had been in this apartment ten years ago for Gordon's retirement party and not much had changed. The dining room chairs had been refinished in a bold blue-green brocade and the walls were painted a deep navy blue. There was a new photographic portrait of the entire Vreeland family on the wall over the fireplace. Every member of the family, from the smallest baby to Gordon himself, was dressed in khakis and a plain black shirt. They were a handsome group—predominantly blond and tall with straight noses, strong chins, and good teeth.

Eleanor brought back a silver tray that held a crystal decanter of scotch and two highball glasses. "Did you eat anything at the Pierre?" she asked.

Gordon waved his hand through the air as if eating were a trifle he couldn't be bothered with.

"I'll call the doorman," she said.

"I'm fine," he said.

"Pizza? Steak? Soup? What sounds good?"

"Soup," he said. "Coconut lime soup."

"Thai?"

"Thai Palace. Marvin will know what I mean."

While Eleanor called for food, Gordon took his keys and his phone out of his pocket and set them on the table, loosened his tie and unbuttoned the top button of his shirt, and slipped his feet out of his shoes. When he sat back, his phone rang. He watched it ring three, four, five times, then reached to pick it up.

"Hello?" he said. "Yes, of course. No, I'm fine. Okay. Right. Thank you. I have another call, Joel. I'll call you later."

He paused, then launched into a similar conversation: "Hello? Fine. Yes, thank you. Okay."

He set the phone back down on the table, then shoved it across the glass as if it were a hockey puck.

"People are so nice," he said, as if it were a condemnation.

Eleanor picked up Gordon's phone and turned it off, and then she fished in her beaded evening bag for her phone and turned it off and set it beside his.

"People don't like death," she said. "It makes them uncomfortable."

"Why do you think that is?" Gordon asked.

"Lack of imagination, I suppose," she said. "They can't see what will come next."

A short while later their food arrived. They sat on the couch and drank their scotch and sipped their soup, and talked about Judy and their children and the grandchildren, and how one had autism and one was born with a missing toe, and they talked about the Red Sox and the Yankees, and about the exhibit of Edward Weston photos that had been at the Getty in Los Angeles, and how the price of real estate in Santa Barbara was relatively affordable again. Eleanor got up to make coffee sometime after midnight, but when she came back out to the living room, Gordon was asleep on the couch. She found the linen closet, got a blanket, and laid it over him. She got another blanket and curled up in a nearby wing chair, where she could watch the lights of the city twinkle, and where the light from the reading lamp wouldn't fall on her friend. There were news-papers in a basket by the coffee table, with crosswords that were not yet done. She sat there keeping watch, trying to crack a code that had something to do with college sports teams.

When the sun began to rise, Eleanor got up, splashed water on her face, and went downstairs to ask the doorman where to buy bagels. It had rained during the night and the streets were damp. The air was full of the smell of just-wet cement, freshly liberated dust, and damp garbage. There were people out walking their dogs, and people jogging with gloves on their hands, hats on their heads, and iPods in their ears. There was nowhere better in the world to be on the day after a funeral, Eleanor thought, than New York City. Life was relentless here, on full display. Someone may have died, but someone else would be up at the crack of dawn boiling dough to make the perfect crust on a bagel. She said good morning to the businessman who held the door open for her, and stepped into the light and the heat of the bagel store. Its windows were steamed, and there were four people standing in line at the counter, and two others reading the paper at small tables. She bought a dozen bagels that were still warm from the oven, a tub of cream cheese, lox, and two tall coffees.

The doorman at Gordon's building held the door for her, pressed the elevator button for her, and bade her to send his condolences to Mr. Vreeland. Gordon, however, was still asleep on the couch. He looked so still and seemed so silent that Eleanor got down close to him to make sure that he was still breathing. She could see the flattened tops of his teeth, the gold fillings in his molars, the white hairs in his nose, the places where his skin seemed translucent. She didn't miss living with a man. She didn't miss having a man come home on Friday night to say that they would be having eight people for brunch the next morning. She didn't miss having to talk to the dull wives of men her husband found interesting. She liked spending long hours in her own company, having the entire crossword puzzle to herself, being able to invite whomever she wanted to a party.

She put the food on the coffee table, and felt suddenly very tired. She sat back in the wing chair, pulled the blanket over herself, closed her eyes, and fell asleep.

WHEN she awoke, it was after noon and she was starving. Gordon had showered, eaten a bagel, folded the blanket, and was sitting on the couch with the unfinished crossword puzzle.

She sat up abruptly. "I must have fallen asleep."

"Three hours that I know of," he said, and lowered the paper.

"Three hours! What time is it?"

"Twelve thirty."

"Oh no!" she said, and stood up. "Did Gracie call? I was supposed to meet her for brunch."

Gordon smiled and shrugged. "You turned off the phones, remember?"

"My glory!" she said, and reached to flip her phone on.

Gordon reached forward, clutched her wrist, and said, "Don't."

"Don't?"

"Please. It's been so peaceful."

She sat back. "Okay," she said cautiously. "So you must have slept, too?"

"I did. I think that's the longest I've slept in six months. I'd forgotten how good it feels."

Eleanor nodded toward the crossword puzzle folded on the table in front of him. "Did you figure out the one about North Carolina? Peter Collins is diabolical."

Gordon put on his glasses, picked up the paper, scanned the crossword, and read aloud: "'Jacket material for a mixed-up North Carolina athlete.' Well," he said, "North Carolina are the Tar Heels. Letterman jackets are made of leather. You can get 'leather' out of 'Tar Heel.'"

She reached for the paper to verify his entry on 38-Across. "Impressive," she said.

"I spent an hour on it. I kept wanting to shout out to Judy for help, but then I'd look up and I'd see you sleeping there and I'd remember that she was dead. She's died a hundred deaths this morning."

"That doesn't sound very peaceful."

"It was," he said, and looked straight into her eyes. "Thanks to your being here."

Eleanor felt the heat of his gaze, and she blushed. She raised a hand to her cheek as if she could feel the heat there. Gordon reached out and took her hand and pulled it toward him and pressed his lips to the back of her hand. Her skin was dry and speckled with age spots, and his lips were thin and dry, too, but his lips lingered on her skin and he stared into her eyes, and she recognized that look of longing and desperation and thought, *Oh no.*

•11•

Lily

When Tom and Lily got to Santa Barbara, they slept in Eleanor's guest room and borrowed her sedan until Tom's truck and the Subaru arrived from Vermont. They drove over to their new house, and stood on the deck in the sunshine, looking down at the avocado trees and at the ocean far below, and walking through the empty rooms, thinking of where their furniture would fit and how their lives would be in those rooms. Later that afternoon, Lily offered to drop Tom off at the warehouse while she went out to buy a doormat, a dish drainer, a garbage can, a broom. It was a gorgeous drive along East Valley Road, with its towering eucalyptus trees, fruit trees, and horse ranches, and then they popped out onto the freeway that ran along a cliff above the ocean. The water sparkled in the afternoon sunlight, and across the channel were the islands—Santa Cruz and Santa Rosa.

"Calavo is like a co-op," Tom had explained. "We agree to

sell our fruit to them and they sort it and weigh it and ship it out to retailers. We split the profit, which rises and falls, of course, with demand. Our first harvest should be in about a month."

"That sounds great," Lily said, although she wasn't really paying attention. Her head was full of thoughts about the new house, the drive, the view.

"The Hailwoods didn't try to maximize yield. Nadine says she thinks I should be able to double it, no problem, and that's even taking into account a switch to organic, which will cause a drop in yield as a matter of course."

"Nadine?" Lily asked.

"Our Calavo rep. The one I've been talking to on the phone. She seems like a really nice gal."

Lily knew, before she even stepped into the warehouse, what Nadine would look like. Perhaps not the details, but the type. And she was exactly right. Nadine was about twenty-four years old. Her long red hair was pulled back into a ponytail, her plaid flannel shirt flapped open over a braless blue tank top, her colorless Birkenstocks were caked with mud. She had probably been an environmental studies major, the kind who would hang around Tom's office, soaking up his knowledge, hoping to win his favor.

"How nice to finally meet you!" Nadine sang out when Tom introduced himself.

"Tom's been talking about how much you're helping him learn the ropes," Lily said.

Nadine beamed. "You'll love the community of avocado growers. We're a tight group. We all really look out for each other."

Lily looked across the warehouse, to the industrial scales, the crates of fruit, the skip loaders. This was a temple, and these were the tools of worship. She understood that. She had been in such places many times before, but they were warehouses where fabric was milled and loomed, or living rooms where quilts were being stitched, and where the language spoken had to do with color and pattern, thread and weave. That was a world she knew and loved. She thought back to the summer when she met Tom, in a tiny town called Gothic, on the western slope of the Rockies. He was interning at the Rocky Mountain Biological Labs, and she was taking a break from her graduate studies in Denver to meet a famous weaver who she thought might have something important to teach her about fabric and geometry. Her name was Jenny Wood, and she wove intricate silk twill in the cramped second story of an unassuming wooden shed. Three large looms were positioned in that space, and when Lily saw them crammed together, with spools of yarn set on shelves up under the eaves, she thought of a ship built in a bottle.

"How did you get your looms up here?" Lily asked, thinking of the dirt road, the narrow staircase.

"We built them in this room. My husband, Jacques, and I."

"He's a weaver, too?"

"No, no," Jenny said, "a biologist. He runs the labs in the summer. That's why we come."

Jacques came home that afternoon with one of his graduate students—Tom, a tall, serious young man with a beard and a sunburned face. The moment Tom stepped in the door of the ramshackle house, Lily could feel the high mountain air change, and she wanted to laugh at how improbable it was that in this unassuming cabin in the woods, there were both sophisticated looms and the possibility of love. She smiled at Tom as if she had a secret, and he shook her hand and peered at her. "Do I know you?" he asked.

"I don't think so," she said.

"From Columbia?"

"No," she said, and shook her head. "I went to school in Boston."

"You seem very familiar," he said.

She smiled again. "I know what you mean."

They picked lettuce and tomatoes from the sloping garden out the back door, and while Lily washed the lettuce, and dried it and tore it, Tom stood next to her in the tiny, narrow kitchen, slicing the tomatoes with the precision of a surgeon, and sprinkling coarse pepper and rock salt on them as if he were performing some kind of ancient ritual. She wanted to stop and gape at the dirt under his fingernails, at his elegant hands. She wanted to sit and simply watch. She had traveled all over the world with her mother, visiting beautiful hotel properties and soaring cathedrals, but she felt that evening as if she had traveled to the ends of the earth—to another place and time—and she felt, at long last, at home.

They talked about vegetables and garden pests, about research funding and the job market for mathematicians. They argued about *Star Wars,* and what was going to happen to the relationship between Luke and Leia in the sequel. They stood around Jenny's looms, and watched her demonstrate how archeologists could prove from the pattern in the weft that as far back as the Neolithic era, women worked together to weave cloth. They sat in chairs on the dirt in the front of the house and watched the last licks of daylight fade out from the sky and the mountains cloak themselves in dark, brooding shadows.

Tom paid Lily no special attention. He was, after all, a somewhat shy young man at dinner with his boss. A little after ten, Tom stood and said that he had to go back to his bunk to get some sleep. Lily stood, too, worried sick that she would never see him again. "I suppose I should be going, too," she said. Her mind was racing to come up with something to say, some reason for them to have to meet again.

They said their thank-yous and good-byes to Jenny and Jacques, and walked down the dirt path to the dirt road where Lily's car was parked. While she dug her key out of her bag, Tom looked at his mud-caked shoes. "If, uh, you're free tomorrow afternoon," he said, "there is a little waterfall about three miles from the research center. I've been following the blooming patterns of the columbines up there."

She had to try hard not to throw her arms around him. "I'd like that," she said. "Very much."

He turned and walked off into the night, and she drove in the other direction through the aspen groves and back to the main town of Crested Butte, singing "Rocky Mountain High" at the top of her lungs.

THAT first week in Santa Barbara reminded Lily of those five days in Gothic. They each had only a suitcase full of clothes, and the few possessions that they had decided to carry with them on the plane. They knew virtually no one in town, had nowhere they had to be. On Monday, they went up to the new house and walked through the orchard and picked a crate full of avocados. On Tuesday morning, when it was still dark, they got up and walked the six blocks from Eleanor's town house to the Farmer's Market.

"Why are you going so early?" Eleanor asked.

"That's when the farmers arrive," Tom said, "and the chefs. That's when the real action takes place."

"How does he know that?" Eleanor asked.

Lily shrugged. "That's just Tom."

They picked out yellow heirloom tomatoes with veins of green, tomatillos with paper skin, bulbs of garlic that smelled like heaven, sweet Maui onions, lemons, limes, cilantro, and five kinds of hot peppers. They watched one chef move through the market at the speed of light, buying bushels of vegetables with the flick of his fingers, and another who moved slowly, touching, smelling, tasting everything before she laid down her cash.

Back in Eleanor's kitchen, Lily made coffee while Tom set out his recipes on the marble countertops.

"Avocados," he pronounced, "have been prized for centuries for their high fat and protein content."

Lily minced garlic, grated lemon zest, and listened to Tom go on.

"When the Spaniards came and conquered the Aztecs, they believed guacamole to be an aphrodisiac."

"Those Spaniards were evil, but clever," Eleanor said.

Tom sent Lily out to buy organic, full-fat sour cream, fresh tortilla chips, and a six-pack of Tecate. At lunchtime, he had six different types of guacamole arranged on the countertops, and rating cards for each one. How was the texture, the taste, the balance of flavors, the heat? They ate and debated, and could not agree—but later, when it mattered, they would remember exactly the mix of lemon and spice in the particular mix that Tom most adored.

•12•

Eleanor

WHEN the moving truck arrived, Eleanor came to stand in silent witness with Lily and Tom as the men moved the furniture and the boxes from the truck into the house. The movers were experts; they lifted and turned furniture through doorways and hallways as if they had navigated those exact corners a hundred times.

"Where do you want these?" one of the men asked, hefting a Rubbermaid tub in the air.

Lily glanced at Tom. They had decided to turn the big room off the kitchen into a study, but it was the place where Lily planned to sew as well. She would set up a machine in there, and an ironing board. She would put cork board on one wall so that she could pin up swatches, move around pattern and color. She would be able to work while looking out across the avocado trees, and the ocean, and she would know that Tom was out there, examining bugs, measuring water levels, talking to the trees. She wanted her fabric nearby. It made her feel safe, protected, settled. It made her feel a sense of possibility. "Is the garage okay?" she asked Tom. Her containers would take up so much room that they wouldn't be able to park a car inside; they wouldn't be able to install a workbench.

"Fine," he said, smiling, "but only because I've got the shed."

The men began to parade by with the tubs. "Is *all* of this fabric?" Eleanor asked.

"It's like you and shoes," Lily said.

"You can wear shoes," Eleanor said. "Fabric just sits there collecting dust."

"That's what the tubs are for."

"What's *in* them?"

Lily pictured her green-blue tub, her orange tub, her fuchsia tub, each with gorgeous printed cottons in complementary shades. There were tubs with nothing but black-and-white geometric prints, tubs filled with wool from the Scottish highlands that was so dense it would resist water in a driving rain. There were tweeds and gauzy chiffons, dots and stripes and solids. "Just fabric," she said.

"It's just like my mother," Eleanor said. "I never understood it."

Lily looked at her mother—at the lines that fanned out from her eyes, at her earlobes weighed down by silver earrings, and her sun-spotted skin. "It's because you never learned to sew," she said, and then lowered her voice and added, "which I always thought was strange."

"My father owned a mill," Eleanor said. "He wanted so badly to make it in the world, and he understood how much depended on appearances. My mother never did. She insisted on sewing her own clothes. She'd go to Boston's fanciest parties in a homemade gown. Other wives wore the latest outfits from Filene's or Bonwit Teller, but she insisted on homemade. She never understood how society judged her for it, and how it embarrassed my dad."

"And you?" Lily asked. "It embarrassed you?"

"Of course it did," Eleanor said.

They stood there, watching the parade of tubs go by as if it were a river and they were watching from the bank. Tom walked in with a floor lamp. He plugged it in, then unplugged it, moved it across the room, and plugged it in again.

After a while, Lily said, "I was proud of the clothes Grandma made me."

"That was obvious," Eleanor said.

"I carried her lace on the plane with me," Lily said, "because it's one thing I couldn't bear to lose."

"A piece of old lace?"

"It's not just lace," Lily said. "It's our family history. Does that mean nothing to you?"

Eleanor shook her head. "No," she said. "It doesn't. It's only proof of how stubborn my mother was."

"Stubborn? I think it's sentimental. A man brings this piece of fabric home from the war for his wife, who dies before she ever sees it, and his daughter can never bear to make anything from it because it is so precious to her. She can't even bear to make her own wedding dress. I love that story."

"Being sentimental," Eleanor said, "doesn't get you anything in this world."

"Maybe the point isn't to get something, Mom. It's just to *feel* something. To hold that lace in your hands and feel something."

Eleanor had been excited that Lily and Tom were moving to town. But standing there watching those tubs go by, she wondered if her excitement had been misplaced. What, besides blood, bound them together? Lily was not a woman Eleanor would choose as a friend. She was her daughter, but they were nothing alike. Eleanor would never hold on to a piece of fabric for fifty years just because of the story it carried in its threads. She would never have stayed married to someone as long as Lily had stayed married to Tom. Being that sentimental, after all, left you wide open for all kinds of hurt. "Feeling," Eleanor said, "is overrated."

Lily burst out laughing. "You're impossible, Mom."

ON their second Saturday, Eleanor hosted a welcome party. She invited people to Tom and Lily's back deck for cocktails and grilled scallops, stuffed mushroom caps, and endive with herbed cream cheese. Eleanor's employees were there, and her friends from the museum, and her friends from the pool, and

Lily and Tom's new neighbor, Mary Hazelton, who lived in the house down the hill. Two women whom Lily had known in high school came, and after reminiscing about the time one of them wrote a paper on the history of the ukulele and about how good the peanut butter cookies in the cafeteria had been, they invited her to play bunco with them on the first Tuesday of the month. The Hailwoods stopped by, and raised a toast and said how glad they were that Lily and Tom had come. Nadine arrived with two men from the warehouse. Her hair was washed, her jeans clean, a bra still not visible under her beaded tunic.

Lily smiled and shook Nadine's hand and offered her wine.

"Just water," Nadine said sweetly. "Thanks." Lily wondered briefly why Nadine didn't drink wine. Was she a recovering alcoholic? Or did it give her migraines, the way it did Lily? Before she could start a conversation, another woman rushed up to her and said, "Lily? I'm Shilpa. I'm Eleanor's yoga instructor at the club, and I've found the perfect dog for you."

Lily watched Nadine make her way toward Tom, who was leaning against the railing and looking out over the sweep of water.

"It's an Australian shepherd," Shilpa said, "about ten years old. From a family who will be moving to Brussels next week. This dog will love it up here on the hill."

Lily smiled. "We've never had an Australian shepherd," she said. "Ours were always German."

"This is a special dog," Shilpa said. "She has one milky blue eye and one brown. A spirit dog. A protector."

Lily continued to watch Tom talking to Nadine. "A protector?" she asked. "That sounds good."

13

Lily

BUNCO turned out to be a simple game of probability, and the point of the evening seemed to be to complain about men. One woman's husband had recently walked out on her because he had fallen in love with her sister. Another woman had just hired a detective because she suspected her husband was carrying on with someone at work. And then there was the endless parade of powerful men in politics who had fallen for their interns, their secretaries, a call girl, another man's wife. "Men are all a bunch of assholes," someone said, and Lily was jolted from her complacence.

She set down her wine. She looked at the woman who had just made the proclamation. "Not all," she said.

The room went quiet. Everyone looked at her and waited for an explanation. Were men in Vermont different from men in California?

"It's just that I know a lot of good men," she said. "Men who would never cheat on their wives."

"Just give 'em time," someone said. There was laughter, and more wine was poured, and Lily's defense was soon forgotten.

But her old friends from high school had gotten to her. Over the next few weeks, she couldn't help but notice how eager Tom was to ask Nadine for help, how eager she was to give it. One night, Tom and Lily were slated to have dinner with Eleanor, and Tom stayed late at the warehouse to help Nadine with some formulas for compost. He called Lily at the house. "Go on without me," Tom said. "I'll come by later."

Lily drove down the hill to her mother's house, and sat nervously while Eleanor prepared gazpacho and chilled shrimp salad she had picked up from the gourmet deli. She felt as if she were on trial, sitting there without Tom.

"Where's Tom?" Eleanor asked.

"At the warehouse," Lily said, "with some of the other growers. He can't get enough of it. He loves it so much." She had told her tale, and her mother had believed it, but Lily could barely touch her food. She hadn't known Tom was tired of her headaches. She hadn't known that Tom wanted to be a farmer. Maybe she didn't know a whole lot else about Tom as well.

TEN days after their arrival, they met Shilpa on a Wednesday evening at the animal shelter in Goleta—Tom and Lily, and Eleanor, who had never owned a dog, but still considered herself an expert in identifying good disposition. The shelter was a small bungalow, with a maze of dog runs out the back, and the moment they stepped outside, the dogs started to howl.

"She's waiting for you," Shilpa said of the Australian shepherd. "I told her you were coming. Her name is Luna."

Tom looked at Lily and she smiled, because she knew that Tom didn't believe that dogs could understand human speech, although he believed they could understand something else about humans—their moods, their desires, their souls. Eleanor saw the look pass between Tom and Lily and felt a flash of envy at that kind of wordless communication, that depth of understanding between two people. She'd never had it. She wondered what it was like.

Luna was large, with three colors of fur spreading out across her head and chest. She had brown speckles on a white muzzle, and just as Shilpa had described, one milky blue-white eye, and one brown one. She came right up to them when they opened the door, and licked Tom's hand, and nuzzled Shilpa's leg, and circled Lily and Eleanor with her tail wagging.

"The family says she's high-spirited. She chases blackbirds. She apparently likes Popsicles."

Tom knelt down to look more closely in the dog's mismatched eyes, and to look at her teeth and her paws. "She's beautiful," he declared.

"I told you that she's ten years old," Shilpa said, "didn't I? Her life expectancy is about four more years."

Lily nodded. "That's okay," she said, "because we're old, too."

Eleanor coughed in an exaggerated way, as if to say, *If you're old, then what am I?*

"You could count your age in dog years, Eleanor," Tom said, "and no one would be the wiser."

They all laughed, and walked back to the front office to complete some paperwork, and to pick up Luna's dog dish and leash. There was a man behind the counter, who hadn't been there before. He looked up. "Lily Peters," he said, and grinned. "I'd recognize that smile anywhere. What the hell are you doing here?"

It was Jack Taylor. She hadn't seen him in thirty-four years but she would have recognized him anywhere, too. He was fit and tan. His blond hair had gone gray and was cropped close to his head. He squinted out from blue eyes that had spent a lifetime looking into the sun. In high school, Jack used to skip classes when the winter swells were breaking at Miramar Beach, and Lily, who went to class even when she was sick, would note his absence as if part of her own body were missing. She rarely spoke to him, would have sworn that he hadn't known who she was—the small, pale girl who was devoted to math and never went to dances.

"Oh," Lily said, feeling nervous again. Her heart was beating hard in her chest. "We just moved back, actually. My husband, Tom, and I." Lily glanced at Tom, who was holding the dog on a tight leash. "This is Jack," she said. "Jack Taylor. We went to high school together."

"She used to beat the crap out of me in math," Jack said.

"She tends to do that," Tom said, smiling.

"And this is my mom," Lily added, waving her arm toward Eleanor.

"What a pleasure," Eleanor said, holding out her hand as if Jack might kiss it. He leaned over the counter, took her hand, and pumped it.

Lily remembered exactly the feeling of walking into calculus and looking forward to seeing Jack. He used to sit slumped in his desk chair, his long hair flopping, but whenever Dr. B called on him, Jack had the answer. He couldn't be tripped up. Lily used to love the power play between teacher and student, and would secretly cheer for Jack. It was far more interesting to listen to the two of them wrestle with math than it was for Lily to give Dr. B exactly what he was looking for, and to receive his empty praise. "Did you go into math?" Lily asked. "After high school? I always thought you might."

Jack laughed. "I went into surfing," he said.

"Did you?" Lily said. She wasn't sure whether or not he was kidding.

Shilpa chimed in to explain. "Jack's head of the sports ambassador program for Patagonia," she explained. "He travels all over the world for them."

"Shilpa," Jack teased, trying to call her off, "what's the harm in these people thinking I'm just a surf bum?"

Shilpa lowered her voice and, in a theatrical whisper, said, "He's actually a VP. He has an office at the headquarters in

Ventura. And he volunteers with stray dogs every other Sunday. He's no maverick."

"I *surf* the big water at Maverick, baby," Jack said with a sly grin. He turned his gaze on Lily, and she felt his eyes boring straight into her, and her cheeks grow hot. "And you?" he asked. "What brings you back to paradise?"

"Avocados," she said. "We bought an avocado ranch up near Sheffield Drive."

"You're a rancher, then?"

"Tom taught biology at the University of Vermont for twenty years," she said. "This is a second career."

Jack nodded. "Nice," he said, and stood up and came around to rub the dog behind her ears. "And now you're taking home this great shepherd. She's a beauty."

"She really is," Tom said.

Lily felt suddenly embarrassed, with Jack standing so close to her on one side, and Tom so close to her on the other. She could lean one way and brush the skin of her husband's arm, and that was accepted, allowed, and she would feel nothing but the familiarity of his touch. She could lean the other way the same number of inches, and brush the skin of this former golden boy, and that was illicit, forbidden, and she would feel . . . what? She didn't know. She had never dared such a thing. She was appalled that the question had even entered her head—and sickened by what the bunco ladies would say about it—and couldn't wait to get out of that dog shelter and away from Jack.

"See you at the beach," Jack said, and Lily knew that he must say the phrase to everyone he met, that it was as benign as saying, *Have a nice day, we should have lunch,* but she found herself thinking about Tom meeting Nadine for lunch, and Tom working late with Nadine at the warehouse. She found herself thinking about Jack.

Before they even made it to the car, Eleanor spoke up. "I don't remember that boy from high school. I think I would have remembered such an attractive boy."

Lily opened the back of the car for Luna; she scratched the dog's ears. She remembered how every time she used to mention anything having to do with a boy—that she was studying with one, working on a science project with one, going with a group of them to get root beer floats at A&W—Eleanor would question her about whether the boy was handsome, available, interested. It got to the point where Lily stopped mentioning boys at all, and then Eleanor grilled her about *that.* "He wasn't my friend," she finally said, in response to the comment about Jack. "He was just a boy from math class."

Tom spent the afternoon in the orchard with Luna, while Lily went to the pet store to buy some chew toys and dog food. She looked for Jack at the end of each aisle, behind each cash register. She was disappointed and relieved when she didn't see him. When she got home, she wandered through the trees calling out to Tom. She finally found him at the compost pile behind the shed. He was turning the pile with a pitchfork, and sweat poured from his brow. The dog was chasing birds that neither Tom nor Lily could see.

"She's crazy," Tom said, nodding at the dog with a smile.

She was so crazy, in fact, that after the sun went down, she raced around the house like a puppy. Lily gave her the chew toy, which helped for a little while, but the dog was wound up as tight as a top. Tom took her out for a walk, which seemed to calm her a little, but by the time they got back, he was exhausted.

"Go to sleep," Lily said. "I'll stay up with her."

Lily sat with her laptop on the living room couch, and Luna sat at her feet, alternately putting her chin on Lily's knee, and leaping up to bark at the moon as it rose in the sky. It was a full moon, big and bright, and Lily didn't mind having to stay up. She scrolled through websites of art quilters, finding one whose designs of aspen trees looked like a photograph, and another whose abstract patterns reminded her of Escher.

The dog was so transfixed by the moon out the window that, by midnight, Lily understood exactly why she was named the way she was. Soon after, Lily dragged the dog bed she had just bought into the bedroom, where Tom was asleep. Luna followed, but she refused to go near the dog bed. Lily closed the shades so that there was no sign of the moon, and no light whatsoever. The dog finally leapt onto the bed, settled on Tom's feet, and went to sleep.

LILY dreamed of Jack. She dreamed that she had gone down to the beach to help save the birds who had been covered with oil, and that Jack had been there, too, out on his surfboard, immune somehow from the black goo that lapped at the shore. In 1969, in actual fact, the birds made Lily nervous, and the oil stank, and she thought her mother was only doing it to make a point. In her dream, however, she was the hero. She was saving the birds. And Jack, who appeared the same way he looked in 1969—young and tan, his long blond hair flopping over his face—walked up the beach to Lily, took her in his arms, kissed her without saying a word, and then he peeled her clothes off, and he gently laid her on the sand, and it was a tropical island then, and there was no oil, and they were alone, and she gave herself up to him.

When she woke, she rolled toward Tom with guilt and desire. She fitted her body into the curve of his spine, and kissed him where her face pressed into his shoulder blades. She reached her hand around Tom's body and placed her palm over his heart. He rolled over, pressing his chest against hers, his belly against her belly, his thighs against her thighs. They had been married for so long that there was no mystery in the way they touched. It was as if they had agreed to play a symphony, and she knew her part, and he knew his, and they both knew how things would sound when played together, but they played, still, for the pleasure of knowing.

But at a certain point, that morning, in the middle of a certain movement, Lily stopped playing the part she normally played. No longer the eager wife, the grateful wife, the bored wife, the playful wife, the conciliatory wife, the merely willing wife, she wasn't a wife at all. She was an earnest girl on her way to study math, and the man in bed with her was a boy named Jack who planned to study the waves, and it was Jack who was kissing her and stroking her, and it was Jack who made her hips insist on more, and Jack who made her cry out.

"Wow," Tom said. "Retirement suits you well, Mrs. Gilbert."

She laughed nervously, but inside her head, things were popping—bubbles of guilt, little pockets of shame.

14

Olivia

As soon as Brooke learned that her grandparents had a dog, she wanted to visit them. She loved dogs. She chased small white dogs in the park, laughed at the long, lean ones on the street, tried to offer the big, mean ones a Cheerio. Ryan was gone every weekend scouting at high school swim championships up and down the state, and so Olivia thought a trip to Santa Barbara to see the new dog was a good idea. It would, at least, be a diversion; instead of asking endless questions about where her daddy was and when he was coming home, Brooke was asking endless questions about the dog and where it was going to sleep and who was going to feed it.

They began to pack twenty-four hours in advance of their trip—Olivia so that she didn't forget some crucial piece of toddler gear, and Brooke so that she didn't forget her bear, her blanket, the Cheerios she intended to give to the dog.

"You can't feed the dog the food that you eat," Olivia said.

"Why?"

"It will make her sick."

"Why?"

"Because dogs like dog food, not people food."

"I want dog food."

"No, silly," Olivia said. "You eat people food."

"Why?"

"Because you're a person."

"Anna cooks it."

"Well, yes," Olivia said, realizing that, in addition to stopping the mail and the newspaper, she had to call to cancel meals for Thursday and Friday. "Anna cooks our dinner sometimes when we're here, but she won't be cooking our food at Grandma's house. Maybe Grandpa Tom will make you some guacamole."

"'Molee!" Brooke sang out.

ON the night before they left, Ryan called from Mission Bay. He and Olivia hadn't spoken in two days.

"Hey," he said. "It's me. Is Brooke still up?"

"No," Olivia said.

"How are you guys doing?"

"Fine."

"Up to anything fun?"

"We're going down to see your mom and dad," Olivia said,

as if she were a reporter reciting the news, "and to meet the new dog."

"Oh," Ryan said. "Okay. I wanted to stop off and see them on my way down here, but I didn't have time. How long will you be there?"

"I don't know," she said.

"If you're mad at me, Olivia," Ryan finally said, "why don't you just say it."

"I've said it."

"You're mad that I have a full-time job, is that right? That's the complaint? That I'm not home for dinner every night?"

"This isn't what I wanted," Olivia said.

"Believe me, it's not what I wanted either," Ryan said. "I'm out here busting my butt and nothing seems to make you happy. A bigger paycheck, being able to stay home, food from my grandmother . . . none of it makes you happy?"

She paused for a moment to let the thoughts in her head come together, but they were like high, thin clouds, dispersed by the wind. She couldn't pull them into shape. "I don't know," she said, and pressed her lips together and squeezed her eyes shut and wondered if she would ever feel like herself again.

SHE had planned the drive so that Brooke would sleep, but Brooke didn't sleep. She wanted to listen to *Baby Beluga* over and over again, she wanted to know what the big truck next to them was carrying and where it was going, she wanted to know when they were going to go past the cows. Olivia drove, and answered, and drove, and answered, and when she drove up the narrow road that led to Tom and Lily's house on the hill, and saw the avocado trees spread out before her in neat, shimmering lines, she felt a sense of deliverance; someone would be here to help her.

The dog came bolting up to the car, barking, and Brooke started to chant, "Luna, Luna, Luna."

Tom came around the side of the house, waving and carrying a rake. He grabbed Luna's collar and pulled her back from the car. Olivia got out, kissed her father-in-law on the cheek, opened the back door, unlocked Brooke from her car seat, and hoisted the child on her hip. Brooke leaned over precipitously to try to pet the dog, so Olivia set her down and said, "Let Luna come to you, sweetie."

Luna stepped up to Brooke and sniffed her and circled her, and wagged her tail, and Brooke laughed, and Olivia never took her eyes off Luna's speckled snout or her mismatched eyes, alert to any sign that the dog would lunge, bite, attack. Olivia quickly realized that there would be no deliverance— not here, not anywhere, at least not until Brooke was five, or ten, or sixteen, or twenty-one.

Lily came out and threw her arms around Olivia and lifted Brooke into the air, where it seemed she didn't want to be. Lily set her down. While Brooke and the dog continued to circle each other and sniff each other out, and Tom and Olivia monitored them, Lily took the duffel bags from the car, and carried them into the guest room, which had new Bertasi sheets on the bed, a new bedspread, a big, red stuffed chair from the house in Vermont, and wildflowers in a vase beneath the window.

Olivia came in, hauling the port-a-crib. "This is a beautiful room," she said. "You've done such a nice job with it."

"It doesn't feel real," Lily said. "That this is our house, that's our dog, and you can just drive down to see us." She smiled. "I love it."

"It's wonderful to have you so close," Olivia said, "and the dog is obviously a big hit. Brooke would give anything for a dog."

"You're not a dog lover?"

"Oh I am," Olivia said. "We had Saint Bernards growing up. Five of them, over about ten years. It's just that . . ." She stopped, and turned toward the window so that Lily couldn't see her face, which had cracked open. She busied herself with unzipping the portable crib, composed herself, then stood up and faced her mother-in-law with tears in her eyes. "It's just that I can't handle a dog," she said. "I can barely handle Brooke."

Lily stepped up to Olivia and embraced her. The two women were nearly the same height and build, and Olivia fit in Lily's arms as if she were her own child. Olivia stepped back and sobbed. "It's just so hard," she said. "I'm so tired. And Ryan, you know, he's gone a lot. For his job. And when he's home, we're mad at each other all the time."

"Remember how after you gave birth to Brooke, you were

shocked that no one had warned you how much it would hurt?"

Olivia nodded.

"It's the same deal with a toddler. There must be something in our brains that doesn't hear the stories other women tell, because everyone warns you how tired you're going to be. Everyone talks about how hard it is to keep your marriage whole. But every new mother is shocked. It will get better. I promise."

They heard Brooke begin to wail, and the sound got closer, and then Tom was there with Brooke in his arms and Luna at his heels. "Luna licked her face," Tom said.

Brooke reached out her arms for her mother, and Olivia took the girl, and felt her body shaking and heaving. "Shhhh," she said, "you'll be fine," and then to Tom and Lily said, "She skipped her nap. She was so excited to see you. I'll just lie down with her until she goes to sleep."

Tom and Lily left the room, and Olivia lay down with her overwrought child on the crisp new sheets, and fell asleep before Brooke did.

15

Eleanor

BUCKY Harrington hosted the Red Sox Opening Day party at his house on Charles River Square in April. Everyone arrived when it was still dark and the temperature hovered at 33 degrees. The caterer they used had hot coffee and strudel at the ready, and soon the voice of Jerry Remy warmed everyone up.

"Sounds like summer," Gordon said, and everyone smiled and nodded.

They watched as Dice-K took several pitches to warm up his arm, and as Manny helped settle the team down with a home run in the fourth inning. They grumbled when Keith Fouke stepped up to the plate for Oakland, since he had been a Red Sox not so many years before. In the eighth inning, Jacoby Ellisbury went up for a catch, making a huge leap into the wall and coming down with the ball. The crowd in Bucky Harrington's living room went crazy.

Throughout the game, other parties and other baseball games were relived. Eleanor could no longer remember the name of a certain friend's child or the title of a book she read or which street she needed to turn on to get to a favorite restaurant, but she remembered events from college and her young life in Boston with crystal clarity. It was as if she were retaining only the memories that really mattered.

Gracie used a walker because she couldn't risk a fall. She sat in a big wing chair behind the couch, and never touched the strudel or the fruit salad or the hot dog that was presented to her. Eleanor wasn't sure Gracie was even following the game. During a commercial break, Eleanor pulled up a folding chair next to her old roommate. "We've never had an Opening Day quite like this one, have we?" she said.

Gracie turned and looked at Eleanor. "No, ma'am," she said.

"You're not eating your hot dog."

"I'm dying," Gracie said.

"I know that," Eleanor said, "but that's no reason to ignore a hot dog."

"I think it will be soon," Gracie said.

"Poppycock."

Gracie reached out her hand and took Eleanor's in hers. Gracie's skin was paper thin, and her hand shook. "I'm trying to say good-bye," she said.

Eleanor shook her head. She felt frantic. "I'll come to New York," she said. "I'll sit by your side."

"No," Gracie said, "I couldn't stand that. It will be easier this way."

Eleanor leaned over and put her arms around her friend. She could feel the thinness of her frame, the laboring of her breath. "Damn you, Gracie," she said.

"Next year at Fenway, have a hot dog for me, will you?"

"Until they cart me away," Eleanor said, and she pulled back and squeezed her friend's hand softly, being careful not to crush her bones.

The game came back on, and Eleanor couldn't watch as Papelbon attempted to close it out. She went to the kitchen for a Bloody Mary she didn't want, stepped outside to the small patio out back. She took a gulp of air and closed her eyes to keep in the hot tears. Suddenly, she felt a hand on her shoulder. It was Gordon.

"She's in terrible pain," he said.

"I know," Eleanor said, and wiped the tears that had run down her cheek. "Are you doing okay today? Judy would have loved this crazy breakfast, although she wouldn't have let on. She would have pretended to be offended."

Gordon shrugged. "I hardly sleep anymore," he said, "which is just as well. I hate waking up and having to realize, again, that she's gone."

"It was always something of a blessing to me," Eleanor said, "to realize I was finally rid of my husbands."

Gordon laughed. "You weren't easy to be married to," he said.

She smiled. "I always said love never lasts."

"You still playing the field out there in Santa Barbara?" Gordon asked, and Eleanor had the distinct sense that he was nervous. He shifted his weight from foot to foot, and swirled his Bloody Mary around his glass.

"Good God, no," Eleanor said.

Gordon cleared his throat. He looked at his shoes. "Eleanor," he said. "Before Judy died, she told me I should remarry."

"That's just like Judy," Eleanor said. "Always thinking of everyone else first. You have any prospects? A distinguished navy man like you would be quite a draw, I would think. That, and the apartment on Seventy-third Street."

Gordon looked up. "She told me I should marry you," he said.

Eleanor was holding her drink in her right hand in a crystal highball. She dropped it on the patio and it smashed and sprayed tomato juice on her black patent flats and on Gordon's khaki pants. People came to the door to see what had happened, and to see if everyone was all right, and then the caterers came with sponges, and a maid came with a mop. They eventually all went back inside, and by that point the game was over, and the after-game interviews were going on, and people were talking about going back to their hotels for naps, or going over to the museum of art to see the Winslow Homer exhibit or going over to the Harvard baseball field to see what might be going on.

"Will you join me for lunch?" Gordon asked Eleanor.

"I'm sorry," Eleanor said, "I'm going with Gracie and her nurse to the train station."

"I'll have them hold us a table at the M Bar," he said. "They do a great poached lobster."

She closed her eyes. What could Judy possibly have meant by doing this? "Fine," she said.

SHE and Gracie sat on the benches at South Station and watched the people coming and going.

"The world has gotten faster," Gracie said.

Eleanor smiled. "I think we've just gotten slower."

"Look at everyone," Gracie said, "headphones and cell phones. It's ridiculous. They never get a moment's peace."

"It's fantastic," Eleanor argued. "I have a new BlackBerry. It has its own little global positioning system. Tells me exactly where I am in any city in the world." She fished the gadget out of her bag, and held it out on her palm.

Gracie scowled. "What on earth are you doing with a thing like that?"

"Luke gave it to me for Christmas. Look," she said, pressing the screen. "Look, here are pictures of Brooke, and of the house on the avocado ranch. I can even play hearts."

"Against a computer?"

"Try it," Eleanor said, holding out her phone.

Gracie waved her hand dismissively. "I'd rather just watch the passersby."

Eleanor turned off her phone and slipped it back into her bag. "Gordon says that Judy told him to marry me," she said.

Gracie chuckled.

"Why would she do such a thing?"

"Oh come on," Gracie said. "She probably just wanted to know he'd still be loved."

"Loved? You can't suddenly decide to love someone because someone else said you should."

"Why is that any worse a reason than any other?"

"Since when are you so philosophical?" Eleanor asked, and immediately wished she hadn't.

In the light of the station, Gracie's skin looked translucent. Eleanor thought she might be able to trace one of her friend's veins from her hand, up her arm, and straight into her heart. "I'm dying," Gracie said. "It tends to make you wax on about things."

"And what do you know about love anyway?"

"I know I never had it," Gracie said. "Nothing like Gordon and Judy. I was too damn stubborn. Just like you."

Eleanor looked at the board announcing the train arrivals and departures. The train Gracie would be taking back to New York was only seven minutes away. "What am I going to do?" Eleanor asked.

Gracie looked at her. "Say yes," she said.

"I've known him practically my whole life as Judy's husband. And I've botched every relationship I had. What good would it do him? And what good would it do me?"

"You might surprise yourself," Gracie said.

Her nurse stood, and said it was time to make their way to the tracks. Eleanor stood and helped Gracie to her feet. They walked slowly through the terminal, toward the archway leading to the train, and then down onto the platform. They felt the warm wind of the train as it pulled into the station, and Eleanor thought of the moment she first laid eyes on her friend. She was eighteen years old. Her mother had driven her out to Wellesley, and carried her suitcases to Room 28 in Tower Court. When they stepped into the small room with the sloped roof, there was a blond-haired girl sitting on a chair, her suitcases on the floor in the middle of the room. She was wearing a plaid skirt, a blouse with a Peter Pan collar, a navy blue sweater. She leapt up. "I've been waiting for you," she said. "I'm Gracie Dooley from Charleston, South Carolina. We're going to be great friends!"

"Good-bye, Gracie," Eleanor now said.

"Good-bye, Eleanor."

Eleanor stood on the platform while everyone settled onto the train, and she watched Gracie sit by the window in a first-class seat. She waved while the train pulled out of the station, and then she walked slowly out to the street and called a cab to take her to the Mandarin.

GORDON stood when she walked in. He pulled out the wicker chair for Eleanor, and called the waiter over to order her a drink. "Black coffee, please," she said. "It's only twelve thirty and I'm exhausted."

"Opening Day will do that to you," the waiter said, and Gordon laughed and raised his glass.

They talked about the game and about their friends who had been at the party and about the city of Boston and how good it was to be there. Eleanor told Gordon about the whale that had died on the beach in Santa Barbara, and how it reminded her so much of the oil spill of 1969, and how she couldn't stop thinking about it—oil-covered birds, and the great hulking carcass of the whale. She chatted like a nervous schoolgirl through soup and sandwiches, until finally, when the waiter brought coffee for the second time, Gordon circled around to the reason for their being there together.

"Judy made lists for each of us on a yellow legal pad," Gordon said. "There were lists of things she wanted each of the children to have, and lists of things she wanted them to remember—*stand up straight, look people in the eye when you speak to them.* That was for the grandkids."

Eleanor nodded.

"My pages were letters about various things," Gordon said. He reached into his pocket, took out his wallet, and unfolded a piece of yellow lined paper. "She gave me this one last."

Dearest Gordon,

I can't bear to think of you being alone. You have been such a good husband, and your talent should not go to waste just because I'm leaving this earth. You should marry again.

*Soon. And you should marry Eleanor Peters. Good friend-
ship is a fine foundation for good love, I think. You won't
have to defend your obsession with the Red Sox to her, and
you won't have to explain why you sometimes break into
songs by Gilbert & Sullivan, and the kids won't have to take
time to get to know her since they've known her all their
lives. I suppose that she will try to say no; I don't think she
feels that she has been very good at love. But love, as you
surely know after so many good years together, is a choice.
There is no reason why Eleanor can't choose it, and I hope
you can get her to see this. It would give me great peace to
know that you are not alone.*

Forever,
Judy

After he finished reading the words, he handed the piece of
paper across the small table to Eleanor. She read Judy's familiar left-leaning scribble, noting how erratic her lines were, how
lightly the pen had moved across the page. She folded it and
handed it back. "It's a lovely letter, and you know how I trea-
sure our friendship, and how I treasured Judy's, but you can't
expect me to just say yes, Gordon. You can't."

"I know that," Gordon said, "but I wanted to show you the
letter, and to tell you that I think she was a genius."

"No woman has ever been more adored by a man," Eleanor
said.

"I mean that I think she's right."

"About which part?"

"That love is a choice."

"Even if I agreed to marry you, Gordon, which I'm not agreeing to do, falling in *love* with you is a whole other matter. People don't just decide to fall in love, and then that's that. I mean, we're talking about love, Gordon! People search for love their entire lives and never find it."

"I don't think it's that hard," he said, "and I don't think Judy thought so either."

"Not that hard?"

"We made a decision every day that it was going to work."

"You were extraordinary. You must know that. You were gifted, blessed."

"It's true," Gordon said, "but it could be true for you and me, too."

She shook her head. "All my husbands either dropped dead or walked out on me," Eleanor said, "or both. And I was happy every time they left. There was always someone else I found more attractive, more interesting."

"You liked the hunt."

"I suppose I did."

"But you said you weren't playing the field in Santa Barbara. There are no other men in the wings, are there?"

"I swore off men," Eleanor said. "It was my New Year's resolution."

"I see," Gordon said, and he put the yellow piece of paper

away, but Eleanor had the distinct feeling that the conversation was far from over.

ELEANOR took a nap that afternoon and then met the others for a walk around Harvard Square and hamburgers at Charlie's Kitchen. Gordon kept his distance the rest of the day, giving no indication of the conversation they had had at lunch. They shared a cab back to the hotel, and when they got into the elevator, Gordon said, "What floor, Eleanor?"

"Twenty-two," she said.

They rode in silence to her floor, and he held the door while she stepped into the vestibule, and he stepped out behind her, and walked by her side to her room.

"You're like a puppy," she said when they got to her door.

He shrugged. "I've come to loathe the night," he said. "I can't sleep, and when I do, I have nightmares. Are you good for one more drink?"

"Come in, come in," she said, relenting, and she led him to the sitting area by the window.

She sat down on the bed and took off her shoes while he called room service to order something from the bar. She was so tired, she didn't care about propriety. They talked for a while about dinner, and the view, and when the drinks came, Gordon went to the door to pay the bellman. When he turned around, Eleanor was resting on the pillows, asleep.

He debated leaving. It was a tricky question because

Eleanor was a tricky woman. She was the most spontaneous woman he knew, on the one hand—a lover of parties, of travel, of early morning swims in the ocean and of love affairs that did not take into consideration the rules of the world. She was, on the other hand, someone who stood by ceremony—who believed that men should open doors for women, pay for dinner, and mix a strong martini, and that women should know how to wear pearls and set a proper table. She might think nothing of his sitting up all night in her room, or she might take great offense. She had recently sat up all night in his living room, so he was inclined to think she wouldn't mind his returning the favor. Besides, he felt desperate. When Judy gave him the note on the yellow legal pad, he immediately understood her impulse. He would have wanted to do the same for her. A good, long marriage made you believe in love. It made you depend on it. It made you crave it. Judy's directive to him had brought them both a measure of peace in her last days, and had brought him a sense of hope in the days that followed her death. If Eleanor refused him, however, he felt certain he would be completely lost.

He pulled the comforter across the bed and laid it over Eleanor. He turned off the main light in the room, and turned on the reading lamp by the window. Then he sat down, picked up the newspaper, and began the long wait for morning.

16

Lily

On the morning of that same day, Tom got up at 6 a.m., made a cup of coffee, and immediately went out to be with the trees. There was a shed at the bottom of the hill—a small house, really—filled with wooden crates and picking poles and racks and clippers. He went through trying to understand the purpose of each of the tools, and he studied the irrigation system, and the compost pile behind the shed. At lunch, he came in and gave reports to Lily.

"There's a raccoon family that lives under the shed," he said. "The trees on the downhill side of the slope have more fruit. There's some kind of beetle in the bark on some trees by the eastern fence line."

At four o'clock, he called Lily to say that he was going to work through dinner at the warehouse with Nadine.

"You've been spending a lot of time there," Lily ventured. There had been early-morning trips to the warehouse, lunch at the warehouse, meetings at the warehouse. And except for when she had instigated it, there had been very little sex in their new bed. When they moved into their first apartment in Vermont, they had made love in every room, on every surface, and they had laughed, and gone out into the world each day filled with each other, and smug about their love. Now, it was as if they were brother and sister.

"Nadine's putting together a presentation on the benefits of organic composting," Tom said, "and I'm just helping her out."

Lily couldn't help it. She pictured Tom slowly stripping the flannel shirt off braless Nadine. It was a hot day and her skin would be sweaty, and his skin would be sweaty, but they wouldn't care because their desire for each other would be so great.

"We'll probably order something in," Tom said, "so you should go ahead and eat without me."

"Okay," Lily said, but what she was thinking was, *Of course.* What she was thinking was, *Love is just an illusion.* What she was thinking was, *I am such a fool.*

SHE put Luna into the back seat of the Subaru and headed down the hill. She would never have admitted that she was going to the beach to look for Jack, but that was exactly what she was doing. She wanted to know what it was like to act on a whim. She went to Eucalyptus Lane, parked the car, and walked down the shady street to Miramar Beach. Cement steps with a rusted railing led down from the end of the lane to the sand. She held Luna on a tight leash and made her way down. When they hit the sand, Luna went wild. She pulled on her leash, leaping at the seagulls who darted on the ground and flew through the air. She lunged toward a little terrier, whose fur was wet and matted.

"Whoa, girl," Lily said. She scanned the crowd. There were families with umbrellas and coolers, who looked like they'd been camped out all day, and couples lying bronze and sleek side by side in the late sun. In the water, there were toddlers running in the froth, kids with boogie boards, body surfers. A few surfers bobbed in the waves farther to the south. She turned in that direction and walked just beneath the houses that lined the sand. *It's a beautiful afternoon,* she told herself. *I'm just taking my dog for a walk.* When she got closer to the surfers, she slowed down, and scanned the people sitting on their boards, bobbing in the waves. Luna yelped, struggling to move toward a pile of seaweed abuzz with flies. She reached down to pet Luna on the head, and when she stood up again, she heard someone behind her calling, "Lily!"

She turned. It was Jack. She had come to find him, but she hadn't expected him to actually appear. She was startled and embarrassed. She thought about pretending not to hear him, or turning and running back to the car, but Jack was jogging toward her, waving. "Hey," he said when he caught up to her, "I recognized the dog." He leaned down and took Luna's nose in his hand. "How you doing, girl?" he asked, and then he let Luna lick his salty skin.

Lily felt her heart leap. She felt an electric jolt, and it was so strong that she was certain Jack felt it, too. How could he not?

Lily swallowed. "She's crazy," she said, "barks all the time. But we've already fallen in love with her."

"Excellent," Jack said. "I can't own a dog because I'm gone so much, but dogs are so much easier to be around than people, don't you think?"

"They can be," Lily said.

He looked her full in the face, and she thought she wouldn't be able to stand the intensity of his gaze. "You look exactly the same as you did in high school," he said. "Your smile, it's exactly the same. The years have been good to you."

She looked at the sand, at Luna's paws. "Thank you," she said very quietly.

"I always liked you," he said. "You were so serious, so dead set on going out into the world. Did you find whatever it was you were looking for?"

Lily swallowed. It felt like an incredibly intimate question from a man who was essentially a stranger. But she had come here for this. She had come to the beach for exactly this. "I'm not sure," she said.

He put a hand on her arm, and his skin felt hot and charged—the way it had in her dream. She didn't flinch or pull away. She noticed how Jack's arms were so much thicker than Tom's, how they were darker, stronger, more firmly set in their sockets. She was lost for a moment, in the fact of Jack's hand on her skin, and then he stepped back.

"Our offices are in Ventura," he said. "Come by and see me sometime."

She swallowed. Her throat was dry. "I will," she said in a quavering voice, and then she turned on her heel and walked quickly back to the car.

SHE burst into her kitchen, opened a bottle of the zinfandel left over from her mother's welcome party, poured herself a glass, downed it, and stood at the counter waiting for the moment when she would begin to feel weak, when her heart would begin to pound and her head would begin to throb. Red wine did that to her. She was counting on it.

IT was ten thirty when Tom got home that night, and still hot. The moon was high in the sky, and the stars were coming out strong. Luna was wound up again, and the moment Tom walked into the house, Luna came bounding up to him, circling him and yelping.

"Hey, Luna," he said, squatting to nuzzle her nose. "How's my girl?"

Luna trotted toward the back deck, and when Tom saw a light on outside, he followed. Lily was sitting on a chaise longue, part of a teak set they had purchased from the Hailwoods, with apricot-colored pillows.

"What are you drinking?" Tom asked, thinking he might join her. When she didn't answer right away, he picked up the bottle. "Red wine?" he said, as alarmed as if she had been drinking arsenic. "Why are you drinking red wine?"

"I guess I just felt like flirting with danger."

"I think that's a decision you're going to regret," Tom said.

She turned to look at him and, with great tenderness, said, "You know that, don't you?"

Tom picked up a wedge of cheese. "Know what?" he asked.

"How I can't drink red wine. Exactly how sick I get. I mean, you know that very specific thing about me."

"It's not a big mystery, Lily."

"Oh, but it is," she said, and gulped more wine. "It is. I mean I could tell someone that red wine makes me sick, but they wouldn't have any idea what that meant. You know all about how ice helps, and when it's time to go to the emergency room. You know all that."

"Why don't you just go to bed, Lily," he said. He didn't know if she would get a headache or not, but either way, he loved his wife. He was the kind of man who faced whatever came to him, who handled things, who got things done.

"I'm not tired," she said. "I'm the opposite of tired."

"Well, I'm exhausted," he said. "I'm going to go to bed."

"For the first time tonight?" she asked.

"Now you've completely lost me," he said.

She sat forward in her chair and spoke quietly. "Have I?" she asked. "Lost you, Tom? Do we not love each other anymore? Did we make this whole move for nothing?"

"Lily," he said, and his voice was gentle and pleading. He wanted her to stop babbling, to go to sleep, to try to cheat the headache she had invited into the hot night.

"Well, it's true," she said. "It's like we're roommates. I mean, we moved across the country together. We picked up and moved, and you hardly want to touch me anymore, and you spend all your time with Nadine and maybe we don't really love each other, or not enough anyway. Maybe we never did. Maybe it was all just convenience."

Tom lowered himself into the chair next to Lily, and Luna came and put her nose on his knee. "Roommates?" he ventured. "I never had a roommate who acted the way you did the other night."

She felt the blood rush to her creeks, and awkwardly waved her arm across the night. "Usually when I touch you now, it's like you're not there. I thought this move was going to help us, but now I'm thinking I was wrong." Silence settled over the back deck and the stars seemed to crackle in the hot sky. "I've been wondering if you've been sleeping with someone else," she said.

"What are you talking about?"

"Nadine," she said. "I'm talking about braless Nadine."

Tom got up from the chair so abruptly that it had the effect of a punch to Luna's nose. The dog reeled back and howled. "Are you kidding me?" Tom asked.

"About which part? Her being braless?"

"No," Tom said, "about what just came out of your mouth."

"I wasn't kidding," Lily said. "We walked away from our house, our jobs, our whole life because I thought somehow this move might be good for us, but all it did was free you up to hang out with braless Nadine."

"That's not fair," Tom said, "and you know it."

Lily threw back some more wine. "I don't know what I know anymore," she said. "Especially about you."

"Come on, Luna," Tom said. "We're going for a walk."

Tom and Luna walked out the front door, and into the parched hills. There was a trail that went up the bone-dry creek bed and cut off onto the shoulder above the house. It was speckled with the shadow of oak trees swaying in the wind and alive with the sounds of summer—frogs thirsty for water, crickets wondering about the heat. Unaware of anything but the night, Luna put her nose into the unseasonably hot wind, and followed Tom up the trail.

Lily sat for a moment on the back deck, stunned at what she had done and what she had said, and stunned that Tom had actually walked out. She missed Luna's presence by her side, and felt an irrational sense of gratitude that Luna would not be able to tell Tom the secret of what Lily had done on the beach—why she had gone, who had appeared, what she had felt. She got up and made her way to the front door.

"Luna?" she called. "Luna?" She listened to the air moving through the brush, and to the crickets.

"Tom?" she called. "Tom?"

When there was no answer, she went back to the bedroom, got into bed, and waited for the headache to come find her.

•17•

Tom

Tom had friends who had taken lovers, who had swapped wives, who had taken advantage of the proximity professors have to young, eager girls, but Tom had never been interested in making a mess of things for a few small, extramarital pleasures. He didn't think it was worth it. He wanted what he had now: a comfortable, familiar marriage; an earthbound challenge that stimulated a dormant part of his brain; and a driveway that did not need to be shoveled. He realized that he had no idea anymore what Lily wanted. She had wanted to move. She had pushed for it. Why was she so suddenly unhinged?

When Tom got back to the house, he went immediately to the deck to see if Lily was still there, and if she was okay. He picked up the bottle of zinfandel, which still had a glass left in it, then set it down, and walked toward the bedroom. Lily was curled into a ball under the covers, her arms tucked under her body like fine-boned wings. She was a small woman who looked even smaller when she was asleep. The accusation she had made seemed to be hovering around her, like a tangible thing, thick and black. He stood over the bed for a while, watching, as Lily slept and Luna curled up on the carpet by the door. He was so sweaty and hot, he couldn't imagine climbing into bed. He walked out back to the deck, lay down on a lounge, finished off the wine, and after studying the stars, closed his eyes and fell asleep.

At two o'clock in the morning, Tom swam up out of a deep sleep, awakened by the barking of a dog. He sat up slowly, confused. He couldn't remember why he was alone and outside, wearing jeans and a T-shirt. He didn't understand whose dog was barking, and why. He opened his eyes and saw Luna standing there giving short, sharp bursts of warning. In seconds, Tom was on his feet. "What is it?" he asked the dog, and began to walk through the dark house. He could hear things—groaning, something loud like thunder, and he had the thought that it could be raining—and still Luna kept barking and barking.

He found Lily crouched in front of the toilet, vomiting and sobbing and gasping for air.

"It will be okay," he said to her, and then to Luna, "It will be okay." They had been here a hundred times before, and they knew how it went: Lily would stay in the bathroom, sobbing and vomiting and pleading for the pain to stop, and when the pain ebbed, she would say she was sorry for drinking the wine, and then the cycle would start all over again, perhaps with a new twist this time: she would say she was sorry for what she had said, and Tom would say not to worry about it, and they would go back to the way they were—bound together, connected by the way they felt pain and the way they gave pleasure and by the fact that they had chosen to love each other for so long.

The dog was standing in the doorway, barking even more urgently, inching backward into the bedroom. She bolted out to the living room, and circled back. She did this two times before Tom realized that Luna was trying to tell him something more. He followed her back through the dark rooms, and now he could hear it even more clearly—a kind of insistent hum, and then he could smell it: something burning, something on fire. Tom left Lily retching in the bathroom and walked to the windows by the front door. Luna padded after him, still barking madly. He opened the door, and smelled the smoke—which smelled sweet and benign, like a campfire. It was, after all, fragrant stuff burning in the hills: sage, manzanita, eucalyptus. He stepped outside, and walked a few steps out into the driveway to see what he could see. The wind was still blowing hot down the canyon, and there was that sound of something buzzing in the air. He thought about helicopters, a swarm of bees. When he got up onto the road, he saw his neighbor, Mary Hazelton, an older woman who lived alone in a house that looked as if it belonged in 1974. She had been at Eleanor's cocktail party a few weeks before. She stood about two hundred feet below him, in the dark, but he knew her by her white hair, and her proclivity for cardigans. Luna raced down to Mary to greet her, and then raced back to Tom, her ears pricked up, her tail alert.

"Can you see anything?" Mary shouted in his direction.

"No," he shouted back. The sky to the southeast was shifting with patterns of light and dark, which could have been fog, or clouds, or smoke. "Maybe something going on across the creek?"

"I expect we better get out," she said. "With this wind, anything could happen."

"Wouldn't the fire department tell us if we had to leave?" he asked. He imagined a bullhorn, a truck driving urgently up and down the road. He had grown up in New York City, where subways failed and buildings burned and sometimes the snow fell in enormous dirty drifts. Once, because of a fire in the incinerator, they had to evacuate the building where his family lived on East Eighty-sixth Street, but they were out of town and missed the drama.

Mary had lived in the Santa Barbara foothills for most of her life. She had friends who had lost houses in the Sycamore Canyon Fire and Painted Cave. "I wouldn't count on it," Mary said. "I'll call nine-one-one, then I'm packing up."

Her use of the word *packing* made him think of suitcases, neatly folded shirts. When he and Lily had packed up the

Burlington house, Lily had carefully weighed each item—*Do we still need it? Do we still want it?* She was glad to get rid of the boys' old ski helmets, old oilcloth jackets, the pasta maker they never used, the textbooks they held on to in case they needed them someday. Tom hadn't been so discriminating. He nodded as Mary turned back to her house. "Wait!" he yelled into the wind. "How long do you think we've got?"

She tipped her nose in the air just like Luna. "I'd say twenty minutes."

He ran back down the driveway and through the front door, with Luna on his heels. He ran back into the study, pulled open a drawer, and started flinging files on the floor—taxes, insurance, and bank accounts—then he left it all and ran into the bathroom, where Lily was crouched in a ball, her forehead pressed against the floor.

"Get up," he commanded. "Get up."

She raised her head and looked at him through small reptilian eyes. He reached out and grabbed her elbow and pulled her up, and she collapsed back to the floor. "Please don't," she said weakly, waving him away.

"Get up, Lily," he said. "There's a fire. We have to leave."

She stood up, then bent over the toilet and heaved.

Tom left her. He ran to the laundry room, grabbed a white laundry basket, and went back to the study to load in the files. He threw in a baseball that was sitting in a stand on his desk— he'd caught it at a Yankee game on his twelfth birthday—and a framed card that Ryan and Luke had made for him one Father's

Day when being a father was something he *did* rather than something he was. He carried the basket out to his new truck, hoisted it in the bed, and ran back to the bathroom. Lily had gotten up, pulled on a pair of sweatpants and a T-shirt, slipped on her old sheepskin slippers, and was sitting on the edge of the bed, holding on to the mattress as if she were at sea.

"Come on," he said. He lifted her, propped her up. She moaned while she shuffled along: "It hurts so much, it hurts so much." When they got outside, the hot wind and the smell of smoke hit Lily full in the face, and she put her hand over her eyes to try to shut out the assault on her senses. She groaned. She stepped to the Ford and held on to the edge of the truck bed, and then her stomach seized again.

Tom pointed at Luna. "Stay," he said. "Stay with Lily."

Luna sat on the driveway at the door of the truck, whining as if she, too, were in pain.

Tom flew back into the house, to the bedroom to grab his wallet and car keys, and then pulled down a duffel bag from the top of the closet and bolted for the study. He shoved in the mortgage papers, their passports, and their laptops, and then he started pulling out Lily's bins of fabric. He riffled through them until he found the Matisse tablecloth and cardboard tube Lily had carried by hand from Burlington, and he shoved these in, too. He hoisted the duffels on his shoulder and walked as fast as he could out to the truck, ignoring the sweat that poured from his face and soaked his clothes, and the fear that pumped through his veins.

Lily was sitting in the front seat, feverish and reeling from the pain, and Luna was sitting on the ground beside her door, exactly where she had been told to stay. Tom dumped his load in the back, pressed the car keys into Lily's hand, said, "Don't move," to Lily and Luna both, then turned and ran back into the house through the front door. He thought he would get some books, the photo of the boys that hung in the front hall-way, but when he got inside, there was smoke swirling in the air, and he coughed, and he changed his mind about trying to salvage anything else. He headed out the side door to get the hose to water down the roof, but when he rounded the corner, a hot ember the size of a baseball pelted his leg. He stumbled back from a wall of flame. The fire hissed and crackled and seemed to suck the hot night toward it like a black hole. He stood there, unable to move, and thought, *So this is how it will end,* but then he heard Luna barking in the driveway, and a siren wailing, and he turned and ran back around the side of the house to see Lily standing in the driveway yelling, "Tom! Tom!" Luna bolted through the front door, where he had dis-appeared just moments before.

"Start the truck!" Tom yelled to Lily, and then he took off after the dog.

Luna followed the path Tom had taken through the house. She skidded straight through the living room, out the side door, and directly into the fire.

Tom stopped again in the doorway.

"Luna!" he called, but the fire roared so loudly in his ears that he couldn't hear his own voice. He turned to go back the way he had come, but all he could see was smoke and all he could take into his lungs was smoke. He got onto his hands and knees and crawled across the hardwood floor of the living room toward the front door. He knocked the edge of the glass coffee table with his head, and realized he had gone the wrong way. He gulped the thick air. He coughed, and gasped, coughed and gasped, and then everything went black.

18

Ryan

When he got the call at 5 a.m., Ryan was eating a bowl of cereal in the dark kitchen of his cold apartment. He had on his swimsuit, sweatpants, a fleece top—a uniform that felt like a second skin after twelve years of competitive swimming. On the mornings he swam with the masters' team, he came back to the apartment for a second breakfast with Olivia and Brooke, and then drove back to the pool to run the morning workouts for his college team.

"Hello?" he said. He was expecting a swimmer to be calling to say that she was sick, or that his car wouldn't start.

"He's still at the house," his mother said—her voice rushed, panicked, raspy. "It was engulfed in flames, Ryan. Totally engulfed."

His mind was still foggy with sleep. "Mom," he asked, "what's going on?"

"A fire," she said, and then she coughed, and sobbed, and whatever she said next was incomprehensible.

He stood up. He could hear voices in the background. "Where are you?" he asked.

"Emergency room," she said. "Daddy went back in the house; it was totally engulfed."

"Okay," he said. "Okay."

She moved away from the phone, and he could hear her retching.

"Mom," he shouted. "Mom."

She came back on the line, and moaned.

"Have you called Nana?"

"She's gone," Lily said, and Ryan felt a wave of panic move through his body, the hot flush of knowledge that no one else was in charge.

"What about Luke?" Ryan asked, but he couldn't hear what she was saying. "I'll be there in two hours," he said. "Hold tight, okay? Hold tight."

HE threw some shirts in a daypack, then went to wake Olivia.

"Stop it," she mumbled when he put his hand on her freckled shoulder. Brooke was up in the middle of the night every night now with nightmares—about alligators, sharks, a giant gorilla—and Olivia was living in a state of total sleep deprivation. He no longer touched her for anything less than an emergency.

"Wake up," he said, shaking her again.

She pulled a pillow over her head.

"Olivia, wake up," Ryan demanded. "Something's happened to my mom and dad."

She recognized the sound of terror. It was a sound that reverberated in her own head now, all day long, and all night long. Was Brooke eating enough, was Brooke sleeping enough, would Brooke fall into the pool, was the babysitter trustworthy? People always said that staying at home with a toddler was the hardest job in the world, but what they never said was what averting disaster all day long did to your soul—how it lost some of its protective coating, and became raw, exposed. She sat bolt upright. "What's wrong?" she asked, swinging her legs over the side of the bed, ready to solve the problem.

"It's my mom," Ryan said, and Olivia stopped midstride; she hated to be so callous, but she had to conserve her energy. This wasn't her problem to solve.

"There was a fire," Ryan said. "I have to go."

"Right now?" Olivia asked.

"My dad might not have gotten out."

"Oh my God," she said, and stepped toward him and threw her arms around him. She was wearing a thin nightgown, with spaghetti straps. He could feel her breasts and her soft tummy pressed against his body. She felt warm and she felt as if she weren't his anymore. It wasn't that long ago when the slightest touch from Olivia sent him into a frenzy. They couldn't kiss without ripping each other's clothes off. They couldn't sleep through a whole night without climbing on top of each other. Now he held his wife in his arms with a kind of caution.

"You'll be okay?" he asked. He wasn't sure what Olivia and Brooke did every day. There were groups of moms they met with, and some kind of class they went to that had something to do with music. Olivia bought organic fruit and vegetables at the local market, and cubed and steamed them for Brooke. When Brooke was asleep, or watching something on TV, Olivia transcribed notes for a medical office. He figured they would be fine without him. He wondered if he would even be missed.

She nodded. "We'll be fine."

"I'll call you when I get there," he said.

WHEN he got on the road, he felt a cold sense of dread. He dialed his parents' new phone number—a phone at a house where he had never lived—but there was no answer. He knew his parents had an answering machine. It had his father's voice on it: *We're not here right now, but leave us a message and we'll be sure to get back to you soon.*

"Fuck," Ryan said.

He plugged in his iPod and listened to Sting. He was used to seeing his mother distraught. When he was younger, she used to get migraines all the time—three, sometimes four times a month. She would cry out in pain, vomit. He couldn't stand the smell, or the fact of his mother being ill, and he would go in his room and put his music on. Luke took after their dad. He would wade right into the storm with a bucket and an ice pack.

While Sting's mournful voice filled his head, Ryan tried to imagine his dad caught in a fire. His mind wouldn't let it happen. His dad was quiet, reserved, a guy who planned everything out in advance, considered everything that could go wrong, and focused on whatever problems arose until they were solved. Ryan remembered a time when he had accidentally cast a fish hook through Luke's thumb. They were in the middle of a remote lake in the White Mountains in the heat of summer. While Luke howled, and Ryan sat there pale and stricken, his dad calmly assessed the wound, opened his tackle box, got out a pair of needle-nose pliers, broke off the barb, and slipped it out the way it had gone in.

Olivia won't come, he thought. *If something's happened to my dad, she won't come to Santa Barbara.* And he realized that his marriage, which was so new, was never going to last as long as his parents' had. As he drove over the pass into Santa Barbara, he saw the smoke that blanketed the hills like a shroud and he stared out at the mocking blue sky, the sunshine, the sparkling sea. When he got down onto the freeway, he could see actual flames on the hills—angry lines of them, marching along the hill—and he could see people driving in both directions, their cars hastily piled with whatever belongings they had grabbed before they fled.

WHEN he got to the hospital, Ryan bolted inside and demanded to see his mother. A receptionist directed him upstairs; a nurse walked him down a hallway. He found her lying in a hospital bed. Her eyes were closed, and her face, usually so pretty and composed, looked as if was bruised. Her dark gray hair, which usually swung around her ears and her chin, was matted against her head. There was an IV stuck in her arm, and a bag of clear fluids on a post near her head. Luke was sitting on a chair beside the bed, slumped forward, the whole weight of his head in his hands.

Luke looked up. "He's dead," he said quietly. "The doctor just told us. The firemen got him out but there was nothing they could do."

19

Eleanor

WHEN Eleanor woke up at daybreak the way she always did, she was startled to find that she was still fully clothed, and that Gordon Vreeland was asleep in the chair by the window. She was irritated that he had stayed. He was mooning after her the way all the rest of them were, and in one of her oldest and dearest friends, it was pathetic. She got off the bed, showered, and changed into a pair of slacks and a sweater. These things took her longer than they used to, because her bad knees made it hard to bend down in the morning. Getting her shoes off the floor required her to sit first, and if she dropped the soap in the shower, she would be in real trouble. She had a flight to catch at eleven o'clock, and she refused to eat breakfast at the airport. She would have a proper breakfast downstairs before catching a cab. When she was packed and ready to leave, she placed a hand on Gordon's shoulder and shook him awake.

"Get up, Gordon," she said.

"What?" he said. And then, "Oh, right, good morning, Eleanor."

"Why are you here?" she asked, her hand on her hip.

He sat up. "I was watching you sleep," he said, as if it were the most normal thing in the world. "I must have fallen asleep. I'm sorry."

"I'm going down for breakfast," she said, and she began to collect her keys, her purse, her suitcase.

Gordon stood up and asked if he could use her bathroom. He washed his face, and smoothed down his thin gray hair, which stuck straight up from his head like a little boy's. He followed Eleanor to the elevator.

"Look," she said while they stood there waiting in the hallway, "I'm sorry I can't accept your offer."

"Does that mean I can't have breakfast with you?"

"Of course you can have breakfast with me," she said, "for crying out loud."

After they had ordered, she pulled out her phone and switched it on. Sometimes the airlines called with flight information, and she quickly scanned her messages. There were fifteen messages from yesterday alone. She wrinkled her forehead and studied them—and then she panicked. Both her grandsons had called, and they usually only did that on her birthday. She listened to just two frantic messages from Ryan— *Where are you? Answer your goddamn phone!*—before she excused herself from the table, stepped out of the restaurant into a vestibule in the lobby, and dialed Ryan.

"What's going on?" she demanded.

Ryan's voice was void of any emotion. He sounded flat, hollow. "There's been an accident," he said. "A fire."

"What?" Eleanor whispered.

"There was a wildfire in the hills."

"Are they okay? Lily and Tom?"

"They knocked her out. She was hysterical."

"Are you *there*, Ryan? In Santa Barbara?"

"We've been trying to reach you for hours, Nana. We didn't know where you were."

Eleanor began to walk back to the table in the restaurant, still talking on the phone. It was a habit she loathed when she saw other people doing it—carrying on conversations in public. "It was a wildfire?" she asked.

"The house is gone," Ryan said. "She doesn't know yet."

"Dear God," Eleanor said.

Gordon was standing, leaving money on the table, wheeling Eleanor's suitcase.

"And Dad . . ." Ryan said.

Eleanor had heard enough bad news in her life to know what was coming. Something in Ryan's tone, in the way he said that one word—*Dad*—said everything.

"Dad didn't make it out," Ryan said.

She felt something snap inside—some thread, some stitch that held her heart in place. She stopped in the middle of the restaurant, where the other diners were now staring at her, aware that something dramatic was happening while they ate their waffles and bacon. "Are you saying Tom's dead?"

"Yes," Ryan said.

"I have a flight in two hours," she said. "I'm on my way."

Gordon pressed his hand on her back and guided her into the lobby. He took her room key and dropped it at the front desk, then led her out the front door into the busy morning air. She was shaking. Her teeth were chattering, and her heart was pounding. She gulped in a drink of air, and when she let it out, it came out as a shuttering sob. Gordon put his arm around her and asked for a cab. When the cab pulled up, he got in next to her in the backseat and said to the driver, "Logan Airport, please."

They were in the tunnel before she spoke.

"There was a fire," she said, "in the hills. Lily's husband was killed."

Gordon pressed his lips together, and looked out the window of the cab at the tiled walls of the tunnel, and the dim light. Sometimes hours would go by when he forgot that Judy had died, or forgot to remember that she was dead, but mostly, he was reminded of it time and time again, and the pain never diminished. It was the same hurt, time after time. He had begun to recognize it, to see it coming, to brace for it. But sometimes—like now—the pain crashed over him unexpectedly, and he felt as if he were drowning. He drew in a large breath and let out the air in a kind of sputtering gasp.

Eleanor had been trying to be matter-of-fact. She thought

that if she could just get to the airport and get on the plane and get to Santa Barbara, it would somehow be okay. But when she heard Gordon sigh, she could not hold it together anymore. Tears spilled from her eyes, and she reached out and squeezed his hand in solidarity, and in thanks.

Once they got to the airport, Gordon used his phone to find news about the fire. It was only 80 percent contained. Eighty-three structures had burned. There was a shelter set up at the high school, and the insurance companies had already rolled in mobile units to help people process their claims. He fed her this information in small bits as they stood in line, and she only nodded in response. She had lived in Santa Barbara through several fires. She knew how it went: the hot winds whipped down the canyons at sundown, the eucalyptus trees burst into flame, the fire raced along the ridges like a voracious beast and the only thing you could do if you were in the way was to run. She'd known people who escaped from their homes with nothing but the clothes on their backs. She'd known others whose house was left standing while every structure around it was burned to the ground. The power of the fires was so awesome that the entire population of the town entered into a kind of reverent hush. Smoke filled the sky, ash filled the air, and people sat in front of their televisions transfixed by the images of flame and the specter of burned houses. They listened as their fellow citizens talked about their great good luck at being alive, and proclaimed their resolve to continue to live in the fragrant hillside chaparral, despite the fact that fire might come again.

When Eleanor had a boarding pass in hand, she made her way to the security line. Gordon followed her as far as he could, but then there was a uniformed security guard asking to see ID and boarding passes, and he was unable to continue.

"Will you call me when you arrive?" he asked.

She nodded dismissively, and turned to go, but then she stepped out of the stream of people, and turned back to face him. "Tom and Lily were like you and Judy," she said. "They were one of those couples that made you believe in marriage. It used to drive me crazy that she had exactly the thing I had never been able to get. I had husbands die and husband disappoint, and I took lover after lover trying to fill the void, and she just sort of fell into this beautiful, lasting relationship like it was nothing. I know I shouldn't have thought this about my own child, but I didn't think it was fair." A rim of red rose up around her eyes as if someone had drawn it in, and her nostrils flared. She gulped at the air, once, as if she was going to dive underwater and needed her breath.

"You'd better go," he said. He put his hand on her back, and gave her a small push toward the gate.

She turned into the sea of people surging toward the security check, slipped off her shoes, and was gone.

SHE normally loved to ride on planes. She loved the hum of the engines and the clouds out the window and the way the entire country seemed within grasp when you were thirty thousand feet above it. But the trip to Santa Barbara that day was torture. She had one flight from Boston to Denver, and another from Denver to Santa Barbara. She felt faint on the first leg of the trip, and nauseous. The flight attendant brought her a 7Up, and some crackers and a warm towel.

She knew what it was like to have a husband suddenly die. She had been with Billy when his heart stopped. They were on their way home from Buenos Aires, where he had been playing an exhibition baseball game. They were at the airport, walking along, and then suddenly he was no longer next to her. He was slumped on the floor at her feet, and she knew before anyone could tell her that he was dead. She was secretly relieved. Once he made the major leagues, his love of baseball eclipsed his love of anything else. Eleanor didn't know yet how easy it was for a woman to walk out on a marriage, and sudden death was an elegant solution to her dilemma.

Elliot Taft must have sensed her glee. A Harvard classmate of Billy's, who did not have the good fortune to be on the Great Date, came calling within weeks of the funeral, and said he had been trying to keep his hands off her ever since they had met. He was married, with three children, and Eleanor took him as a lover. One day that fall, Lily came home early from school and found them naked in bed. Eleanor could see confusion and betrayal flash across her daughter's face, and so she told Elliot that he had to marry her, or leave her. By that point, Elliot couldn't give her up. He left his wife and children, got Union Oil to transfer him to a new city, and started a new life with Eleanor and Lily. But Elliot Taft wanted it all—his first wife, his new wife, and any other woman that struck his fancy. When he died after the oil spill debacle, Eleanor thought that he got exactly what he deserved.

Her third husband, Jacques, walked into her office one day and said he wanted a divorce. He had been a stately, polished man, an architect, an art collector, and he had picked Eleanor much the same way he would have picked a painting—for the way it would look in his home, for the prestige, for the invest-ment. Many of his friends and colleagues were architects and designers, and through them, she was able to broaden the reach of Bertasi Linen all over the world. "That sounds rea-sonable," she said, and she called a lawyer, and he was gone within a matter of weeks.

As her plane touched down in Denver, Eleanor kept trying to imagine what it would be like to lose a husband with whom you were actually in love.

In Denver, she watched the planes taking off and landing as she waited for her flight, and she kept imagining them fall-ing out of the sky, and people raining down. She checked her phone, and saw that Gordon had called three times, but she did not call him back. She called Luke, and Ryan, and heard that they were waiting to see the body, and deciding what to do with it.

The trip to Santa Barbara took forever. She felt as though

the canyons below her and the clouds above continued to go by as if on a conveyor belt, as if the landscape was moving in a circle, and they were just standing still in the sky. She didn't know what she would do to help Lily through this, but she would come up with something. Despite all the ways they had let each other down over the years, and the distance between them, and the fact that it was, in so many ways, her fault that Tom had been in the path of the fire, Eleanor would come up with something.

20

Olivia

OLIVIA'S nerves were frayed. That was the word she kept saying to herself, and the picture she kept imagining—the end of a rope, frayed, its individual threads exposed. A strange array of thoughts flitted across her mind like static on a TV screen—*we need to call a plumber about the drain in the bathtub, maybe Franny can watch Brooke on Wednesday, if Ryan's dad is hurt what will happen to Ryan's mom?* She couldn't remember the last time she'd slept through the night. Every night, as she brushed Brooke's teeth, changed her diaper, changed her into pajamas, read her *Harold and the Purple Crayon* again and again and again, she thought, *Maybe tonight.* But every night, Brooke awoke because her diaper was wet, or she'd had a bad dream, or she was thirsty, and Olivia would get up and stumble through the dark house to do whatever had to be done, and she would lie in bed and, instead of going to sleep, would wait for the next assault.

Things were easier with Ryan gone. She didn't have to wash her hair, didn't have to come up with something to say when he asked how her day had been, didn't have to feel guilty when she got in bed and he reached out for her and she rolled away and said, "No." She could concentrate, simply, on getting through the day. All morning, Brooke had been asking where Ryan was, and all morning, Olivia had been lying to her.

"Where's Daddy?" Brooke asked.

"He had to go away for a little while," Olivia said.

"Where?" Brooke asked again.

"He went to see Grandma and Grandpa."

"Why?"

Olivia panicked. Why? What could she possibly say that a two-year-old would understand? "Because they needed his help," she said.

"Why?"

"Because Grandpa Tom isn't feeling well."

"He's sick?"

"Yes," Olivia said. "He's sick."

She put Brooke down for her morning nap and backed out of the room so as not to disturb her. She sat down at the computer to search for plumbers. When the phone rang, she jumped. "Hello?" she said softly.

"It's me," Ryan said, and she could tell from his voice—gravelly, hollow—that something was very wrong. The thought she had just had—that things were easier without Ryan—was swept away, and she felt a wave of concern and affection for him.

"What's wrong?" she said. "What's happened?"

"It's my dad," Ryan said. "He's dead."

She sucked in air and instantly felt the burn of tears in her eyes. "Oh my God, Ryan," she said. "Oh my God."

He hadn't cried until then, but the sound of Olivia's voice made him remember that he had his own family now. He was a father. And he needed to be there for his child the way his dad had been there for him. "There was a fire," he said through his tears. "In the hills. I guess he went back for something. He was trying to get something out."

"He was trapped?" Olivia whispered.

"The firemen said it was the smoke," Ryan said. "It was the smoke that killed him."

She had seen pictures of California wildfires. From her home in Boston, they had seemed like exotic, far-off catastrophes. But here was something very specific—smoke, probably black, probably toxic, smoke that could kill. Ryan was sobbing, and Olivia realized that she had never heard him cry. She closed her eyes. "Oh Ryan," she said. "How's your mom?"

"Fucked up," he said, "totally fucked up." And then, "Olivia? Will you and Brooke come down?"

Her eyes welled up with tears again at the way he asked—as if she might not say yes. "Of course," she said, "of course we'll come down." She looked around the apartment at the diaper bag spilled on the floor, the food left out on the counter, the laundry that still needed folding. She imagined just picking up Brooke and walking out the door. "Should we come right now?"

"Tomorrow might be better," Ryan said. "We're meeting with the coroner. We have to get Mom into Nana's house. You should fly, don't you think?"

"That'll be expensive."

"It'd be stupid to have two cars here. Just fly. And can you bring me another pair of jeans?"

She got up, got a piece of paper, started a list. "Anything else?"

"My razor, I guess. Deodorant."

She nodded. She remembered when she and Ryan first started spending nights together. The presence of a razor in her bathroom was momentous. The presence of deodorant meant everything. She remembered wanting the tokens of Ryan's life to be a part of her life, too—to belong in her bathroom, to mingle with her lavender lotion and her peppermint soap.

"What's my mom going to do?" Ryan asked. He spoke so softly now that she could barely make out the words.

"Your mom will come through," Olivia said. "She's a strong woman. Did the house burn down?"

"Burned to the ground. A fireman told me. A guy in a yellow rubber jumpsuit just like you see on TV. I kept wanting to say, 'Are you for real?'" Ryan laughed then, a sick, hollow sound. "I kept wanting to say, 'Dude, it's not Halloween.'"

She laughed along with him, just to make him feel better.

"Kiss Brooke for me," Ryan said.

"I will."

"Tell her I love her."

"I will."

"And you, too," he said. "I love you so much."

She licked the tears that ran down her face and they tasted salty. She hated to admit it in light of everything that happened, but they tasted good. "I love you, too," she said.

21

Lily

LILY and the boys slumped down the hall and into the white room where Tom's body lay under a sheet. Gritting his teeth, Ryan stepped forward to lift the edge of the sheet. Luke put an arm around his mother's shoulders and ushered her forward. He was glad to have something to do with his hands.

Tom's skin was smudged with ash, covered in soot. He smelled of smoke. Lily's first thought was that Tom would sit up and shake off what was ailing him and go back to being Tom. She counted her own breath—in, out; in, out; in, out; in, out—and when he didn't breathe during that whole time, she thought, *Okay. They're right. He's dead.* She lifted his hand and held it, and with her other hand, brushed her fingers lightly on Tom's cheek. "He's so cold," she said, and squeezed her eyes shut because she could hear him in her head saying, *I don't think I would miss the cold.*

"You know what I keep thinking about?" Luke asked. He was tall like his father, not as beefy as his brother. "How much he loved his stupid garden, all those goddamn peas and kale."

"I keep thinking about how much he loved Mount Mansfield," Ryan said. When Ryan was in high school, Tom set out to climb every peak in the state of Vermont over four thousand feet. Luke accompanied him on almost every climb, but because of his swimming, Ryan was rarely free to go. In August, when the swim team took its only break, he joined his dad and his brother on the last big climb. *We saved the best for last,* his dad declared, and when they got to the top of Mount Mansfield, he grew very quiet as he looked out over the scoured valleys and the green-padded hills. After a while, he said, *"When I die, cremate me and throw my ashes from this peak."*

"He's *dead*," Lily said, and neither of the boys said, *"Smart, Mom,"* or *"Good observation, Mom,"* the way they might have under other circumstances. They just stood there over the body, feeling small and fragile, as if they, too, could at any moment simply stop walking and talking and breathing.

Ryan cleared his throat. "I'll take his ashes to the top of Mount Mansfield," he said. "I can do it before the snow falls, unless you want to come with me, Luke. We could do it next summer."

Luke nodded. Surely his grandmother would give him enough time off to help scatter his father's ashes. "Maybe we could take some of the ashes over to Apple Tree Point, too. To that cove he loved. Mom could come with us, and Olivia and Brooke."

Lily rested Tom's hand back next to his body, and stepped away from the table. Tom's family had a plot at Mount Auburn Cemetery in Boston—a neatly manicured row of granite tombstones shaded by elm trees and hydrangeas in the lush green park where proper New England families buried their dead. The Gilberts had a relative who had been an astronomer and a telescope maker. His was the first grave in the family plot at Mount Auburn—*Charles Gilbert, 1755–1838, Patriot, Scholar, Scientist*. But Tom didn't like Mount Auburn Cemetery. He didn't like the dates carved in granite, the gargoyles on the mausoleums, the way the gardeners so carefully manicured the ancient, haunted leaves. "Just cremate me," he always used to say after a visit to Mount Auburn. "Scatter my ashes in the garden where they'll do some good, or on a mountain where they'll blend into the scenery."

Lily had always intended to do as he wished. She and Tom had thought their deaths through with as much attention to detail as they lived their lives. They had generous life insurance policies, an airtight will that would preserve the family money in a trust, durable powers of attorney so that each of them could pull the plug on the other should they end up in a vegetative state. When the boys were young, they had long, somber conversations about the importance of staying the course if tragedy were to strike. If one of them were to slip on the ice and hit their head, run off the road and hit a tree, receive a sudden diagnosis of pancreatic cancer and be gone in a month, the surviving spouse would stay in the house, stay in Burlington, keep everything as stable as possible. Death itself might be unknowable, but Lily Gilbert thought she knew just what to do if Tom—who never got sick, who never complained, who never seemed as if he were even susceptible to death—were to be the first to die: she would simply follow the plan they had made as if it were a road map. Now here she was, alone, somewhere far off the map. *Damn him*, she thought.

She looked at Tom's blackened body and it seemed to her as though it was already on its way to ash; it didn't have that much further to go. "No," she said, and both boys looked up as if someone else had walked into the room and spoken that word. "We're not going to cremate his body. I'm going to bury him at Mount Auburn."

Ryan felt as if his whole body were a high-tension wire. It seemed to vibrate, to sizzle. "You can't do that, Mom," he said sharply.

She stared at her son as if he were underwater and the sound he'd made had been too distorted to hear. He'd been a quiet teenager, the kind of boy who slipped out of bed on dark winter mornings to get himself to swim practice, who holed up in his bedroom listening to music for hours on end, but when he decided he had something to say, he said it with force and conviction, and he found that he often got his way. He was never the loudest member of the team, or the one who stood out in a crowd, but he was always elected captain. He had a sureness about him that drew people in. Now that he was in his twenties, that sureness had hardened into something sharp-edged that Lily found suddenly ugly.

"You can't do it," Ryan repeated. "Because it's not what he wanted."

"It's what *I* want," she said.

Ryan turned away from his father's body to the white wall of the hospital, and then he turned back to his mother. "But it's not what he asked us to do."

Lily looked again at Tom's body—cold, inert, lifeless. "He's not here anymore," Lily said.

"Which is why we have to honor his wishes."

Lily shook her head. "No we don't," she said. She looked into her son's eyes—hazel, flecked with gold, totally different from his dad's solid green eyes. "We couldn't save him from the first fire," she said. "But we can save him from this one."

Luke looked again at his dad's body. Tom's hair was matted with ash. His fingernails had half-moons of black under the rim. "She's right, Ryan," Luke said quietly.

Ryan looked up, shocked that his younger brother had spoken, shocked to see that Luke was a man, too, grown-up and opinionated. They were so old, so suddenly.

"Dad would never break someone's trust," Ryan said, "and I don't see how we can break his now."

Lily jerked her head up. Why had Ryan chosen those words—*Dad would never break someone's trust*? Had he emphasized the word *Dad*? *Dad* would never break someone's trust—but *Mom* was another story? Mom would go to meet another man, fantasize about another man, imagine leaving a perfectly good marriage to a perfectly good man just because *good* somehow didn't seem like it was good enough anymore?

"Let it go," Luke said.

"I can't have any more fire," Lily said.

Ryan pressed his teeth together again. He thought of Olivia and of Brooke, and of everything slipping through his fingers like water. "Fine," he said, and turned away from his dad's lifeless body, and his mom's battered face.

SHE made arrangements for Tom's body to be embalmed and shipped back to Boston, where they would have a small family ceremony to put him in the ground. She liked the idea of him resting under all that snow, in a place that would be green and leafy all spring. She thought of all the things that burn—books, photographs, rugs, furniture, walls, flesh and bone. It gave her some measure of comfort to think that nothing could burn the piece of granite that would bear Tom's name.

"What about a funeral out here, Mom," Luke asked, "or a memorial service of some kind?"

Lily imagined sitting in a borrowed dress in a borrowed church, and then she thought of guacamole. All spring, Tom had thrown himself into the study of avocados—their history, their uses. *"The preferred way of eating avocados has always been to mash them up. The Aztecs called this mix ahuaca-mull."*

Lily would look up from her computer, or from the soup she was stirring on the stove, and say, "Really? I had no idea." When their knives and cutting boards and mixing bowls came off the moving truck in Santa Barbara—safely arrived, after all—Tom began to cook. He had never shown any interest in cooking before, but suddenly, he was bringing back exotic peppers from the Farmer's Market and slow roasting them over an open flame, mincing garlic and cilantro, and buying specially curved knives with which to deseed heirloom tomatoes. He set down bowls of guacamole in front of anyone who walked into the house, pushing baskets of chips across the table, cracking open cold beers. It was a strange invitation from a man who wore wool socks with his sandals.

Within the first week, Tom developed a favorite recipe. It was the one that elicited the most praise, for its chunky texture and its lively taste. Even Eleanor, who usually preferred more refined fare, said that it tasted like summer.

"What's in it, Tom?" Eleanor asked.

"Ah," he said, pleased to have piqued her interest. "A man who shares his secret guacamole recipe is a man who is a fool."

Now he was dead, and Lily imagined re-creating his guacamole. It would taste like summer, and they would all stand around and remember how much Tom wanted to become a gentleman farmer, and how he had gotten his wish, however briefly. "I think we should just have a small gathering for now," she said.

W<small>HEN</small> they left the hospital in the late afternoon, the sky was orange and opaque. The fire was still burning in the hills and smoldering in the canyons. Hundreds of families had fled, and were huddled on friends' couches watching the news, crouched in front of other people's computers scrolling through lists of burned properties, camped out in the Red Cross shelter at the high school giving thanks for dinner and a blanket. Lily and the boys got in Luke's truck in solemn silence. It was Lily, sitting in the front passenger seat, who spoke first.

"What happened to Dad's truck? Someone drove me down the hill in it, but then an ambulance came because I couldn't stop vomiting."

"It's parked up on Sheffield Drive behind the police line," Ryan said. A fireman had come up to him in the hospital to tell him about the truck and to tell him about the house. *It's gone,* the man had said. *We couldn't save any of it.*

Lily nodded, and then after a moment, she said, "The house is gone, isn't it?"

Ryan cleared his throat. "Yeah," he said. "That's what they told me."

"All of it?" She knew that sometimes it was only a wall that burned, or a room.

"It sounds like it," he said.

Lily laughed, a short, sharp burst of sound. "I'm homeless," she said. "I'm a homeless widow."

"Nana's on her way," Ryan said, because it was, at least, an answer to the question of where they would sleep. "She said to go to her house."

Images flashed into Lily's mind—the socks in her sock drawer, the washing machine and dryer that had just been delivered, the stack of books in the study. Was all of it really gone? And if so, where did it go to? She looked out the window of the truck at the greasy sky, and at the ash that gathered on the windshield like snow. Was that the remains of her teapot, her kitchen table, the blown-glass ornaments she brought back from Venice? "I don't have a toothbrush," she said.

Luke turned on the ignition. "Grandma probably has one," he said.

"I don't have underwear."

"Then I'll go to Target," Luke said. "I'll get you whatever you need."

When they got to her mother's house, Lily went straight to her mother's office. It was on the first floor, just beyond the entryway, with a window that looked out onto a patio with bougainvillea-covered walls. There was a drawer with pens and paperclips and stamps and tape and scissors, and a wooden tray for correspondence. She took a piece of blank paper out of the printer, wrote "Bedroom" at the top, and started to make a list:

Cherry spindle bed

Organic cotton flannel blanket

Susan Sargent Blue Birds duvet cover and pillow

L.L.Bean cotton flannel sheets, blue

L.L.Bean cotton flannel sheets, green

Bertasi Linen cotton sheets, navy blue piping

Bertasi Linen cotton sheets, white

Alarm clock

Flashlight

Art Quilts of Lancaster County

A Quilter's Guide to Pattern Design

Organic Farming

The Journal of American Agriculture

Gold-framed mirror

Painting of winter birch trees

Photo of Luke and Ryan

Photo of Ryan, Olivia, and Brooke

Grandma Hattie's pearls

Grandma Hattie's garnet ring

Cashmere gloves

Black leather gloves

Tom's loose coins

Tom's Patriots' hat

Tom's collection of fountain pens—Pelikan Steno (Xmas 1973), Waterman Phileas (20th anniversary), Parker Sonnet (Xmas 1985), the obsidian Montblanc, the silver Cross

She filled up one page, then got out another, and wrote the things she had shipped from Santa Barbara to Burlington and back again:

The new Singer
Gingher scissors—old, new
Box of pins
Ruby red thread

"What are you doing?" Ryan asked.

"I don't want to forget anything," Lily said. It suddenly seemed important that she remember every single thing that she and Tom had purchased, and packed, and moved out to California. If she could name all of those items—the furniture, the clothes, the books, the cups, the toiletries—then perhaps she could know exactly what it was that she and Tom had, all those years together, and what it all meant. She would never have said it out loud, or even admitted it to herself, but she had the tiniest hope that if she could name every single one of the things that brought life to their home, they would somehow add up to Tom himself.

Ryan held open a laptop. "I found the house on a list of lost properties," he said solemnly. "It's on the city's website."

She peered at the screen. There was a list of street numbers. She didn't know whom most of the houses belonged to. She had only briefly met a few of the neighbors, shaken their hands, and said hello at her mother's welcome party.

"There's also a map of the burn area on the *Independent* website," Ryan said, "and I've got Google Earth up so you can compare the two; you can see how the fire came right down the canyon."

They looked at the maps and pointed at the streets and zoomed in on the photograph of the house, which was taken six months ago, when Ted Hailwood was still worrying about bees, and Lily and Tom were finishing up their fall semester classes. "You can see the furniture on the back deck," Lily said, "and the shed at the bottom of the hill. Can you print that out, Ryan?"

"Sure," he said.

Lily turned back to her list. She and Tom had negotiated to buy that patio furniture, because the Hailwoods couldn't take it to the assisted living community where they were moving, and it was beautiful furniture, in fine shape. She wrote "Back Deck," and then added:

Teak table
4 teak chairs
4 teak longues
Carnival striped patio umbrella
Terra-cotta pots
Hummingbird feeder
Wind chime
Sisal doormat

The boys stepped into their grandmother's kitchen to find something to eat. There was hardly anything in the refrigerator—eggs, butter, a chunk of cheese.

"Let's just order pizza," Luke said.

Ryan nodded. He was worried about Olivia and Brooke coming down from San Luis Obispo—he had an irrational fear that their plane would crash—and he was worried about his mother. Her eyes had looked hollow and haunted, and her obsession with writing everything down that she had lost in the house had a creepiness to it that frightened him. He had never actually believed it would come to this—his dad dead? His mother crazy with grief? "Do you think Mom will eat?" he asked.

Luke took a deep breath and let the air out in a loud rush. "Probably not."

"I don't know what the fuck she's doing making all these lists," Ryan said. "It's not like it's going to bring him back."

Luke didn't respond. He was worried about something else. "I don't understand why she got out and he didn't," he said. "It doesn't make any sense. I can't figure it out."

"They were loading things into the truck, right?" Ryan asked.

Luke nodded.

"So he must have gone back for something. Made one last trip."

"Went back for what, though? I mean, what would be that important? His Bean boots? His maps? His pens? He wouldn't be that dumb. Don't you remember how many times he made us come down from a hill because there was lightning, or stop skiing because the visibility was bad?"

"I always thought he was so anal," Ryan said, and his voice broke. "I always used to wish that he would just cut loose and ski after midnight, or stand on a mountaintop in a thunderstorm."

Luke reached out and put his arm around his older brother's shoulders. "Maybe he did," Luke said. "Maybe that's what buying the avocado ranch was for him."

Ryan dropped his head in his hands and wept.

22

Luke

THE next day, Luke was desperate for something to do—anything that would make his head stop spinning, anything that would help him to breathe. He drove to Target and headed for the toothbrush aisle. He grabbed the first toothbrush that caught his eye—purple, shimmery, with words on the packaging that claimed the bristles would be soft and long-lasting. He selected a tube of the same toothpaste he used, which was the same toothpaste he had used throughout his childhood in Vermont. As he stood there, toothbrush and toothpaste in hand, he remembered the way his dad would stand at the sink brushing his teeth and shaving his face as if precision and control, even in this small daily endeavor, were of the utmost importance. It used to fascinate Luke—that every morning of his life, his dad got up and did exactly the same thing in exactly the same way, whether there was a blizzard outside, or blazing sun, whether he would be going fishing or going to teach a class called Cooperation and Conflict in the Biological Sciences. Once, Luke swiped his brother's swimming stopwatch to time his dad's morning routine. He found that over five days, the routine never varied more than twenty seconds from the norm. When Luke himself learned to shave, he tried to adopt the same precision. He believed it was one of the things that made you a man.

Next, Luke made his way to the area where women's underthings were displayed. He stood on the tile at the edge of the carpet and tried not to think about what he was doing. It was just a chore, an errand, something he had to do. He also tried not to think of Franny Jones and her petal pink underwear and the petal pink bra in tenth grade, and how he had learned to unhook it without even looking. He plunged ahead, trying not to catch the eye of any of the other shoppers. He found a display of Jockey underwear—three pairs wrapped in plastic, one white, one beige, one black. He shuffled through until he found a small. He knew his mother would be a small. He took two packages.

On his way to the cash register, he walked by a display of jeans and sweatshirts at the edge of the women's clothing department. He stopped, and grabbed a pair of Levi's and a plain blue hoodie sweatshirt, then went to pay for his purchases.

The woman in front of him had her cart piled high with toilet paper and paper towels. Underneath the paper goods was a layer of cleaning supplies—dishwasher soap and soap for the laundry, toilet bowl cleaner, and Clorox—and also bottles of shampoo and conditioner. The last item she put on the black conveyer belt was a single can of shaving cream. It was red-and-white-striped Barbasol: the exact kind of shaving cream his dad used. He would shake the can exactly five times, cup his hand, deliver a ball the size, color, and shape of a Ping-Pong ball, set down the can, rub the tips of his fingers together exactly five times, apply the cream to his face, and then, starting on the left side, near the ear, would start his first stroke down.

Luke closed his eyes. He felt them burn. He stood like that—eyes closed, eyes burning—until the cashier asked if she could help him, and then he opened his eyes, brushed away the tears, and set down the toothbrush, toothpaste, clothing, and underwear he had selected for his mother, the homeless widow.

The cashier was a young woman with a name tag that read DARLENE. Luke braced himself for her to look at him with contempt or pity, or for her to ask, "Are you okay?" but she simply scanned and bagged his items, punched the keys on the cash register, made change from the hundred he handed over, and turned to her next customer.

"Thank you very much," Luke said, and hoped she understood how much he meant it.

•23•

Eleanor

ELEANOR'S plane touched down at the Santa Barbara airport a few minutes after ten. Ryan was there to meet her. He was sitting at an outside bench drinking Heineken and watching the strange glow of the lights in the smoky sky. When he saw his grandmother step onto the tarmac, he stood up. He was almost two feet taller than she was.

"Hey, Nana," he said, leaning down to embrace her. His eyes were red, his face heavy. "How was your flight?"

"Longest trip of my life," she said.

He nodded.

"And you?" she asked. "Are you okay?"

He shrugged. "It's hard to believe any of it is real." He took her suitcase and wheeled it along, and led her out to the car.

Eleanor wanted to say, *"Believe it, child,"* because she had lived long enough to know that everything can change in an instant, that people are always dying when you least expect it. "I know," she said, "I know."

RYAN put the suitcase in the trunk of the car, and held the door for his grandmother. When he got into the driver's seat, she looked over at him. "He was doing exactly what he wanted," she said. "At least there's that."

"I know," Ryan said. "That's what Mom keeps saying."

A feeling of guilt flashed across Eleanor's consciousness like a meteor. *It was my fault*, she thought. *It was my fault that they were living in the foothills of Santa Barbara in the sixth year of a drought, on a piece of property that was primed to burn. Were it not for me, they would be back in Vermont, awaiting the spring.* She felt her stomach clench, and grew slightly faint.

"She's doing okay, then?" Eleanor asked.

"She's pretty messed up," Ryan said. "She's just sitting there, making lists."

ELEANOR dropped her purse by the front door and headed directly to the third-floor guest room, where she found Lily with a notepad perched on her knees.

"Oh, my sweet girl," Eleanor said, sweeping into the room. She threw her arms around Lily's neck, and kissed her on the cheek, and clutched her hand as if she would never let go.

"He's dead," Lily said, and even though her body did not move, her face screwed up, and tears spilled from her eyes. "And it's all because of me."

"No, no," Eleanor said, but she didn't say, *You're wrong, it was all because of* me. "No, Lily. It was an accident, an act of nature."

Lily shook her head. "I had a migraine," she said. "I couldn't even see straight."

"A headache doesn't cause a wildfire," Eleanor said.

"I can't live without him," Lily said, looking straight into her mother's eyes in order to make her point as clear as possible. "I can't."

"You can and you will," Eleanor said. "I will see to it." But even as she spoke the words, she knew that there were limits to what one person could do for another. She knew that there was always a space you couldn't cross—a great divide. She had never bridged it with any of her husbands or lovers. She had never bridged it with Lily. She had come the closest with Gracie, who was dying alone in her beautiful apartment in New York City. But she was Lily's mother and she would do whatever it took to help her daughter recover from this blow.

"Have you eaten?" Eleanor asked.

Lily shook her head once.

"What about some Thai soup?" Eleanor said, recalling how that had worked with Gordon on the night of Judy's funeral. "Coconut lime soup?"

"I'd throw it up," Lily said.

"Toast?"

"No."

Eleanor felt panic rise in her like a fever. She wasn't good at doing nothing. "What are you writing?" she asked, nodding at the notepad, and thinking about the piece of yellow legal paper that Gordon had shown her just twenty-four hours before.

Lily tipped the pad so that her mother could see it. At the top of the page was the word "Kitchen." Underneath it was a list:

Walnut cookie jar
2 ceramic mugs from Maine
12 Blueberry Hill dinner plates
10 Blueberry Hill salad plates
9 Blueberry Hill bowls
Cast-iron skillet
Green-handled ice cream scoop
New dish drainer
New garbage can

"I have nothing left," Lily said. "Nothing."

Eleanor nodded, and brushed Lily's dark hair behind her ears. "You have us," she said, and even as she said it, she felt another jolt of guilt. She had wanted this: to have her family near, to have a role to play. She had asked for it. She had orchestrated it. This tragedy was, in many ways, completely her fault.

ELEANOR got up early the next morning and went to her office on the first floor. There were dozens of phone messages on Lily's cell phone—friends and neighbors and relatives calling from all over the country to see if the fires had affected her, to see if she was okay; and people from town—old friends from high school, people from the avocado warehouse. On Eleanor's home phone, there were dozens more. The last one had been from Gordon.

"Please call," he said. "I'm worried sick about you."

She answered all the other calls first. She had learned a thing or two about sudden and public tragedy, and so she knew just what to do: she told everyone about her son-in-law's death, that Lily's house had burned to the ground, and that in lieu of flowers they should send money to the Santa Barbara Fire Department.

Ryan was up early, too. He sat in the office where his grandmother worked the phones—first her home phone, then Lily's cell phone—and looked up information on how to file insurance claims on a house that no longer stood. In between calls, he looked up at his grandmother. "Nana," he said. "What the hell's wrong with flowers?"

Eleanor spoke in the voice of a master passing on a deep secret. She said simply, "They die."

When every call had been made, Eleanor finally called Gordon.

"I miss you," he said.

Eleanor wondered if Gordon had eaten anything besides bagels since she left. She wondered if he had sent his clothes to the cleaners. He was a lonely old man, used to having people around to look after him, cook for him, give a sense of purpose to his days. He no longer worked, was no longer married, no longer mattered in his children's lives. "No, you don't," Eleanor said. "You miss Judy."

"I miss her desperately," he said. "I do. But I also think she was right. What's the point of being alone, when we could be together? You're out there dealing with this terrible thing all alone. It doesn't have to be that way."

"Don't worry about me," she said. "I'm good at dealing with tragedy."

"I'd like to come see you," he said.

Her daughter was locked in the guest room. Her grandson was brooding in her office. There was going to be a memorial party in five days, and she needed to get the gardener to come out and prune the rosebushes on the patio and take the dead leaves off the palm trees. "I don't think that's a good idea," she said, and hung up.

After the phone call, Ryan spoke again. "My dad loved flowers," he said. "He grew these huge sunflowers and he'd

cut off the heads and leave them out on the deck for the chip-
munks. He planted tulips every year along the stone wall at
the edge of the property, even though the deer were the only
ones who really got to see them."

Eleanor looked at her grandson. She'd visited Lily's home
in Vermont every couple of years for Thanksgiving, and occa-
sionally in July when the garden was in full flower. She often
gave Tom things related to the garden for gifts—gardening
books that had been written about in the *Times*, a beautiful
trowel from Smith & Hawken.

"That's right," she said. "I'd forgotten that."

ELEANOR left the house and went to Vons. She got a cart, and
flew through the store, selecting butter, sugar, a box of yellow
cake mix, and a bottle of Mount Gay Rum. When she got back
to the house and started mixing the ingredients in a bowl,
Luke came and stared. "You bake?" he asked.

"Usually only when people die."

Lily came downstairs when the cake was almost done.

"This is for Tom?" she asked. "The cake is for Tom?" Eleanor could see a thousand emotions flicker across Lily's face,
and she wasn't sure whether Lily was going to wail or scream
or laugh or burst out in an angry tirade.

Eleanor nodded.

Lily didn't speak. She walked directly over to her mother, and
collapsed into Eleanor's body like a flower falling off its stem.

Eleanor was not used to her daughter's body in her arms. She was not used to the weight, to the smell, to the look of her graying hair, to the feeling of her shoulders shaking. She put her arms around Lily, first one, then the other, as if she were trying to feel her way.

24

Lily

THE jeans and sweatshirt reminded Lily of ones she'd had in college. There was something comforting about getting up every day and putting on the most basic, generic clothes. Her mother kept offering to go to Saks or Nordstrom to buy her a nice pair of pants or a skirt, but having her mother pick out clothes for her brought back too many memories of being a child in her mother's house, and so Lily just kept wearing the clothes Luke had bought, and she kept saying, "Please don't."

Lily slept on and off during the day, and at night, she sat up cataloging. Once, when she heard sirens, she went to the front door, and then settled again on the couch, across from where Luke had fallen asleep. Around 4 a.m., she stopped writing down things she remembered from her house on the hill and began to write out guacamole recipes. Some had three roasted peppers, and others had four. Some used lemon and some used lime. Tom had begun experimenting the moment they got to town, using ingredients from the Farmer's Market, and pushing the guacamole on everyone he met. At dinner, he would recite the recipes to Lily, and she realized now that she hadn't really been listening. She remembered the peppers—Anaheim, Pasillo, Serrano—but she couldn't remember whether Tom had paired the mild chiles with lemon, or the hot ones with lime.

"The avocado is considered the most highly nutritionally evolved of all food plants," Tom once told her. *"With the biochemical profile of a nut rather than a fruit, the average avocado provides enough protein to replace the meat or cheese in a light meal."* He had started a journal that he wrote in every night—notes about the trees and the weather, the soil and the fertilizer. It was a black Moleskine notebook with blank pages, and he poured his thoughts into it like a modern-day Ben Franklin writing the almanac. *Old Tom's Almanac.* She turned back to her list and wrote at the bottom of one column:

Tom's Moleskine farm journal

SHE awoke at 8 a.m to the smell of frying eggs and immediately felt nauseous. She imagined throwing up—just sitting there and throwing up, the way second graders sometimes do at their desks, when they are totally overcome by sudden sickness. She remembered the red wine she'd drunk on the back deck, and how Luna sat with her under the hot sky, and she remembered the cold tile on the bathroom floor when Tom came in to say that there was a fire and they had to leave.

Underneath all her thoughts, like an infection that won't back down, were thoughts of Jack. She had gone to look for Jack. She had sought him out. And her skin had buzzed under his touch. She drank the wine because of Jack. Maybe Tom had died because of Jack. And the truly insidious part of the thought was that she wasn't sure she regretted it. Maybe there was some divine plan at work. Maybe the move to Santa Barbara wasn't supposed to buoy up their marriage. Maybe the move was meant to end it. Maybe the move was meant to deliver her into the arms of someone new. Maybe she had been given an excuse to behave the way her mom always did— tossing out one person for another, acting on what felt good in the moment.

She was horrified at her own thoughts. She threw off the covers, took a freezing cold shower as punishment, and then charged down the stairs to the kitchen.

"I want to go see the house," she said. She needed pain to yank her back to a proper place of mourning. She needed to see where the house had been, where Tom had died.

Her whole family turned to look at her. Ryan put down a cup of orange juice, Luke swallowed a bite of pancake, Eleanor turned off the stove.

Luke cleared his throat. "I can take you up there in my truck," he said.

"Nana and I can follow in her car," Ryan said, "and one of us can drive Dad's truck back."

Lily had forgotten about Tom's truck and the ride down the hill, and the transfer to an ambulance. Her head had been exploding. The firemen had left the truck at the side of the road when the ambulance met them. At the time she had thought, *When Tom comes down, he'll see it and he'll bring the truck down to the hospital. He'll bring Luna.*

Eleanor looked at Lily's slippered feet. "You'll need shoes," she said. Lily nodded, because this time her mother was right.

WHEN they got to Nordstrom's shoe department, Lily went straight toward the clogs. They were heavy, practical. They would last fifteen years. She asked the sales clerk if she could to try on a black pair, size 6 1/2, and when the salesman brought them out, she was pleased at how compact they seemed. She slipped them on and walked a few steps around on the carpet. She listened to the discussions the other shoppers were having with each other—*that was a steal, they're so cute, you look amazing in them.* Living with Tom had permanently cured her of shopping for pleasure. He was a true New Englander, the kind of man who valued owning the same pair of Bean boots for thirty years, and who thought nothing of depending on a twenty-year-old hat. Tom could patch an oiled canvas jacket, caulk an old wooden boat, rewire a washing machine that got stuck on the rinse cycle. Lily fell into his thrifty ways. She would spend money on a beautiful wool coat, but with the intention of owning it for fifty years. She would buy a length of fabric to make a skirt in a timeless cut, knowing that it would look good for decades.

"What about these?" Eleanor said. She approached Lily carrying a copper-colored sandal similar to the ones she had on her feet, and a black patent leather ballet flat.

"I'm getting the clogs."

"You can get more than one pair of shoes, Lily."

"I don't need more than one pair of shoes."

"For goodness' sake, you lost everything. Buy a few pairs of shoes!"

"I don't need them," she said.

Eleanor handed the strappy sandal and the pretty flat to the saleslady, dramatically rolled her eyes, and said to everyone and to no one in particular, "How on earth did I end up with a daughter who doesn't love shoes?"

THEY drove in silence toward the police line on East Valley Road, and when they got there, a policeman leaned into view and asked them for ID.

She handed him her driver's license, and while he checked it against the list on his clipboard, she remembered Tom carrying boxes, thumping them in the bed of the truck. She remembered him yelling at her to get in the truck, and ordering Luna to stay by her side. When the policeman came back, he said, "Officer Tippet will accompany you to your property."

Luke noted how the man said *property*, not *house*. "We also have a truck," Luke said, "a white Ford, parked on Sheffied Drive."

The policeman looked at another page on his clipboard, then stepped away and spoke into his walkie-talkie. There was crackling, a conversation. The policeman confirmed that the escort would take them to the truck as well.

Luke followed the black-and-white police car for a mile through an unscathed grove of trees, and Ryan drove his grandmother's Lexus behind them. They could smell the scorched ground, and they could feel the looming blackness, even though they couldn't see it. It was an aching emptiness, a void, a place where there had recently been something and now there was nothing. Lily remembered taking the boys to see the Grand Canyon when they were in middle school. They drove out to the South Rim very early one morning, scattering elk in the darkness. Tom kept saying, "Can you feel it coming?" and the boys, wild with excitement despite the hour, kept saying, "What? What?" But they knew; you could feel it—something big out there. A big space. And then there it was—the canyon, the ground falling away, the eons of time exposed before them, the void.

This was exactly like that.

THEY came first to the pickup truck. It had been pulled onto the dirt at the side of the road, by a row of scraggly orange trees at the edge of someone's property. It was wrapped with yellow caution tape and there was a sticker slapped onto the windshield warning people that this was police property. Officer Tippet parked his cruiser, got out, snipped the tape. Lily climbed out of Luke's truck and walked to the back of Tom's Ford. She stood at the tailgate and peered into the back. "This is what he saved," she said in a small voice. "This is what he chose to save."

There was a laundry basket filled with paper and a duffel bag, all of it smelling of smoke and covered in fine white ash. She spotted the Matisse tablecloth and the cardboard tube that contained her grandmother's lace, and she closed her eyes. She saw again the wall of fire coming around the side of the house, saw Tom disappear into the smoke and the flames. She turned away from the truck and sank to the ground, squatting like a child, her face in her hands. *He saved all this for me,* she thought. *He saved all this for me.*

LUKE walked over, pulled down the tailgate, pulled his mother to her feet, and guided her to sit down. He sat next to her, weeping, too, his arms tightly around her shoulders. Ryan, watching his brother, suddenly thought what a good father

Luke would make. Luke would be just like their own dad—calm, kind, connected. Perhaps Ryan didn't have what it took. Perhaps he hadn't paid close enough attention to how it was done when his dad was still alive to show him how. He put both hands on the side of the truck, as if he might push it away, and closed his eyes.

Eleanor walked toward them all and began to gather up the caution tape, because she knew someone was eventually going to have to drive this truck somewhere when all the crying stopped. Later she and Lily would argue about it—how Eleanor was always fixing things, always doing things, how she couldn't stop and just *feel*, how crazy she was, how cold, and how it had always been that way.

25

Lily

THEY left the truck on the side of the road, got back in the cars, and drove up into the hills. They waited in silence for the scorched earth to present itself, and then suddenly it was before them—bald and blackened hills, half-burned trees, the gutted-out houses of people who just days before had been making toast in those houses, folding laundry, writing bills, arguing about dinner, touching each other with hands that weren't entirely honest. "Oh my God," Lily said. Cement foundations marked out their phantom rooms, and chimneys stood as tall as giants in a black Lilliputian land. Everything was absolutely gray and absolutely still.

Luke drove slowly up the road thinking that this was the way the moon must look, that this was the way a landscape looked when it had been bombed off the face of the planet. He took a turn to the left, then a fork to the right, and Mary Hazelton's house stood before them, miraculously whole and untouched. Across the street, Tom's avocado orchard, with its neat rows of bright shiny green trees, continued to do its work of turning sunshine into chlorophyll, and chlorophyll into green-fleshed fruit.

Lily couldn't help thinking that everyone had gotten it wrong: her house did not burn, her husband did not die. She would round the corner, and Tom would be there with Luna on the front step, talking about bark beetles or the latest news on global warming. She would run up to him and throw her arms around his neck and say that she was sorry for what she had said and what she had done and what she had thought, and he would say, "It's okay." They would go on comfortably ignoring each other and counting on each other, drawing on the investment of love they had made as if it were a bank account.

On the other hand, she kept imagining the lot where their house had been, wiped clean as if by a giant's hand. She pictured it smoothed over. She remembered seeing footage once of a house that had been lifted off its foundation by a tornado, exactly like Dorothy's had been. This one, however, had been a real house, a little two-bedroom cottage built on the banks of the Missouri River. The owner stood on the threshold, talking to the TV cameraman, saying, "As God is my witness, we went to bed in this house a full half mile away and woke up right here where y'all are standing." Maybe her house had been lifted away like that, by the fire.

She held her breath. Luke drove on, and when they rounded the final bend, she exhaled.

It was all true.

She sat holding one hand over her mouth and nose, because ash was still falling from the sky like snow, and she didn't want to breathe in burned pieces of people's homes, of pine trees that had lived a hundred years, of someone's flesh and bone. Her eyes stung, her nostrils flared. There was the place where Tom had died, there was where she had sat in the truck waiting for him to come out of the house, there was where the fireman who saved her had stood as he pushed her out of the driver's seat. She sat next to Luke, saying nothing, until Ryan came and opened her door, and the smell of smoke and ash and charcoal, which had been strong enough inside the car, exploded with full force upon them.

Lily stepped out of the car. She waited a moment, expecting Luna to come bounding out of the flattened house, barking her greeting, but there was no sound besides the soft rustling of the wind in the avocado trees, which stood there, green and mocking. The policemen had cautioned them against doing anything more than taking a brief look at the property. There were live embers, open gas lines, toxic smoke. In a few days they could come back to sift through the ash to see if anything could be salvaged. For now, they just stood in the driveway, staring at the wreckage, trying to comprehend everything that had been lost.

After a while, when the silence and the stench became too much to bear, Eleanor said, "Why don't we go now?"

Ryan was quick to agree. "You can drop me off at Dad's truck," he said. "I'll drive it down to Nana's."

Lily shook her head. "I want to stay," she said.

Ryan and Luke glanced at their grandmother, because someone had to dissuade Lily, and they figured it would be Eleanor.

Eleanor coughed. "Sweetheart," she said, "I don't think that's a good idea. The policemen said—"

Lily cut her off. "I know what they said. I'm not going to do anything stupid. I just want to pick some avocados so they'll be ripe for the party."

Luke was the first to speak. "Maybe we should wait, Mom," he said.

"For what?"

"For everything to cool down." They could hear hissing and popping where things still simmered. There was a palpable sense of instability. But there was also the knowledge that Tom had died in a spot just a few feet in front of them, and that knowledge bore down on them in a physical way. It seemed like it might be difficult to stand there very much longer and not get crushed.

"I'll just be a few minutes," Lily said.

Luke coughed—his lungs protesting the gritty air. "I'll stay with you," he said.

Ryan, relieved to be released from the strange scene, said quickly, "Nana can take me down to get the truck."

Luke stepped up to his mother and took hold of her hand. "Come on," he said, and led her toward the trees.

26

Luke

THEY walked around the smoldering remains of the house to the orchard. The first two rows of trees were charred and stripped of leaves. The damaged trees stood out like skeletons against the rest of the orchard, which was still green and vibrant, dusted with ash.

"You want to pick the ones with the blackest skin," Lily said as she walked down a row of trees. "They should fall right off in your hands."

Luke squinted up. "Is there something we can put them in? A bag or something?"

"There are crates in the shed," she said. "If the shed is still there."

They walked to the bottom of the hill, and the shed stood before them, unscathed. For a moment, Lily thought that Tom would step out from behind the shed and say something about raccoons or beetles or red-tailed hawks. She stood there, waiting, and then Luke rolled back the big barn door and stepped inside. He grabbed a crate, and one of the long poles with a picking basket on the end. "You want one?" he asked.

Lily nodded.

They went back into the trees, and set the crate on the ashy ground. The air was acrid, and they coughed as they worked. They reached into the trees and pulled down avocados, one by one. When their crate was full, they took it to the shed and used the hose—neatly coiled against the outside wall—to rinse the ash off the fruit. Luke carried the crate up the hill and put it in the back of his truck.

Lily stayed by herself at the shed and touched everything that was still there—the hose that Tom had coiled, the old rake that Tom had brought from Vermont, the ball of twine that Tom had barely begun to use. She thought of things she had lost over the years—glasses, keys, a white enamel casserole pan, a scratchy green wool shawl given to her by a friend in college whom she never really liked. She was forever losing pens, which was her argument against owning anything other than a simple Bic ballpoint, but Tom always said that if you invested in fine writing instruments, you wouldn't lose them. Their mere expense would keep them safe.

But she had lost expensive things, too. She once lost one of a pair of black pearl earrings her mother had lent her to wear to dinner in Milan. One minute, they were adorning her ears, the next, the left one was gone. The waiters searched the floor under the table while Eleanor grew more and more dismayed, but nothing was ever found. Eleanor forgave her, but Lily never forgave herself.

"They're just *things*," people always said, to soothe the dismay of loss. "You can replace things."

That was true about a Bic pen. But why, then, did she remember that casserole pan, with its chips on the handle? Why did she remember that shawl—its exact color of pea soup green, its bulky knit-purl pattern, the loamy way that it smelled when it was wet? Could the loss of an object give it meaning?

"Ready to go?" Luke asked.

Lily jumped. She placed her hand over her heart, which was beating wildly. "You scared me," she said.

He put his arm around her, and she noted how he had the same build as Tom, the same long arms, the same smell. "Sorry," he said.

They walked back up past the charred remains of her home—the washer and dryer warped and twisted, the kitchen reduced to nothing. It was as if someone had come and carried away the refrigerator, the sink, the bay window, the cabinets, the pots and pans and plates they had so carefully covered in bubble wrap so that they wouldn't be damaged on their cross-country trip.

"Remember when Oreo ran away that one Christmas?"

Luke nodded. "That was the worst," he said. "How Ryan made up those flyers and walked around on Christmas Day posting them everywhere."

"But it worked."

"Yeah," Luke said.

Lily stopped right in front of Luke's truck—right in the spot where Tom had told Luna to stay, and where she had stood and yelled at Tom not to go back into the house. "I think Luna must have died," she said. "They never found her body, but she ran straight into the fire. The flames were huge on that side of the house." She pointed to her left. "She was probably incinerated."

"Why would she have run into the fire?" Luke asked.

"Because Tom went in. She was going after Tom."

"Maybe she got out. Maybe someone found her."

Lily shook her head.

"There must be people who rescue animals after a fire, some kind of shelter. I'll find out. I'll go look."

BACK at his grandmother's house, Luke searched for information on animal rescue. It only took him two phone calls to learn that there was a central holding area for animals rescued from the fire.

"Luna had tags, didn't she?" he asked his mom.

"Yes," Lily said, "and mismatched eyes. You can't miss the eyes."

He grabbed a cold piece of pizza, got back in the truck, and drove out to Goleta. He walked through the pens and the dog runs for forty-five minutes looking for an Australian shepherd with one blue eye and one brown, but there was no such dog to be found.

WHEN Luke reported that he hadn't seen Luna, Lily thanked him for trying, and she had to stop herself from thinking, *I have to remember to tell Tom how Luke took on the search for the dog, how hard he tried, how good he was.* She had to stop herself from thinking, *I have to remember to talk to Tom about Ryan and how worried I am about him.* Instead, she got out her list and added a page:

Luna
Dog bowl
Dog mat
Dog brush
Dog bed
Gnawed rope toy
Leash

27

Ryan

RYAN sat on the same airport bench where he had greeted his grandmother, and waited for Olivia and Brooke to arrive. He drank Heineken in the warm night air and thought of his wife and child hurtling through the sky. He thought of a girl he used to know who set a school record in the 500 Free, and how she had died on the plane that hit the Pentagon. She had gone back to school late that year, because on the day she was originally planning to fly, she'd had an acute attack of appendicitis.

When the little plane touched down, Ryan stood up. Brooke had called Tom Pop-Pop. Olivia said it was because making the *Grr* sound at the beginning of the word *Grandpa* was something that didn't develop in children until later. Olivia had read this in a book. Everything Olivia knew about being a parent she'd read in a book. She didn't have much of a relationship with her own mother, and so she set out to learn it all herself. Ryan loved Brooke. He liked the way she smelled and the way she climbed onto his lap and curled into a ball when she was tired. But he wasn't a student like his brother, Luke. He wasn't a scholar like his dad. He didn't want to have to work so hard to understand why Brooke called his dad Pop-Pop.

He saw Olivia at the top of the stairs that descended from the plane. She had Brooke's pink backpack slung over one shoulder, and her enormous canvas bag in the crook of her arm. She held Brooke on her hip, and held the railing of the stairs as she descended. Ryan felt as if he might jump out of his skin as he waited for them to make their painstaking descent down the stairs, and walk across the tarmac.

When they stepped through the gateway, he swept Olivia and Brooke into his arms, and there was a subtle transferring of weight so that he held Brooke now and he breathed in the scent of her soft hair.

"How was the flight?" he asked.

"Good," Olivia said. "Brooke had a snack and we read some stories."

"We read *Olivia*," Brooke said, and Ryan knew she was referring to the book about a pig who thought she was a diva, "the *other* Olivia."

This was something Brooke always said when she spoke about this particular book—the *other* Olivia—and so Ryan laughed, and Olivia laughed, and Brooke beamed.

227

THEY collected all the luggage, and strapped the car seat into the back of Nana's car, and then Brooke said she wanted juice.

"You can have juice when we get to Nana's," Ryan said.

"But you promised," Brooke said, and Ryan could hear her voice escalating in tone and intensity, and he felt the muscles in his neck tighten.

"I did," Olivia said to Ryan, and then to Brooke, "I promised you could have the juice when we got to Nana's."

"I want my juice," she said, and her voice now began to waver. She was on the verge of throwing a fit. "You promised!"

"I did," Olivia repeated, and then she turned to Ryan and said, "I promised."

Ryan turned to look out the driver's side window as Olivia unsnapped her seat belt, got out of the car, went around to the back, and unloaded all the suitcases he had just loaded in. She dug around until she found the juice, and then she unwrapped the straw, thrust it through the hole, and handed the box to Brooke.

Olivia got back into her seat, Ryan started the car, and before they even got out of the parking lot, the juice was gone.

"I want more," Brooke said.

Olivia turned backward to face Brooke. "I'd like it if you said, *Please. Please may I have more juice.*"

"Please may I have more juice," Brooke said, and Ryan thought he might scream. The feeling of happiness and connectedness he had felt when Brooke had talked about the pig book was gone, replaced by the familiar dread of his child's demands, his wife's endless calm, and his own place outside of their circle.

LATER, when Brooke was telling her uncle Luke about her airplane trip, and Ryan and Olivia were taking the luggage in from the garage, Ryan lowered his voice and said, "My mom's been obsessed with making these lists. She's pretty messed up."

"What kind of lists?" Olivia asked.

"Stuff that was in the house."

"She has to do that for insurance, right?"

"Yeah, but these lists have everything on them. You know that drawer everyone has with scissors and rubber bands and the twisty things from plastic bags? She has a list for that drawer. And a list of all the cleaning stuff. The toilet cleaning brush and the Clorox."

"I'd do the same thing," Olivia said.

"You would?"

She nodded. "Write it all down so that your memory doesn't surprise you later, so that the story is all right there."

Ryan rolled his shoulders backward and then rotated his left ear toward his left shoulder to try to stretch out his neck. "I think she's crazy," he said, and then he added, "I don't know how much patience she's going to have for Brooke."

"She's not crazy," Olivia said. "I totally get it. I'd do the same thing. And I bet she'll be fine with Brooke."

"I'm just saying you might want to wait until morning before Brooke goes in there."

Fifteen minutes later, Brooke started asking when she was going to see her Nana and Pop-Pop, and Olivia launched into a careful explanation of how Pop-Pop had died and that's why they had come on the trip, and how Nana was sad and didn't want to see them right now. She had said the same words, or words like them, a dozen times since they started out on their trip.

Brooke went to her lime green duffel bag and pulled out Bear, the stuffed teddy bear she slept with every night. "I want to show Nana Bear."

"Nana's sleeping," Olivia explained. "She's just down the hallway in her own bedroom, asleep, and we should go to sleep, too. You can show her Bear in the morning."

"I want to show her Bear now."

"Sweetie . . ." Olivia said, but before she could continue, Ryan said, "Oh for God's sake."

"What?" Olivia snapped.

"The answer is *no*," Ryan said. "Just tell her no. She can't do it."

"Ryan, she doesn't understand what's going on. You can't just tell her *no*. You have to explain . . ."

"You can just tell her no. My mom has refused everything that's been offered to her for the past two days—tea, soup, toast, back rubs, sleeping pills. If Brooke goes in there—"

"Can I finish my sentence?" Olivia demanded.

"If you'll let me finish mine."

While her parents stood locked in battle, Brooke turned and bolted out the door. She ran down the hallway, glancing in each door, and when she got to a door that was closed, she opened it and ran in. The shades were drawn, the room was dark. It smelled of fire, and of sweat, and of despair. Lily sat on the bed, propped up by two thick pillows. The white down comforter was drawn up to her chin. To Brooke, her grandmother looked similar to her bear. Her hair was dirty and limp. The light in her eyes was dim and flat. Her limbs looked as if they were incapable of holding her up. She had been intending to introduce Bear to Nana—to say, "This is Bear." But Brooke had a child's instinctive understanding of pain. She stopped at the side of the bed and wordlessly handed Bear over.

Lily smiled. She reached out and accepted Bear with one hand, and with the other, she reached out and gently stroked her granddaughter's silken hair.

"Thank you," she said.

28

Lily

Lily got up in the middle of the night, left the teddy bear, and went down to her mother's garage, where the things Tom had saved from the fire were sitting on the cold cement floor. The boys had immediately gone through the documents to locate the insurance papers they needed to file claims, and they had begun to sort through the rest of what was there. It was all covered in a white ash, which looked benign, but left a greasy residue whenever it was touched. Next to the duffel bag and the laundry basket were a pile of microfiber rags and a bottle of Simple Green, which they had been using to try to clean things off.

She turned on the light and saw that one of the boys had tried to clean the cardboard tube that held Hattie's lace. It was no longer dusted with ash, but there were dark, greasy streaks down its sides. She snapped off the plastic end of the tube and peered at the lace. It was still neatly wound inside archival tissue, totally undisturbed. The cardboard tube had done its job—as cocoon, as armor, as shield. She felt a wave of gratitude for the simple tube, and for her grandmother's impulse to preserve the piece of cloth, and for how well her husband had known her and loved her. As the fire bore down and the danger closed in, he had thought to save the one object that meant the most to her—that defined her. It was a piece of possibility. She closed the tube back up and set it down again on the garage floor.

Next, she found the Matisse tablecloth and took it inside. It hadn't fared as well. It was covered with ash, it smelled of smoke. She carried it through the dark house to the laundry room. She carefully set it in the washing machine, turned the dial to "cold" and to "soak," measured out a capful of Ivory, and pushed the start button.

While the washer started its work, she grabbed her purse, snuck out of the house into the still-dark morning, and went to the Farmer's Market.

SHE hadn't been paying attention to Tom's guacamole obsession. She had minced garlic when he asked her to, chopped onions, held a Pasillo chile over an open flame to char it, but she hadn't read his recipes, didn't know the alchemy that went into his successes. She was determined, however, to re-create the guacamole he had thought was best. She remembered that it had been chunky and smoky, with a kick of lime and a wave of heat that followed the first cool taste.

She bought limes first, then onions, garlic, and three kinds of chiles. She walked by three tables piled with red cherry tomatoes and thick beefsteak tomatoes until she got to a stand offering a wide variety of shapes and colors. The banner on the awning read TUTTI FRUITI FARMS: HEIRLOOM TOMATOES. She stopped to taste the samples the farmers had set out on a folding table. There were a dozen glass bowls of sliced tomatoes, with toothpicks for sampling. She speared a small green tomato, a piece of thick yellow striped tomato, and one that was pear-shaped and golden yellow. The one she liked best was a small round red one labeled JAPANESE. It popped in her mouth—a burst of sweet, vibrant flavor. She bought three pounds, and felt a thrill when the farmer beamed at her and said, "These are very good in guacamole."

THE only person awake back at her mother's house was Eleanor. She was sitting at the table reading the newspaper. "You missed Ryan," she said. "He went out for a swim. I figured you were on a walk."

"To the Farmer's Market," Lily said, and held up her bags. "I'm making Tom's guacamole."

"He had one that tasted just like summer," Eleanor said.

"But a little smoky? With a roasted pepper?"

"And lime."

"Can I help wash things, or chop?"

Lily nodded. She knew her mother didn't have the patience to cook. She took Eleanor's offer for what it was—a gesture of solidarity. "Maybe you can start by squeezing the limes and chopping the garlic," she said. "I've got a tablecloth in the washing machine I need to rinse."

"I did that," Eleanor said, and instead of being worried that her mother had done it wrong, or that she had done it at all, Lily just nodded, and thanked her.

They chopped and sliced and mixed things in different combinations, trying to match what was in front of them to what they remembered Tom had made. They argued about the amount of lime, the degree of charring necessary for the pepper. By the time Olivia and Brooke and Luke came out to the kitchen, there were six large bowls of guacamole. The smell of garlic filled the air, and the tang of roasted pepper.

"'Molee!" Brooke squealed.

"*Huevos rancheros?*" Luke asked.

"How long have you two been *up?*" Olivia demanded.

"Too long," Lily said, "but I think we got it."

"Got what?" Luke said.

"Daddy's favorite guacamole."

The mood in the room suddenly shifted. Tom's spirit had been alive in the chopping and the mixing, but now that they were done, it was clear that it would take more than a recipe to bring Tom back. Lily washed her hands, and announced that she was going back to bed.

"What about your tablecloth?" Eleanor asked.

"I'll get it," Lily said.

She walked slowly to the laundry room, got out the clean, damp tablecloth, and took it to the guest room upstairs. She spread it out on the bed to dry, and then climbed underneath the sheets and cried herself to sleep.

•29•

Nadine

Nadine was bereft. She hadn't known Tom for very long, and she hadn't known him very well, but she felt his death keenly. She circled around Tom's ranch for days before she got the courage to drive up the hill, and turn into the driveway. She wanted to see if the trees were still standing. She sat in her truck, tears rolling down her cheeks, and scanned the blackened scene. There was Tom's stone fireplace, still ready to warm the night, and the foundation of the house still sturdy and whole. Beyond where the house had been was a row of burned trees, looking naked and gnarled, and beyond them, the untouched orchard. After a few moments, Nadine became aware of a high-pitched yelping. She got out of her truck and tried to piece together what it was. A baby crying? A woman yelling? A siren coming up the street again to fend off another fire? Yes, she decided, it was an inconsolable baby suffering from colic, caught in a rhythmic wail, but then she remembered that there were no babies in this neighborhood; there were no people; there were no houses.

A moment later, Luna appeared from the thick light like an apparition. Thin, her fur matted and soiled, she seemed to float out of the trees as if she, too, were made of smoke. "Luna?" Nadine asked, and blinked. She stepped forward and held out her hand. "Luna," she said softly. The dog raised her head, stepped slowly toward Nadine, and changed her howl to something that sounded more like weeping.

Eleanor's defenses were so strong that when Nadine called in the afternoon about the dog, she almost didn't get through. "It's *Nadine*," she finally said. "Nadine from the Calavo warehouse. We met at the cocktail party."

"I know who you are," Eleanor said.

"Then may I please speak to Lily?"

"She's indisposed at the moment," Eleanor said. Lily had barely gotten out of bed for the last forty-eight hours. She hadn't showered, had only eaten a piece of toast, a scrambled egg. Whenever anyone asked her if she wanted some soup, or to go on a walk, or to watch TV, she just shook her head no, and continued to stare out the window at the charred hills.

"I have Luna," Nadine said.

It took Eleanor a moment to process what she was hearing. "Dead or alive?" she finally asked.

"Alive," Nadine said. "But barely."

Eleanor felt a jolt of joy—a sudden belief that redemption was at hand. Dogs were better suited for grief than people were. They didn't try to talk to make things better. They didn't ask how things were going or if they could help. Luna could give Lily what Eleanor never could.

She took the phone up to the third floor, tapped on Lily's door, and stepped in without waiting to be invited.

Eleanor held the phone out toward her daughter.

"No," Lily mouthed, and shook her head. She didn't want to speak to anyone. She didn't want to hear them say they were sorry, didn't want to hear them wonder what they could do to help.

"It's Nadine," Eleanor said, "from Calavo. She has some good news."

Lily sat up. She took the phone. "Yes?"

"Luna came home," Nadine said.

When Lily didn't respond, Nadine offered more: "I went up to check on the trees, and she was there."

"She's dead," Lily said.

Nadine reached down and stroked Luna's back. Her fur was singed and matted and she was covered with burrs. "She's sleeping right here on my kitchen floor."

Lily sat up higher on her pillows and looked wildly around the room. She hadn't slept more than a few hours in a single stretch since the fire. She felt like everything was folding over on itself—time and reality and even the organs inside her body, which gurgled and churned in protest of food she wasn't eating. Several nights, in the middle of the night, she could have sworn she heard Tom calling to her. She strained her ears, got out of bed, opened the windows, walked down the stairs, only to be reminded by the emptiness and the darkness that Tom had died, and Luna had died, and their house and everything in it had burned to the ground.

She had the odd sense that Nadine had conjured Luna up like a witch doctor, or a shaman. She believed it was Nadine's doing somehow that the dog was alive. And she remembered how Tom had been with Nadine on the night of the fire—how Tom's staying at the warehouse had been the reason Lily had gone down to the beach in the first place. It was Nadine that had justified Jack in her mind. Nadine and the whole crashing reality of how you can never know what your husband is doing or thinking. You can never be sure that love is real. You can live with someone for almost thirty years and love them and be loyal to them and feel loved in return, but you will never know how they truly feel about you, how much space they leave open in their heart for other people, other things.

"It can't be her," Lily said.

Eleanor was still standing by the bed, waiting to spring into action—to go get the dog, to bathe the dog.

"It can't be her," Lily repeated.

Eleanor walked over to the bed, took the phone from Lily's hand, and spoke to Nadine. "This is Eleanor," she said, "Lily's mother. I'd like to come see the dog."

Eleanor rummaged in a drawer for a piece of paper and a pen, but while she was writing down Nadine's address, Lily spoke up.

"It can't be her," she said.

"Just a moment," Eleanor said to Nadine, and she looked over at Lily and saw that there were tears streaming down her face, falling from the edge of her face to her collarbone.

"Eleanor?" Nadine was calling. Her voice was coming through the receiver of the phone. "Eleanor?"

"I'm sorry," Eleanor said to Nadine. "We're going to have to call you back." She hung up.

"Tom ran back after her," Lily said. "She ran through the front door, and he ran in after her. She can't be alive."

"Dogs have a sense for danger," Eleanor said. "She may have escaped. She may have tried to help Tom escape."

Lily could picture Jack leaning down to scratch Luna behind her ear. She could hear him saying, *I'd recognize that smile anywhere; See you at the beach; Come by and see me sometime.* She could see herself smiling back, and going to the beach, where she knew she would find him.

"I don't want to see her," Lily whispered.

Eleanor sat on the edge of the bed, and reached out to smooth Lily's hair behind her ears. Lily turned her face from her mother's touch.

"It would remind me too much of him," she said, and although Eleanor did not know it, the *him* she was talking about wasn't just Tom—it was also Jack.

•30•

Lily

AFTER the phone call about the dog, Lily got out of bed, eased her wedding ring off her finger, and set it on the bathroom counter. She usually never removed it, and the skin underneath was pink, and dented to fit the shape of the platinum and gold band. The ring featured a two-and-a-half-carat diamond, a miner's cut that had originally been set in a man's platinum dinner ring. "A hideous old ring," Eleanor always said. It had been in her father's family for generations. When Billy Edwards proposed to Eleanor, he did everything the proper way. He asked her parents for permission, and when they gave it, they gave him the dinner ring to do with as he wished. Billy removed the diamond from its ornate embrace and had a spectacular ring designed—a band of diamonds, a swirl of platinum and gold that held the diamond aloft. He had the jeweler remake it three times before he deemed it acceptable for his young bride. Eleanor always said that she liked the ring better than the man; she continued to wear it on her right hand through her second marriage. She wore it until Lily brought Tom home. At dinner that night, Eleanor slid the ring off her delicate finger, and handed it to her daughter.

"What is this?" Lily asked.

"Following a hunch," Eleanor said, "that you're going to be needing that ring soon."

"Mom!" Lily cried. She loved the ring; it was the one thing of her mother's that she wished was hers, but she was mortified that Eleanor was behaving this way in front of her boyfriend. She tried to hand the ring back.

"Okay, then," Eleanor said. She took the ring from Lily's hand. "Have it your way." She slid it into Tom's palm. "That is my gift to you," she said, "should you decide to marry my daughter. Should you decide otherwise, I expect you'll return it. And if your marriage doesn't last, I'd like it back, as well."

LILY and Tom argued ceaselessly about the ring. Lily felt guilty about accepting it, and she felt strange about slipping something on her finger that her mother had worn for so long. She also worried that the ring would be bad luck to her marriage, since her mother's marriages had all ended so badly. But Tom was planning on their marriage lasting forever, and thought the ring was beautiful on her hand. "Besides," he said, "I like the idea of a family stone. It gives it a certain meaning, a certain weight that we couldn't get just walking into a jewelry store."

"The weight," Lily said, "comes from the fact that it's two and a half carats."

"What if there was some way of putting our own stamp on it? Making it a talisman of lasting love."

She burst out laughing at his corny statement. "A talisman of lasting love? You've got to be kidding me."

But he wasn't. Tom took the ring to a jeweler to be engraved. When he got it back, he marched her outside, got down on his knees, and said, "Say I do."

"About what exactly?"

"About marrying me."

"I do," she said. "Of course I do."

He handed her the ring and a flashlight so that she could see how he had changed the family heirloom.

Lily took the ring, took the flashlight, and read the immortal words that Yoda had uttered to Luke during his Jedi training:

Do or do not—there is no try.

She threw back her head and laughed. "Okay," she said. "You win." She helped him up out of the snow and he slipped the ring on her finger. She hadn't taken it off—until now.

AFTER she slipped off the ring, she called her friend Elizabeth back in Vermont. She had been thinking about fire—about what burns and what explodes, and what melts and what survives. It seemed important for her to know more concretely about the reality of fire's impact on rock and metal, wood and skin, on paper and leather, fabric and hair, on pots and pans and refrigerators.

"How hot does your kiln burn?" she asked.

"Three thousand degrees," Elizabeth said.

"Is that as hot as a wildfire, or hotter?"

"About the same."

"So if I put in a fountain pen, what would happen?"

"If there was air caught inside, it might explode. Otherwise, it would turn to ash."

"What about a leather shoe?"

"There would be nothing left."

"A fork?"

"Nothing left."

"But it makes the clay stronger, that kind of heat?"

"Yes. The molecules realign themselves into stronger chains."

"And besides clay, what doesn't burn? What can't burn?"

"Diamonds," Elizabeth said.

What Lily loved was that Elizabeth never asked why Lily was asking. She never said, *I'm worried about you.* She never indicated that she had any concern at all for her friend's sanity. A few hours later, Elizabeth called back to say that there was an artist in Mission Canyon—a friend of a friend—who was willing to let Lily come work in her studio a few mornings a week, if she was interested. Her name was Shelley, and she was waiting for her.

WHEN Lily got to Shelley's studio, she felt transparent, as if Shelley knew that she had come to play with fire, as if she knew what was in her pocket.

"What type of work are you interested in doing?" Shelley asked.

Lily looked at the bowls and cups and vases on the studio shelves. She thought about how her boys used to play with fire when they were young. On the Fourth of July they'd light red rocket firecrackers and she would watch them from a safe distance back and think, *Boys*. When Luke was in eleventh grade chemistry, he developed a fascination for hydrogen and helium and dry ice and baking soda, and was constantly making small explosions in the garage. That was before fire became something that toyed with them instead of the other way around.

"I don't know," she said. "I didn't really think about that. I just thought it would be a good thing for me to do."

"To work with clay?" Shelley asked.

Lily nodded. She felt like an idiot.

But then Shelley said, "It can be very healing."

They took a chunk of fast-drying clay and set it on the worktable. It was red and cold and smelled of dampness and something organic.

"What about a house?" Shelley asked. "We can make a house from a block of clay."

Lily shook her head. Her house had been obliterated. She wasn't interested in resurrection.

"An angel?" Shelley asked. "You can shape one from a simple cone."

"I don't believe in angels," Lily said. She didn't believe that Tom was floating around somewhere, looking over her. He was in a box that would be buried under the ground at Mount Auburn Cemetery, marked by a piece of granite that would never burn.

They were silent for a while. Lily watched her hands working the clay, and she felt the warmth of the clay as it took heat from her fingers.

"What about a little round bowl?" Lily asked. "With a lid."

Shelley nodded. "A very sensual shape," she said, "very organic. Perfect."

They rolled the clay into a ball, and then pinched and pulled it, being careful to avoid stretching it too thin so that it wouldn't collapse. Lily felt the way the clay moved and turned as she pressed and kneaded, and it felt good in her hands. She liked how it yielded, how it took the shape she gave it. Shelley showed her how to cut a lid to match the opening of the bowl, which was like cutting dough for cookies. When she was done, Lily had something that looked like a lumpy teacup.

"I'd like to put something inside," she said, and pulled her ring out of her pocket.

Shelley stared at the diamond ring. She didn't have to ask if it was real. She could tell by the way Lily held it, and by the way the light hit it, and by the energy that seemed to come off it. Elizabeth had told her that the woman who was coming to her studio had lost her husband in the fire, and her house, too, so she had expected strong emotion, but she hadn't expected this—a sacrifice, a cremation.

"It will burn to ash," she said.

"I know."

"Not the diamond, of course, but the ring. The band."

"I know."

"You're sure you want to do it?"

"I am," Lily said.

Lily dropped the ring onto the wet clay. Neither woman said anything while they washed their hands and cleaned up the worktable, but when Lily was ready to go, Shelley stopped her. "The bowl will take a few days to dry," she said, "and I will put it into the first bisque firing. Then you can come back to glaze it."

Lily nodded. "Would you do it?" she said. "Put a clear glaze on it?"

"Sure," Shelley said, and then: "You're sure about the ring?"

"Yes," Lily said. "Very sure."

31

Lily

An hour before the guests were set to arrive at the house, Luke was sitting with Brooke looking at pictures of his father that friends from Vermont had e-mailed when they learned that all of Tom and Lily's photos had burned. There was Tom at the tops of mountains, in the garden, in the snow, in the classroom, with Lily, with the boys, with their dogs. Luke had printed out some of the photos and arranged them on a poster board, the way he had done for projects when he was a boy. Lily thought that Luke had chosen the photos well; you could look at the board and see the things that had made up Tom's life, the things he had loved.

In the kitchen, Olivia chopped onions and garlic for the guacamole, carefully following the instructions Lily had left for her—mince the garlic very finely; strain the lime juice; leave the pits of the avocados in the guacamole to keep it from turning brown. Whenever Lily walked by, Olivia offered her a taste, but Lily just kept saying, "I'm sure it's fine."

Around dusk, flowers were delivered to Eleanor's door. There were forty large white rosebuds packed into a square of glass like perfect sugary confections. Eleanor set them on the marble counter not far from where Lily was mincing cilantro, and although Lily had paid little attention to the cards and bouquets that had been arriving all week, she looked up from the cutting board at the spectacular roses and instantly thought: Jack. *Jack has sent me these flowers because he loves me, he can't live without me, and I will no longer have to bear this grief alone.*

She reached for the card, which was tied on a white silk ribbon, and tried to pretend that her heart wasn't beating wildly.

With sympathy, Gordon Vreeland

Lily held the card out to her mother. Her hand, which was wet and stuck with small bits of herbs, was shaking. "It's for you," she said.

Eleanor took in everything—her daughter's crestfallen face and the vast amount of air between them—and quickly glanced at the card. "No," she said gently, "they're for you, Lily."

"His wife died, what?" Lily asked. "Two weeks ago? Three?"

"Lily," Eleanor said.

"No," Lily said. "I just want to know what the rules are, you know? Because it used to be that you had to wait three or four months after your spouse died before choosing a new one. That was considered a polite period of mourning when Dad died, wasn't it, Mom? So now it's just a week or so, which I guess means I should keep my eyes open today when everyone comes to help me get over the fact that my husband just died trying to save our fucking dog, because Prince Charming might walk through the door and sweep me away. And oh," she went on, "you always said you wanted the wedding ring back when my marriage was over. Perhaps you're wanting it now for yourself? For marriage number four?"

Eleanor said nothing. She just stood there, mouth agape.

"I burned it," Lily said. "It's gone. Ashes to ashes and dust to dust."

A wave of incredulity swept across Eleanor's eyes. She had never had a marriage like Lily's marriage to Tom. She didn't know what that kind of love and that kind of loyalty felt like. But that didn't make her worthy of such derision. That didn't make her unable to provide her child comfort during a tragedy. "Don't you dare speak to me that way," she hissed.

"Why?" Lily asked. "Because it's too close to the truth? Because you're hoping to snatch Gordon Vreeland up?"

"No," Eleanor said. "Because I may not have been as lucky in love as you were, and I may not have been the mother you hoped for, but I was never cruel."

Eleanor swiped the florist's white card off the counter, turned, and left the room so fast she seemed to disappear into thin air.

32

Eleanor

ELEANOR climbed the stairs to her rooftop deck. In one direction, you could see out across the red tile roofs of Santa Barbara to the courthouse bell tower—a tiled square tower modeled after the Alhambra in Spain. Beyond the courthouse was the harbor, with its curl of seawall and its sea of masts. To the west were the mountains, charred now, but Eleanor knew that fire was what renewed the chaparral. Even now, under the scarred earth, seeds were shaken loose from their hard casings and roots were primed to grow in the spring. People would rebuild their houses and their lives, and the hills would grow green again. One thing you figured out when you'd lived as long as she had was that it always happened that way.

She stepped out into the shadowy night, sat in one of the wrought iron chairs, and called Gordon in New York.

"Well, you put me in a fine pickle," Eleanor said.

"The flowers?" he asked.

"Lily thinks I've gone and plucked a widower straight from his wife's funeral. She thinks this is what I've done all my life, you see, so it fits into her vision of me."

"She thinks you've chased widowers?"

"She thinks I've been opportunistic when it came to men. It's because all the men I married were rich, and because many of the other ones I became involved with were married."

"So she's right, then," Gordon said.

Eleanor sighed. "But look what it's gotten me. I get to sit here in my old age and remember all the adventures, all the good times. I chose my path, every step of the way. It's not her right to judge it after the fact."

"Eleanor," he said. "She's just had something yanked away that you've disregarded your whole life."

"You're on her side?"

"Well, no," he said. "But I understand what she's feeling."

"You think I've disregarded love? I've loved, Gordon. I've loved extremely well. And it's presumptuous for you to assume that you know anything about it. In fact, I'm offended."

"I know I'm going out on a limb," he said. "I do. And I'm sorry if I've offended you. But time is running out for both of us."

"I can't replace Judy," Eleanor said.

"But have you ever let anyone love you, Eleanor?" Gordon said softly. "Do you know what I'm offering? Do you know what it feels like to be cherished?"

She thought, strangely, of Gracie, and the friendship they had shared for sixty-four years. Gracie had cherished her, and she had cherished Gracie. But it was easier with friends than it was with lovers. There was a natural distance that never had to be bridged—and Eleanor needed that distance, because without it, she was afraid she would lose herself. "I don't think I'm going to answer that question," she said.

"But will you at least think about it? Can you promise me that?"

"I will," she said, and then there was just silence between them. They might have hung up; it was a natural break in the conversation, but neither was ready to end it. Gordon spoke into the silence.

"I sent the flowers because I just wanted to send my sympathies," Gordon said. "It's how I was raised."

"I know," she said. "As was I."

"I miss you," Gordon said.

She stared out across the darkened city. She had come to Santa Barbara during her second marriage, when Lily was still young, and it had felt like home from the start. She loved the feel of the air and the smell of the sea and the way everyone in town, whether they were locals or visitors, seemed acutely aware that they were in on something good.

"Are you still there?" Gordon asked.

"I am."

"I haven't been able to sleep since you left. I haven't been able to complete a crossword puzzle."

"You miss Judy," she said.

"I miss you, too," he said. "May I come visit?"

"It would be too awkward, Gordon, to have you here court-
ing me when you know I don't really want to be courted. This
is Lily's home now, too," she said. "And it would just be awkward all around. I'm sorry."

33

Olivia

OLIVIA dressed Brooke in a navy blue dress for the memorial party, and patent leather Mary Janes. She braided her hair, and made sure Brooke washed her face. For her own part, Olivia just threw on the same black wrap dress she'd worn for every party, funeral, or function she'd been invited to since giving birth. No one at this party would know the difference, except for Ryan. A number of Tom and Lily's close friends and colleagues were flying in from Vermont, and there was an aunt and uncle from New York, and some cousins from the Midwest. Most of the people coming today seemed to be friends of Eleanor's who had known Lily as a child. Olivia couldn't help wondering how many more people would have come if the party had been held in Burlington. Tom could never go out in that town without running into people whom he was teaching, or had taught, or had worked with, or hiked with. The house was filled with letters from them, and cards, and flowers.

"Is there going to be a party in Burlington, too?" she asked Luke. He was the safest person to talk to, the only one who didn't seem brittle.

"I have no idea," Luke said. "I guess if Mom wants one."

"Will she stay here, do you think?"

"I wouldn't, if I were her."

"You'd go back?"

"I'd go somewhere, that's for damn sure."

BROOKE followed her great-grandmother around the party, to the delight of everyone gathered, but when anyone spoke to Brooke, she would say, "Pop-Pop died," and they would all grow silent, for fear of saying the wrong thing.

At one point, Brooke broke away from Eleanor to come up to the island where the guacamole was set out. "'Moleee," she said.

"You want to try Pop-Pop's guacamole?" Lily asked.

Brooke held her hands up in answer, and Lily took a chip and scooped up a bit of the guacamole. "It's hot," Lily said. "Hot, hot, hot."

Brooke took the chip and bit it, and her brow wrinkled as she tried to reconcile the cool dip with her grandmother's warning about it being hot. Then the taste hit her tongue, and she began to hop up and down. "Hot," she said. "Hot, hot, hot!" And then she looked back up at Lily and said, "More 'moleee!"

Lily laughed, the first time all week, the only time that night, and handed her another chip.

RYAN drank margaritas all night and talked to anyone who would listen about camping in the Vermont woods with his dad. He told one of Tom's New York cousins about the things his dad had saved from the fire—the jumble of paper and the old baseball and the duffel bag stuffed with fabric.

"That's a hell of a thing," the man said. "Having a few minutes to choose what to save from a whole house full of memories."

Ryan shrugged. "I'd just get my car keys and walk," he said.

Olivia was standing nearby, rocking Brooke back and forth on her hip. The child was on her way to sleep, her thumb in her mouth, her eyes closed. Olivia turned to face her husband.

"You'd walk away from Brooke's room?"

Ryan shrugged. "You can always get another crib."

"What about Bear or her blanket?"

"It's all replaceable."

The cousin caught the eye of another guest and moved toward the bar, leaving Ryan and Olivia alone.

"Us, too?" she said softly.

Ryan swigged the end of his margarita and didn't answer,

which was answer enough for Olivia. *I came out here because Lily lost her husband,* she thought, *but I think I may have lost mine, too.*

AFTER the enchilada dinner Eleanor had brought in to go with the guacamole, she stood up and thanked everyone for coming, and for the donations they had made in Tom's name. She told the story about Tom and the engagement ring, and about the look on his face the day he first saw the avocado farm. Ryan was afraid he might cry, and so he held Brooke on his hip like a shield, and spoke quickly about how he hoped he could be as good a father as his father had been. Luke surprised everyone by reading a prepared speech that wove together remembrances of Tom in the garden, in the woods, and in the classroom. It ended with a vow that Luke was going to learn how to grow something, in his dad's honor, even if it was just a houseplant—a line that made everyone laugh.

Lily did not speak. She couldn't speak. She sat on the couch in between her sons, wearing the teal dress her mother had purchased, smiling at her friends and family, and holding back her tears the way she might hold off a headache in the middle of teaching a class. She kept thinking about getting up and pouring herself a glass of red wine, and cutting herself a slice of the chocolate torte her mother had ordered from the bakery, because physical pain seemed to her the most appropriate thing to feel right then, but she held off doing that, too.

At the end of the night, after Brooke had gone to bed, Olivia sat with Lily on a couch by the window, alone.

"You okay?" Olivia asked.

"I used to love to go to parties with Tom," she said, "because he would remember everything that I forgot. I would just have to turn to him and ask, and he would whisper the name of a neighbor, or where someone's child ended up moving, or how I knew the woman in green. It's like half my memory is gone."

Olivia nodded. She thought she understood.

"But the worst part," Lily said, "is that, with the house gone and everything in it, there's no proof that I lived my life."

"You don't need proof," Olivia said.

"Maybe you do," Lily said. "Maybe that's why we all rush around collecting things and cramming our house full of things. So that we'll have proof."

"Did anyone ever tell you that you think too much?"

Lily looked up at her son's wife and nodded. "Tom," she said. "He used to say that to me all the time."

Olivia pressed her lips together and looked at the ground. "I'm sorry," she said.

"It's okay," Lily said. "I miss him. It's unspeakable what happened to him, and my own part in it is unforgivable." She stopped, and breathed in and breathed out. "But I'm not sure our marriage was okay," she said quietly. "I'm just not sure."

"What do you mean?" Olivia asked quietly.

Lily shrugged. "Sometimes I think the only reason we stayed together was because we were afraid of coming apart."

"There could be worse reasons."

"But it didn't feel like what I imagined a long marriage to be—rich and vibrant and passionate. It just felt . . . familiar."

"But that sounds lovely, actually. I would like that—a marriage that felt familiar. Mine feels like it still needs to be broken in. Or maybe like it's the wrong fit altogether."

Lily looked up, surprised. So it was true. Her son and his wife were having trouble.

"Sorry," Olivia said quickly. "I shouldn't have said that to you. We'll be fine. We're just going through a rough patch because of the baby. We'll be fine."

"I guess you can't ever really know if you're going to be fine or not," Lily said.

They could hear Luke and Ryan downstairs watching a ball game. There were occasional shouts at the television, waves of cheers.

"What did you mean when you said that your part was unforgivable?" Olivia asked. "Weren't you sick when the fire broke out?"

Lily had told no one what had really happened that night. She said she'd had a migraine. She said she'd never smelled the fire, never heard it, never sensed it, never would have gotten out if Tom hadn't come for her. Everyone knew the things that Tom had taken out of the house—they were stacked in the garage downstairs, dusted with ash and with tragedy. Everyone knew that Tom went back in for the dog. But the fact that the last time Lily had slept with Tom, she had imagined another man in his place? The fact that Lily had gone to the beach to see that man in the flesh? The awful things she had accused Tom of doing before she saw him disappear into the hills, the dog trotting by his side? No one knew.

"It's just unforgivable," she said, "that after all this time, I can't control my migraines." She knew Olivia would buy her lie, and she was right.

"Don't be so hard on yourself," Olivia said, and Lily just pressed her lips together and nodded.

34

Lily

THE next afternoon, Lily told her family that she was going out, and then she walked out to the curb and got in the truck. Before she could close the door, Olivia appeared with Brooke. They had been walking around the block because Brooke had been crying, and Olivia thought a little fresh air might help calm her down.

"Hey," Olivia said. "Where are you off to?"

"To do some errands," Lily said, but the way she said it, it sounded more like a question than a statement.

Olivia cocked her head. "Did you tell the boys?"

"I told them," Lily said, "and my mother. Living here is like being back in high school, only worse. Everyone watching my every move, everyone gauging every word that comes out of my mouth."

"We're all so worried about you," Olivia said.

"Worried about what?" Lily said. "That I'm not sleeping? That I'm not eating? That grief might make me insane?"

Olivia shifted Brooke from one hip to the other. The girl had her head on her mother's shoulder, her thumb in her mouth, and a glassy look in her eyes. "Well, yes," Olivia said.

"So what if I am?" Lily said. "Please tell the rest of them when you go back inside. Tell them to stop watching me so closely. I can't stand it."

"We love you very much," Olivia said.

Lily shrugged, and her eyes filled with tears. "It doesn't help," she said.

SHE drove to the Patagonia world headquarters, which was housed in a series of old industrial buildings a half mile from the beach in Ventura, California. There was a meatpacking building and an old railroad station with brick walls and high, open-beamed ceilings. Patagonia had transformed the warehouses into a hip, eco-friendly campus. All the buildings were painted a bright saffron yellow and acted like a beacon to adventurers, rock climbers, river runners, and surfers who believe that a jacket can last a lifetime and that a clothing company can save the world.

Lily parked her truck in front of the main building and walked up the wide front steps. There was a large mural of a rock climber clinging to a granite wall. The climber looked like a spider, like a monkey, like a creature born to move through the world vertically. Lily stepped through the glass doors and up to the receptionist, who was young and fit and wholesome, which was a prerequisite for employment.

"I'm here to see Jack Taylor," she said.

"Is he expecting you?"

Lily thought about answering, *Yes, he is; he ran up to me on Miramar Beach.* Instead, she said, "No."

The receptionist pressed some buttons, listened at her phone, hung up. "He's not at his desk," she said. "May I take a message?"

"No," Lily said, trying not to look disappointed. "Thanks anyway." She turned and walked back by the spider woman, and toward her car. She had just put her hand on the door when Jack called her name. He was standing on the steps of the building she had just left, shielding his eyes from the sun.

"Hey," she said, and moved back around the car. "I thought I'd stop in and say hello. I should have called . . ."

"No," Jack said. "It's great. Come in."

She followed him past the wholesome receptionist and down the hall, which was lined with more posters of more people doing amazing things in amazing locations—flying through the air in a kayak over a waterfall, trekking across a glacial ridge. He stepped into his office, offered her a seat on a couch, and took a chair across from her.

"I was thinking about you during the fires," Jack said.

"You said you lived in that area. Everything okay back at the farm?"

"Our house burned to the ground," Lily said. It was a phrase she had heard before, but she'd never known exactly what it meant—that every part of a house could burn and everything in it, and that there could be nothing left except the ground on which it was built. She didn't know that when a house burned to the ground, the people who lived there would be forever going to get a certain mug from a certain cupboard, or a certain shirt from a certain drawer, or a certain spool of thread from a certain plastic fisherman's case in a closet where a sewing machine had been kept, and that they would forever be faced with the fact that there was no certainty. She had the urge to add, *But I have lists of everything; I'm making lists.* Because the lists were the only things that were keeping her from flying apart. Her one link to sanity was remembering what was in each room, and where it had sat in relation to other things, and that those things had made up her life.

"Oh my God," Jack said, and leaned back in his chair. "I'm sorry."

Lily took a deep breath. "My husband was killed," Lily said, and looked at the yellow stitching on her Levi's. Her legs were shaking, up and down, up and down.

"Jesus, Lily," Jack said, and stood up and closed the door. Lily could feel her face screw up and she could feel the heat building behind her ears, and then she started to cry. Jack came and kneeled beside her, and when she didn't stop crying, he put his thick arm around her shoulders in an awkward gesture of comfort. He didn't really know Lily. She didn't really know him. But that was why she had come. Jack was someone with whom she shared a blank history. He was a player on the stage of her life, but besides that one strange interlude on the beach, neither of them had spoken any lines or played any scenes. Jack could be whoever she wanted him to be, and what she wanted was to believe that he would rescue her from her doubt and her confusion, from her guilt and her grief.

When he said, "I'm so sorry," she nodded her thanks.

"That doesn't help much, does it?" he asked. "People being sorry?"

"No, it does," she said, looking up. "Of course it does."

"Is there anything I can do, to, you know, help you get back on your feet? Hey, what about some clothes and jackets and things? We've got a whole warehouse."

"It's okay," she said. After all, she had her sweatshirt, her jeans, her clogs.

She wasn't sure what to do next. She thought, suddenly, that she should stand up and tell Jack that it had been a mistake to come, that it had been a terrible mistake, and that she needed to pretend like it had never happened. Then she thought she might confess—explain how she had gone home right after seeing him on the beach, and opened the bottle of wine, and said unforgivable things, and that the reason Tom was dead was because of that. Finally, she circled back to the reason that she was sitting there in Jack's office in the first place: he could love her. She could leap from one love to another as easily as if love were stones on a path. She could make it through the same way her mother always had.

She looked up. "Are you free for dinner?" she asked. "I don't think I've eaten anything in three days."

Jack stood up, leaned back against his desk, crossed his arms. He didn't understand marriage. He had been married briefly once, and thought it was a ridiculous charade. But he understood something about desire. "There's a great burger place down the way," he said. "Burgers and beer."

She nodded, and swallowed. "That sounds good," she said.

WHILE they ate, they talked about people they knew in high school and about the successes and disappointments of their own lives. Jack told how he had started out as a surfer sponsored by Patagonia, moved up to sales rep, did a stint in marketing, and was now in charge of managing the relationships the sportswear giant had with top athletes. Lily explained about teaching, and the textbook she had abandoned, and the decision she and Tom had made to buy the avocado farm. Jack was wide-shouldered, tan, tattooed, his body buffed by wind and water, and she was petite, gray-haired, and as reserved as if she had been born and bred in New England. No one would have imagined they were a couple, and yet as they sat together, they felt the spark of connection. It was the same spark Lily had felt when Jack spoke to her at the dog shelter, and when he had stood near her at the beach—a tugging, a buzzing. She felt nervous and excited and somewhat sickened by it. She remembered making love to Tom and thinking about Jack, and she tried to remember the last time Tom's touch had felt so electric.

They had another beer after dinner, and sat out in the warm night. They were careful not to talk about fire or about sex or about how Lily was living, again, at her mother's house, just as if she were in high school again. Jack paid the bill and said, "My house is just a few blocks that way. We can walk."

Lily nodded, and then she walked with him. She did not touch him as they walked, but she did not change her mind either. She knew exactly what she was doing.

JACK lived in a little bungalow just off Main Street. It had a screen door that banged and surfboards in the garage. His walls were covered in photographs of oceans. There were so many colors of blue and white, and so many kinds of sand, and waves that curled and rose and crashed and sparkled. Lily stood in the center of the room and stared and was about to ask questions the way an academic would—*What are the locations of the photographs? What kind of camera did you use?*—and then Jack was behind her, and his arms were around her waist, and she felt him press against her back. She took a quick breath in, surprised by his touch, and the strength of his arms, and how he wasn't Tom, but she was still Lily.

He pressed his palm flat against her belly, his fingers reaching under the waistband of her jeans, and she did not move, she did not lift her hands or move her arms. She just stood, and let him hold her and stroke her, because that was why she had come. He turned her around so that she was facing him, and leaned down and kissed her on the mouth, and now she pressed back with her lips and her tongue. He slipped his hand under her shirt and around to the small of her back, and she felt him hard against her belly.

"I know how to make you feel alive," he boasted, and he kissed her neck, and her collarbone.

Her whole body was buzzing, from the beer and from the sense of abandon—such an alien, dangerous thing. His touch felt electric, and all she could think of was his fingers and where they were moving, and she wanted to dive into that feeling, to feel only that. She reached down and unbuckled his belt, and unbuttoned his jeans, and he groaned and she thought, *Good*.

He took her into the bedroom, which was surprisingly neat. The bed was neatly made with a chocolate brown cotton comforter, and there were matching pillowcases, and one large photo of a wave on the wall. He lifted off her hoodie sweatshirt, helped her step out of her clogs, slid her Levi's down to her ankles. He flung back the covers on the bed, and she sat on the edge of the sheets. He was still wearing an old plaid pair of boxer shorts, and he kneeled on the carpet and began to suck on her toes, very slowly. She wanted to scream, *No, no, no,* because her brain was about to explode with desire and with fear, and she wanted it to end quickly. She didn't want to *enjoy* it.

Jack's tongue was hot, and his patience was firm. He took each toe one at a time into his mouth, and rolled it around, and licked it. He kissed all the way up one of Lily's legs, over her hip, to her breast, and then he kissed her mouth and moved back down the other side of her body. "Who knew that the smartest girl in the class of 1974 had curves like this?" he said. What he was doing was a kind of performance; she sensed this. She understood that her role was to just lie there and appreciate it. It was different from what she had in mind, but she gave in to it. It was such a relief for something other than her brain to be throbbing.

He climbed on top of her, and rolled his hips, and slid inside, and then he slid out and she groaned—it was a kind of agony—and he kept up the kissing and the licking, moving closer and closer to the center, to the point between her legs where everything converged.

He climbed on top of her again, and rolled his hips again, and thrust inside her, once, twice, three times. This was more what she had hoped for—the urgency and the heat, the pleasure that was so close to pain, and when he pulled out again, she missed it, and she said, "Do that again," in a voice that was a command.

He did, and she cried out, and he cried out, and then her gasps turned into actual sobs, and she was lying under a man she didn't really know, weeping for her husband.

35

Eleanor

WHEN Lily got back, she half expected Olivia to be waiting up for her, but it was Eleanor who was sitting at the dining room table, the *New York Times* crossword puzzle in front of her, and a pen, and a dictionary.

Lily walked through the darkness and stood in front of her mother. When she was a teenager, she would do the same thing, but back then, she had nothing to hide. She was the kind of girl who would stay out all night at parties, drinking nothing. The kind of girl who would go on a date with a boy and just talk. Sometimes Lily thought that her mother was disappointed by her straitlaced ways. Sometimes she thought her mother was waiting up for her with the hope that Lily might actually come home tipsy, with smeared lipstick, a shirt buttoned the wrong way.

"What are you doing?" Lily asked. The light coming in from the night was hazy, gauzy, from all the smoke still in the air.

"You weren't running errands, were you?" Eleanor asked.

Lily raised her hand in the air as if to say, *So what?* and let it fall against her thigh with a slap. "No," she finally said.

Eleanor knew how comforting desire could be, how easy it was to go to it, and to give in to it. She knew how easy it was to get what you wanted when all you wanted was to be held, for a time. She guessed where Lily had gone, and she felt a shock of recognition now that she knew she was right. This daughter, who was so different from her, who had gone through the world on such a different path, had the same impulse in grief that she herself had once had—to reach out to someone else, to find instant comfort wherever you could find it. In the end, maybe they weren't so different after all. "You went to see that boy Jack," she said.

"Jesus, Mom," Lily said. "He's more than fifty years old. He's not a boy."

"Am I right?"

"Right? Right? Of course you're right. And you love that, don't you?"

"Lily . . ."

"You probably actually *love* that Tom died, too, because didn't you tell me it wouldn't last? That he couldn't give me everything I wanted? Well, you're right about all that, too. It's all over. And I have nothing."

Eleanor stood up in the eerie glow. "What I was going to say was that I understand this thing with Jack. I was going to tell you that it's okay. You take comfort where you can find it."

Lily held her breath. The words her mother was saying were so perfect, so exactly right, but she couldn't accept them. It was too much for her mother to be so right. "By the way," she said, "I'm going to fix up the shed and move back up there." Her voice was crisp and matter-of-fact. "I'm going to put a refrigerator and a stove in the front room, and a bed in the back."

Eleanor took a step forward. She wanted to wrap her arms around Lily's shoulders, to stroke her cheek. "You don't have to do that," she said. "You're welcome to stay here as long as you'd like." She swallowed and looked at the ground. "I like having you here," she said quietly.

"I know," Lily said. "I just think it would be best for us both."

She dreamed of fire, of flame, of smoke, of heat. She dreamed of angels—cartoon angels with cartoon wings—who lift people gently from the earth and fly them through the sky like Peter Pan and Wendy, over a glittering lighted earth. She was sometimes in the audience watching with amazement, and she was at other times in the wings of the stage watching with worry to see if the wires might break. In both instances, the angels smiled down at her, but the people they carried just flew; they never looked back.

In the morning, she got out the yellow legal pad. On a fresh piece of paper, at the top in the center, she wrote one word:

Tom

A few days later, Shelley called to say that Lily's bowl had been fired. Lily drove to the studio to pick it up. Shelley had set it on the worktable with the lid on top. It was just as misshapen as when Lily had made it, but there was a sense of permanence about it now, as if nothing could change it. She lifted the little lid, and inside was a ring of ash, and a two-and-a-half-carat diamond.

•36•

Eleanor

AFTER everyone had gone home again and Eleanor and Lily were left by themselves, Gordon called to say that he was in Santa Barbara. He had booked a room at the Biltmore Hotel, and wondered if Eleanor was free for dinner.

Eleanor said, "No, I most certainly am not," and Lily looked up in alarm.

"What was that about?" Lily said.

GORDON called the next day, and again asked if Eleanor was free for dinner.

"Gordon," Eleanor said. "You must stop this."

"Just let me come for a drink," he said. "One drink."

She relented. At six o'clock, he arrived in a crisp Thomas Pink shirt and a pair of khakis with a perfect crease. He leaned down and kissed his old friend on the cheek when she opened the door, and then he stood up and said, "Your place looks good, as always."

"Thank you," she said, and invited him inside.

Lily came downstairs to say hello. Gordon took both of Lily's hands in his own, looked her straight in the eye, and said, "I recently lost my wife of fifty-five years. I know that nothing I can say will make you feel any better, but I did want to say that I'm sorry for your loss."

Lily felt her throat constrict, and her eyes burn. She wanted to fall into Gordon's arms and be comforted, like a child. She pressed her lips together and nodded. "Thank you," she said quietly, and then, in order to change the subject, in order to pay her mother back for all the manipulative things she'd done in her life, in order to throw a rope to this kind, gray-haired man, she said, "So you two are going to dinner?"

"No," Eleanor said. "Gordon just stopped by for a drink."

"I have a reservation at the Wine Cask," Gordon said to Lily, "and no company. Would you care to join me?"

Lily had no interest in eating, and no interest in being out in public, where people might ask how she was doing, or if she was having a nice day, or whether or not her husband would be joining them. But she felt more comfort in the presence of Gordon Vreeland than she had felt in the past ten days. She said yes.

"Fine," Eleanor said. "That's just fine." But she felt jealousy rise up in her like a wave.

37

Lily

THEY ordered the halibut and an expensive bottle of pinot grigio. They talked about Lily's father, and Gordon told stories of the things Billy did in college—how he got an A on a history test he didn't study for, how he once hit three home runs in a row in practice. They talked about Opening Day parties at Fenway Park, and how Lily had never cared much for baseball. Then they talked about death—how final it was, how surprising, how silent.

"Do you think it's better to lose someone slowly, the way you lost Judy, or to lose someone quickly, the way we lost my dad?" Lily asked.

"Slowly," Gordon said. "Not being able to say good-bye is agonizing."

Lily nodded. "It's not only that," she said. "It's that everything's unresolved. I'm not even sure that Tom and I were doing okay."

Gordon set down his fork. "Your mother said you had a very good marriage."

"How would she know?" Lily asked, and Gordon laughed gently.

"Good point," he said. "Your mother was so different from other girls her age. She had this restlessness, this mischievousness. I actually told your father after that first night to watch himself with her. I told him she was dangerous. Billy didn't care, though. He liked that about her."

"Do you think she loved him?"

"Your mother? Love your father?" He took a sip of wine. "Wild horses couldn't keep the two of them apart. Do you know that he climbed out the second-story window of Winthrop House to go see her? Broke about five house rules."

"You're talking about lust, though, not love."

"She wanted him," Gordon said, "as if he were a prize. And he wanted her for the same reason. They were well suited to each other."

"But it wasn't love. It was something else."

"Who can say what love looks like from the outside?" he said. "I think love is only recognizable when you're in it."

The waiter came and took their orders for coffee, and when he had left, Gordon said, "Lily. I want you to know that your mother is not chasing after me. I'm chasing after her."

"It's a familiar scenario, either way," Lily said. "Someone dies, and my mother suddenly has a new man. I thought it would stop when she hit seventy. I thought it would be over."

"You've got it all wrong, sweetheart," Gorgon said. "And I'll tell you why. Do you know what Judy said to me before she died?" he asked.

Lily shook her head.

"She told me I should marry your mom."

Lily looked up. "Why?"

"She thought it would make us happy."

"Would it?"

Gordon shrugged. "I'm an old man," he said, "and I'm not good for much anymore. But I am good at love. I've known your mother for almost fifty years. I've always adored her. It would be a small leap for me to love her. And yes. I think it would make us happy."

Lily thought of Jack, and how she had imagined the same thing—that she could trade one love for another, make a quick swap, stop her grief before it gained steam. She thought of the wedding ring her father had made for her mother, and how Eleanor had worn it for so long, and how Lily had worn it for even longer. She should have given it back to her mother. She should have saved it for someone else. It was a talisman of lasting love and she had willfully destroyed it. "I'll talk to her," Lily said.

"You think that will help?"

Lily smiled. "Probably not."

"Neither do I," Gordon said. "But go ahead. Try. I'm going home on Wednesday."

AFTER dinner, she did not go back to her mother's house. She drove out to Ventura, to the beach cottage with the screen door that banged. It was nine thirty. The lights were blazing in the living room and the bedroom. She rang the bell, stepped back, and waited. She was cold suddenly and wished she had brought a sweater.

Jack opened the door. "I wondered when you would come back," he said.

"You didn't wonder *if* I'd come back?"

He shrugged. "It was pretty hot sex, Lily. Not many people will stay away from that. Are you coming in, or what?"

It was much rougher this time, much faster. He pulled off her clothes and pressed her against the wall, and she felt her skin pull where it was dry and where he thrust against her. When it was over, he asked if she wanted to stay and have a drink.

She shook her head, put on her clothes, and slunk back into the night.

38

Lily

THE news the next morning was filled with reports of an unseasonable cold snap. Citrus farmers were worried about their crops. "My trees can withstand a little frost," one orange farmer said, "but two nights, or more, and the damage will be deep." Lily got up from the breakfast table, agitated and upset. She didn't know a thing about avocado farming, or if the trees were in the same danger, and the only person she thought might know was Nadine.

She called the Calavo warehouse, but Nadine was not in.

"I'm going up to the house," she said, unable to call the charred remains of her home what it was.

"What are you going to do?" Eleanor asked.

"I'm not sure."

"Do you know anything about avocado trees?"

"No," Lily said, "but I'm going to find someone who does. Those trees are all I have left."

WHEN Lily pulled into the driveway, there was an unfamiliar truck already there. It was white, clean, with four doors and big tires. On the back were two bumper stickers: one that said LOCALVORE and one that featured the Sierra Club's iconic sugar pine tree. Lily walked quickly through the rows of trees, peering along them, unsure of what she would find. She felt nervous—as if the person who had arrived before her was an intruder intent on doing her harm.

She walked toward the shed at the base of the orchard, and as she drew closer, she heard footsteps, the crack of someone dropping a wooden crate on the bare cement floor. She stepped into the doorway.

Nadine was at the far end of the shed next to a stack of wooden crates. A picking stick was propped up on the workbench at her side. Her hair was pulled back in a ponytail, and her flannel shirt—red plaid, with tiny black stripes—hung like a flag from her body. She wore Birkenstocks that were flattened and dusty, and she wore, as usual, no bra. Her breasts hung inside her white tank top like ripe fruit. Lily's gaze darted to them, and then came to rest on Nadine's face. "What are you doing?" she asked.

"The fruit will all die," she said. "I'm harvesting it."

Lily peered through the dusty air. She could see dust mites dancing in the shafts of light that came through the old window, and thought about batting them out of the way.

Nadine stepped toward her. "Lily," she said, "I'm sorry about Tom. I'm sorry about your loss."

Lily closed her eyes. Despite the lists she had made on the yellow lined paper, she was tempted to say, *I didn't lose anything*. Losing implied some kind of game, like hockey, baseball, crazy eights—or some kind of carelessness, like keys left in a lock, glasses left behind on a desk. She felt, in that moment, the full flowering of guilt. She felt, suddenly, that she had killed Tom. She had betrayed him, and then she had killed him—by her negligence, her selfishness, her indulgence. She opened her eyes.

"Were you sleeping with him?" she asked. She said it gently, the way you might ask someone if they had recently been ill.

Nadine looked directly back into Lily's eyes. "No," she said. "We were working on a presentation together. He was a smart man, Lily, a good man. He wouldn't have done that to you."

Lily picked up an avocado from the full crate on the workbench, and cupped it in her hand. It was rough and heavy. She let its weight pull her hand down to her side. "But did you want to sleep with him?" she asked.

"Lily . . ." Nadine said.

"It's important that I know the truth," she said.

Nadine shifted her weight from one leg to the other. "Okay," she said. "No. I wasn't attracted to him in that way."

Lily nodded. She set her avocado on the workbench, and it rolled toward the back and stopped against the Peg-Board. A crow called outside the shed, and both women glanced toward the door, as if the bird might be right there, speaking directly to them. When Nadine looked back, there were tears on Lily's face.

"The last time I had sex with Tom," Lily said, "I imagined another man in his place."

She said these words, and then she stood there in the dust and the dim light, letting the tears stream down her cheeks. "I can't seem to forgive myself for that. I can't stop wishing I could have the chance to apologize for that."

Nadine stepped toward Lily and gathered the other woman up in her arms. Lily leaned into her—her free-hanging breasts, her free-hanging plaid shirt, her beaten-down shoes that held her so solidly on the ground—and sobbed.

THE next thing she knew, Luna was there. The dog bounded through the trees, barking, and Lily just stood and watched her approach through the dappled light. Luna circled her, yelping and jumping on her legs, and Lily felt unsteady.

"Stop," she said sharply.

Luna hesitated for a moment, then barreled into Lily, jumped on her, and knocked her down onto the loamy ground. Luna yelped and licked her hands and her face and her neck, and Lily put her hands over her face, and tried to turn away.

"No," she said, "Luna, no!"

The dog sat down a foot from where Lily lay, and waited, panting and whining.

Lily sat up and brushed the dead leaves from her sleeves, and looked into Luna's face, and her mismatched, knowing eyes. Maybe Luna had been with Tom when he died. Maybe she stayed by his side until she knew the firemen had come to pull his body out, and then bolted through the flames to save herself. Lily put her arms around her dog, buried her face in her fur, and smelled the smoke of the fire and the bitterness of her despair.

Nadine turned and walked back into the trees and left them alone.

39

Eleanor

GORDON knocked on her door just after noon on Tuesday.

"Gracie died," he said.

Eleanor backed across her foyer, sat on the kilim bench, and rested her head against the wall.

Gordon closed the door, and came and sat next to her. Neither of them said anything for a long time. They just sat, remembering their friend, and their lives, and all the people they knew who had lived and died.

After a while, Eleanor stood up. "I have to go to the store," she said, "to get the ingredients to make a cake."

"A cake?"

"It's what I do when people die. Make rum cake."

"Can I drive you?"

She closed her eyes. She already had the cake mix, the rum. All she needed were a few more eggs. "Okay," she said.

WHEN they came back to the house, Lily was sitting at the dining room table. She was staring at a vase the size of a large pear, and at her feet was a box, a pile of packing bubbles, and a torn pile of brown paper wrapping. She looked at Eleanor. "It's from my friend Elizabeth," she said. "My old neighbor."

Eleanor stepped closer, and saw that the handles of the little vase were arms. It appeared that the vessel was hugging itself.

"She's a potter," Lily said. "Do you know what that means?"

Eleanor shook her head.

"It means that she knows something about fire."

Eleanor put her shopping bag on the floor, and sat in a chair opposite Lily. Gordon stayed where he was, a short distance apart, as if he knew he didn't belong at the table.

"Listen to what she says," Lily said. She reached into the pot and pulled out a slip of paper like a fortune from a cookie.

"Fire destroys, but it also galvanizes. Tom may be gone, but the love he had for you is fused to you like a glaze."

Eleanor held out her hand, and Lily placed the slip of paper in it. Eleanor read it, laid the paper down, then reached for the vase and turned it so that she could see its perfect symmetry, its human curves. "It's lovely," she said.

Lily nodded. "I love the word *galvanized*. The word *fused*.

I love the way this vase has been burned, but it still feels like it's been loved."

Eleanor nodded.

"I'm choosing to believe it," Lily said.

"What?"

"That the love Tom and I had for each other is fused to me like a glaze."

THAT evening, the three of them gathered in the kitchen. Eleanor had the rum out on the counter, and Gordon asked where the glasses were kept so that he could make them drinks.

"This rum is for making cake," Eleanor said, "not drinking. I've got vodka, gin, and scotch and enough wine for a party, if you'd like."

"But this is good rum," Gordon said. "A little soda, a twist of lime. It could be a new tradition to drink rum while you make rum cake."

"I saw limes on the neighbors' tree," Lily said.

"Aha! A bit of pirating will make this cocktail perfect. Did you know that the British Navy considered rum to be so critical that they gave every sailor a half-pint-a-day ration?"

"And the Americans handed out Hershey bars . . ." Eleanor said.

"We had our fair share of rum," Gordon said. "Don't you worry."

They drank their rum while they beat the cake batter forty-two times by hand. "It has to be forty-two," Eleanor explained. "I don't know why, but that's what my mother always told me."

"She said the same thing about lemon meringue pie," Lily said, "and she made the most amazing lemon meringue pie."

"I'm not a big fan of lemon meringue," Gordon said. "Judy's specialty was a coconut cream. It was divine."

"All I know how to bake is rum cake from Duncan Hines Yellow Cake Mix," Eleanor said. "When I die, you'll know just what to do."

Lily raised her glass. "And I'll drink the rum like the British sailors do and toast a thanks to Gordon."

"I'll be dead, too, no doubt."

"Nonsense," Eleanor said. "You're going to live to a hundred."

Gordon smiled. "Could be. We'll have to see."

"Gracie always wanted to live that long. She used to always talk about how we would drink a bottle of champagne even if we had to sneak it into the hospital." Eleanor sipped her rum, looked straight at Gordon. "Damn her," she said.

The smell of the cake permeated the kitchen now—sweet and powerful—and Lily remembered how she had smelled that on the day after Tom had died, and how she had thought, *That can't be for Tom*, as if it had all been a mistake. "I never imagined Tom would die first," she said to no one in particular. "I never imagined it. Not once."

Gordon stood up and made his way around to the bar stool where Lily sat, and he set his glass down and took her in his arms without saying a word. Eleanor followed him, and came up to her daughter, and leaned over and gently kissed her forehead. Lily took hold of her mother's hand—small and frail, with loose, wrinkled skin—and squeezed it in thanks.

When the cake was done, they put slices on Eleanor's Limoges plates, which she said Gracie helped her pick out at Filene's in Boston when they were just twenty-one years old. They sat out on the balcony, where the air still smelled like fire, and ate their cake and drank more rum until they could no longer keep their eyes open.

GORDON slept that night on Eleanor's couch. When she came downstairs in the morning, she said, "People will talk about us, Gordon."

He laughed. "What people? We're practically the only ones left."

"Is that why you won't leave me alone?"

"It's not a bad reason," he said.

She walked up to him and reached up on her toes and kissed him on the cheek. "You're very sweet, Gordon. I adore you. We will always be great friends."

"But you're not going to marry me, are you?"

"I'm sorry," she said.

"You're kicking me off your couch, then?"

"I am."

"Good," he said. "It's uncomfortable as hell."

•40•

Gordon

He was nearly seventy-five years old, but Gordon had never been rejected by a girl. He had been an awkward, unformed boy when he arrived at Harvard in the fall of 1951, a kid who understood that the long arms and legs that helped him on the baseball field were a liability everywhere else. He stayed away from dances, from drive-ins, from any event where the boys were required to be smooth. When Judy Wyeth wiggled in next to him in the front seat of the Studebaker that day in front of Tower Court, he felt the curve of her hip, smelled the sweetness of her hair, saw the kindness in her eyes, and within moments decided that he wanted her the way he had wanted nothing else in his life. He wanted to hold her, to lie down next to her, to take her in his arms and never let her go. At nights, in his ivy-covered dorm, he would lie awake and dream of having a job, a house, and Judy as his wife.

He asked Judy to marry him on Tupelo Point. It was on a

leafy rise on the path that circled Wellesley's Lake Waban. His knees knocked, his voice shook, and he felt certain that the birds in the trees were there just to mock his intention with their "caw, caw." But Judy threw her arms around him, and she cried, "Oh yes." It was then that he made a vow to himself: he would be a good husband. He would adore Judy until the day he died. He was twenty years old, and he never imagined that she would die first. He never let himself imagine it, until she became so ill that he couldn't ignore it.

And now, Eleanor Peters had kicked him off her couch and told him to go home. He felt crushed, deflated, embarrassed that he had come all that way and failed. It seemed as if the wind had been knocked out of him. As he packed his suitcase to go back to New York, his mind cascaded back through the years, remembering friends whose hearts had been broken. There was a fellow sailor in the navy whose sweetheart had let him go in a letter that arrived on his birthday, who talked of flinging himself overboard. There was a trumpet player at Harvard who sat out in the quad playing Taps when he found out that his girl had betrayed him. Gordon even remembered a boy in the sixth grade clutching a homemade valentine, a look of absolute shock on his face because the girl had shaken her head and said no, she wouldn't accept it. He couldn't remember the boys' names, but he remembered the looks on their faces. Only now did he know what it felt like in the gut.

He wished he could go back to all those moments and provide better comfort to his friends. He didn't know how physical a feeling it was, how strongly it registered in his stomach and his legs and the intricate space behind his eyes. He went to the hotel bar and ordered a drink, and when he told the bartender that he was in town for a girl but that the trip hadn't gone well, the bartender gave him a second on the house. Gordon smiled wryly, understanding, at long last, what a perfect temporary antidote scotch and a sympathetic stranger could be. He was seventy-four years old and still learning about love and life. He was seventy-four years old and alone for the first time.

He was going to fly home the following day, and he knew that when he got there, the doorman would ask if he'd had a nice trip. There was nothing else he could do other than nod, and lie, and say, "Yes, indeed."

41

Ryan

BEER was no longer enough to numb Ryan's pain. He poured himself a shot of tequila as soon as he walked in the door every night, and had another before he went to bed. He didn't try to hide it, and always offered Olivia a shot, too, and that way he nearly convinced himself that he didn't have a problem—not with the drinking anyway.

It was harder to pretend with his marriage. On the night of his father's memorial party, Ryan did not sleep in the downstairs bedroom where Olivia and Brooke were sleeping. He slept on the couch in Nana's TV room. He just stayed there after watching the Dodgers' game with Luke, as if he had passed out from exhaustion, as if he didn't even have the wherewithal to get up and brush his teeth. The truth was that he knew he wasn't welcome in bed with his wife after what he had said, and he wasn't sure he wanted to be there anyway.

"Marriage is fucked up," he said to Luke, during a lull in

the eighth inning, "It's so damn hard to get it right, and when you get it right like Mom and Dad, all you get is heartbreak because someone's always going to die first."

"Mom seems pretty tweaked."

"See?" Ryan said. "It's fucked up."

"But Olivia is great," Luke said. "You and Olivia are great."

"Wrong," Ryan said.

"Wrong? What do you mean, wrong? She's sweet and pretty, and she's great with Brooke."

"She won't let me touch her."

"No shit?" Luke laughed. "And here I thought that was the best part of being married."

"Maybe it is for someone who knows what they're doing, but that's not me, bro. I don't have whatever it is that Dad had."

Luke shook his head. "I can't believe he's gone."

"I know," Ryan said. "It's fucked up."

His grandmother called one night after they returned to San Luis Obispo. She was calling, she said, to check up on them.

"We're great, Nana," Ryan said. "Things are great."

"Don't lie to me, Ryan Gilbert," she said.

"What?" he asked.

"I called to ask how you're doing. I'm quite serious about the question."

Ryan sighed. Olivia was reading to Brooke in the bedroom in the back of the house, but he wanted to make sure they didn't overhear him. He stepped out onto the front porch. "I'm sleeping on the couch. I'm eating food you're paying someone else to cook. My daughter won't let me near her. She constantly says, 'Mommy do it, Mommy do it.' And Olivia is happy to oblige because it makes her feel superior."

"It's that bad?" Eleanor said.

"It's that bad."

"I'll pay for counseling," Eleanor said, "if you think it would help."

"You and your money," Ryan said.

"Well?"

"The truth is," Ryan said, "I won't go. I don't want to sit there and have someone ask me about my family because then I'll have to tell them what a great dad I had and how he was such a great husband, and how he just died in a wildfire and there's just no way in hell I'm ever going to live up to him."

"You don't have to live up to anyone, Ryan. You should know that. But walking away from a marriage . . ."

"I know," he said. "I know. I have no idea what it will cost."

WHEN he got off the phone, the house was silent. He walked down the hallway, pushed open the bedroom door, and saw that both Olivia and Brooke had fallen asleep in the rocking chair. He stood and watched them from the doorway, wondering if he should turn out the light, wake them up, walk away.

After a while, he stepped toward them. He reached down and lifted Brooke out of Olivia's arms. Brooke's skin was sweaty. Her soft hair was matted to her forehead. She smelled like soap. He closed his eyes and held her to his shoulder, and just stood there, holding her, until his arms grew numb, and then he gently laid her on the bed, and kissed her and said good night. He felt like a thief who had stolen something precious.

He walked out of the room, turned off the light, and headed for the couch.

42

Lily

AFTER the avocados were safe from the frost, Lily went back to Beverly Fabrics. She wandered through the aisles, stopping at bolts of fabric that caught her eye, considering the possibilities. There were burnout velvets, Italian wool so fine they felt like silk, silk in a cacophony of color, weight, and texture. Every bolt offered something new to Lily's imagination—a coat, a skirt, a dress—and every possibility reminded her of a piece of fabric she had lost in the fire. There was so much fabric and so many things she had never made! She thought that she could list them all on her yellow pad of paper—Hattie's gray tweed that had not become a jacket, the sage green flea market silk that had not become a skirt, the white dotted Swiss that she had bought in Boston when she thought she might have a little girl. She had one Rubbermaid tub that was stuffed with swatches of printed cotton in different shades of blue. There were stripes, dots, florals, swirls, and geometric prints, and taken all together, they had looked like the sea. Lily had always thought that she would make a beautiful quilt with all that blue. She would design the horizon, the sky and the water, and somehow, it would cease to look like bits of cotton stitched together, and would look, instead, exactly the way the beach did on a clear summer day.

"I should have done it," she said, and she realized too late that she had spoken out loud.

"May I help you?" a saleswoman asked. She wore jeans and a chambray blouse, and her hair was cropped straight across as if she'd cut it herself. Pinned on her shirt was a name tag that said JANET.

"I'm looking for some silk," Lily said, which she knew was the equivalent of walking into a bookstore and saying, *I'd like a story,* but it was all she could manage to say.

Janet looked at Lily kindly. "Ah," she said. "Are you making something for a special occasion?"

"I think so," Lily said.

"Well, let's see," said Janet. "We have some beautiful new dupioni silk, and I think the blue is particularly pretty."

Lily touched the slags in the silk, felt the stiffness of the fabric. "I'm thinking of something that drapes," she said.

"Did you see the Japanese chiffons up front? They're very popular."

"I did," Lily said, "but I don't think I want a pattern."

Through this back-and-forth, Lily figured out what she was looking for. She ended up in front of the wall with the solid-colored silks. She scanned them, and pointed to a bolt above her head—a dark silver gray double-sided satin. Janet brought a step stool, pulled down the bolt, laid it across a cutting table. The fabric shimmered like an iridescent sea creature. Lily reached out to touch it—it was slippery, thick—and the light bounced off it as if it were alive. It looked like mercury, set free. She held it across her body and it moved and flowed over her breasts and over her belly like something magic.

"It looks wonderful with your hair and your coloring," Janet said. Lily couldn't see herself, but she could picture it—the silver gray fabric playing off the gray of her hair, playing off the blue of her eyes.

"This is it," Lily said. "I'd like four yards."

She bought the same sewing machine she had bought just five months before, and needles, thread, scissors, pins. She bought muslin and button forms. She realized, as she made her purchase, that she was amassing things—things that would need to be stored somewhere, things that would be there when she wanted to use them rather than phantom objects that were burned, gone. She realized, too, that these new items would not be shared with Tom. They would be, simply, hers. Everything she bought from here on out would be like that. As Janet rang each item up and put them all in a bag, Lily stood at the counter and tried, unsuccessfully, not to cry.

WHEN she got back to her mother's house, she went to the garage and got the cardboard tube of fabric that Tom had saved from the fire. She spread the pewter silk over the back of the couch, spread the lace out over it, then spread the muslin on the dining room table. She closed her eyes and pictured the dress her grandmother would have made to wear to a dance. She pictured a shift made of silk, an overlay of lace, a dress that would skim over her body like water.

Eleanor came down from her bedroom several hours later, when the muslin dress lay stitched together on the back of a chair and Lily was draping the iridescent silk across her body. Eleanor stopped, startled at the presence of so fine a fabric in the hands of her jeans- and grief-clad daughter. "What are you making?" she asked.

"A dress," Lily said.

Eleanor had never understood the appeal of sewing or felt the impulse to create. It seemed like so much frustration, so much effort, and no matter how good the seamstress was, the result always had the air of homemade about it. She remembered her mother going out with her father to Red Sox games and to the Head of the Charles wearing handmade dresses and suits, and she remembered wishing that her mother would go down to the shops on Newbury Street and buy dresses like the other wives. Her father was a prominent businessman in town, a man who had made it, and his wife still made her own clothes. But at least Lily wanted something new, something pretty. At least she was thinking about how she looked. "Good," Eleanor said, nodding with approval. "That's very good."

THE next morning, there were two muslin pieces—a shift and a piece that would overlay it—and Lily pieced together the silk. In the afternoon, she finished the seams, hemmed, and ironed. The following day, she laid the lace out on the table. She walked around it, considering the scalloped edges, the pearls, and considering all the things that this piece of fabric had never become. Hattie had never danced in it. She hadn't gotten married in it, hadn't dressed her child in it. The life of the lace had been one of longing, of waiting, of stories not told—an experience just the opposite of hers. Life was a risk. Love was a risk. And she saw now, very clearly, that it was one well worth taking. She lifted her scissors and cut right through the lace. Pearls fell to the floor like hail, and Eleanor looked up from where she was sitting and reading, and said, "Sounds like rain."

"It's Hattie's lace," Lily said.

Eleanor got off the couch, came over to the table. "So it is," she said, and then after a moment, she said, "It looks good."

"You can't ever write off a piece of fabric," Lily said, "or the possibility of love."

"What's that supposed to mean?"

"That Gordon loves you. He wants to marry you. I think you should say yes."

Eleanor stood at the table, silently, thinking that Lily sounded like Gracie, and then missing Gracie, and missing Judy and feeling, suddenly, very old.

"Do you have any idea what it feels like to be loved the way he loves you?" Lily asked.

Eleanor walked to the windows that looked out at the blackened hills, where the fire had swept down, and where, even now, the seeds in the soil would be preparing to sprout. She thought about the kind of love that doesn't end, that doesn't bend, that is just there, solid as an oak tree. She had never wanted it before now. She had thought that it would cost her something she couldn't afford to lose—her sense of self, maybe, her pride. Whatever it was, it seemed so silly now that she had lived so long and never allowed love in. It seemed so pointless. It seemed so sad. "No," she said quietly. "The truth is that I don't have any idea."

"I do," Lily said. "Because that's the way Tom loved me. It wasn't flashy, or loud, but it was constant. It was relentless. Nothing was going to get in its way. And I lived with that love for our entire marriage. I came to count on it. To take it for granted actually. But now that it's gone, I know exactly what I had, and I can tell you this, Mom: it feels very nice."

Tears were streaming down Lily's face, but she stayed where she was seated, behind the sewing machine. Eleanor walked back toward her and then Lily stood up and held the dress out in front of her. "It's for you," she said, "from me, and from Hattie, to wear when you say I do."

"You think I should say yes, then? Say yes to Gordon?"

Lily nodded. "I do."

WHEN the dress was pressed and hanging on the back of the door, and when the sewing machine was snapped into its case and the pins all stuck back in the pincushion, Lily drove out to see Luna, whom Nadine was taking care of until the shed was ready for her to move into. She took the dog on a walk along the dirt roads in the hills behind the Calavo warehouse, and sat with her awhile under the shade of one of the avocado trees near where her car was parked. Luna barked at the birds, leapt at the leaves on the ground, full of life. Lily might have been tempted to say that the dog had no clue that Tom was dead— the man who had agreed to take her home, who thought she would be a good partner for tramping through the trees, who went back into a fiery house because he wanted to save her. But there was something in the way Luna behaved around her that convinced her otherwise. Luna seemed to be watching her, and watching the world around her, alert for signs of trouble, ready to head them off. This dog, she thought, whom Tom had touched and loved, was never going to leave her side.

"You're a good dog, Luna," Lily said, looking into Luna's mismatched eyes. "I'm glad you came back."

•43•

Eleanor

AFTER Lily went to see Luna, Eleanor sat on the kilim bench just inside her front door and cried.

She used to always say that love was an illusion. Love always dissolved in the face of everyday pressures, in the face of time. You couldn't pin it down, couldn't hold on to it, couldn't count on it. Something so ephemeral, she used to say, was not a good investment. But she had never been loved the way Lily had been loved by Tom. She had no idea what it felt like to give your heart over so completely that even death couldn't steal it away.

After a while, she got up, and called Gordon. It was evening in New York, and he was getting ready for bed.

"Who is this?" he demanded.

"It's Eleanor," she said. "Calling from California."

"Something's wrong?" Gordon asked. In his experience,

tragedy was the only reason people phoned in the middle of the night.

"No," she said. "I've just been thinking about Judy."

Gordon cleared his throat. So it was tragedy, after all. A reminder of his loss. A moment in the middle of the night when he had to realize, once again, that she was gone and he was alone. He waited.

"Judy and I took a class together our first semester of college. Beginning French. She insisted that we speak nothing but French to each other when we were in the dorm. She said it would be the best way to learn the language. I thought it was just another one of Judy's crazy ideas and laughed at her and told her she was being silly. So she sat in her room every night and spoke to herself. Had conversations with herself. We all laughed even louder at her while we played bridge and smoked our cigarettes. Well, you know it turned out. Judy spoke French like a native, and I always sounded like a schoolgirl. Still do, in fact."

He was more awake now. "Eleanor," he said. "It's the middle of the night."

"My point is that I've been thinking about how often Judy was right."

He sat up straighter in bed. He thought he understood now what was happening. "She was indeed," he said.

"About love, too, Gordon. I think Judy was right about love, too. So I'd like to marry you," she said. "I'd like to accept your kind offer. I don't know how we will work it out with my house and Lily and the boys all here in California, and your apartment and all your children there in New York, but I don't see any reason why we should be alone, Gordon, when we can be together. What I'm saying is, I'm choosing love, just like Judy said I should. I'm choosing you—that is, if your offer is still good."

He smiled. "Will I have to sleep on your couch?"

"Of course not," she said. "I am taking you to be my husband, not my houseboy."

"Good," he said, "because my back ached for days after that night."

HE met her at the airport when she arrived two days later. He stood in the baggage claim area at LaGuardia, his arms filled with white roses. When she came down the escalator, he bent down on one knee, and everyone around him stared at the white-haired man with the white roses who appeared to be proposing marriage, but he couldn't balance there, and then he had trouble getting up, and Eleanor had to help him. He stood up finally, and presented her with the bouquet, and the people who had been watching—who had flown in with her from Los Angeles, or flown all the way from Kyoto—broke into applause. He took her in his arms, and just stood there, holding her and thinking of the ways in which she felt different from Judy, and thinking of the ways in which she felt exactly the same.

Lily

ELEANOR and Gordon planned an early June wedding at the church by the sea.

A few days before the event, Eleanor stopped Lily in the kitchen before she went up to bed. "You'll need a dress for the ceremony," she said.

"I guess you're right," Lily said.

"And you'll need shoes."

"That's true."

"Come on," Eleanor said. "We're going shopping."

"But not to Nordstrom."

"They have the best dresses in town and the best shoes."

"I want something old."

"You mean something used?"

"Exactly. Something with history. Something with a story."

"God help me," Eleanor said.

They walked to a consignment store tucked into one of the

downtown paseos. There were beautiful shoes in the window, and jeweled purses, and a display of couture dresses.

"Can I help you?" the woman asked. "Are you looking for something special?"

"Yes," Lily said. "Something for an afternoon wedding."

The shopkeeper led them to a rack of dresses and began to suggest things—chiffon and silk. Eleanor noted with pleasure the quality of the designers and the range of styles. She and the shopkeeper got into a discussion about how well Chanel holds its value, and Lily slipped off to another rack, and ran her hands along the fabric, feeling her way through the clothes. When her fingers landed on something particularly rich, she stopped. It was a pair of light wool cream-colored palazzo pants. She held them to her waist, and then turned to look for a top. She zeroed in on a crisp, short-sleeved cappuccino wraparound silk blouse. She slipped into the dressing room, tried the outfit on, and walked out, barefoot, into the shop, where her mother and the shopkeeper were still talking. They stopped their conversation and stared.

"Oh," the shopkeeper said.

Eleanor nodded, and bit her lip to keep from crying. "You look beautiful," she said.

A few hours before the ceremony, Gordon was nervously pacing the parking lot outside the chapel.

"How are you doing?" Lily asked.

He darted his eyes at her. "This is a big day," he said.

"It's a very big day," she said, but then she remembered why they were there—because his wife had died, and wanted him to keep loving. "You must be thinking about Judy," she said. She knew it was so, because she couldn't get Tom out of her mind. She kept thinking she would see him, getting out of a car, walking around the corner of the church, walking down the sidewalk, but time after time, Tom wasn't there.

Gordon stopped pacing. "I can't get her out of my mind," he said.

"She can be part of this day," Lily said. And she smiled and added, "Her love can be fused to you like a glaze."

"Like a glaze?"

"That's a line from a potter friend of mine," she said, "who sculpts things out of earth and fire."

"That's good," Gordon said, and his wild eyes calmed down in their sockets, and he stopped moving. "That's very good."

THE gray lace dress appeared to be a part of Eleanor—not so much something she had put on as something she had become. The silk flowed across her small body, and the lace floated over it like flowers scattered on a shimmering lake. Her white hair picked up the silver threads in the fabric and threw off an energetic light. She wore pumps with a strap that buttoned over her feet, and a soft plum lipstick, and everyone said she looked stunning.

Luke was there with a new girlfriend, and Ryan and Olivia, who sat together in willful misery, wondering about dissolution, reconciliation, the myriad paths that lay before them. Lily had made Brooke a blue satin dress with a white bow, and Brooke twirled around like a princess until Lily took her hand and helped her to stand still and watch what was happening before them.

"Nana's pretty," Brooke whispered.

"All brides are pretty," Lily said, and she felt her eyes fill with tears, and her throat constrict as she remembered Tom and the day in Lyon when she promised to love him until death do them part. She had had no idea, then, that she would love him so well, that she would lose him so hard. She'd had no idea that love was so much stronger than death.

"Then how come you're crying?" Brooke asked.

Lily wanted to say that it was because it was such a rare thing to love and be loved, and such a joyful thing, and such a fragile thing, and she wanted to say that she had never thought she would see her mother stand up to receive love like this, and to give it, and that she was grateful to be alive to witness it. She wanted to say how much she had loved Tom, and how much she missed him, and how she woke up every day thinking he would be there beside her again, but there were no words for that kind of longing. "Because," she said simply, "I'm happy for her."

THEY had dinner at the Biltmore, where they could hear the waves of the ocean crashing onto the sand. On the way home, Lily said she would see everyone back at her mom's, and left by herself. Instead of driving north, toward Eleanor's town house, she drove south, to Jack's.

"Ah," he said when he opened the door, "the grieving widow back for more?"

"No," she said, "actually, no. This was all a mistake, Jack. I used you, and I just wanted to come by to tell you that I'm sorry."

"Come on in," he said. "Use me all you want. You look fantastic."

"No," she said, staying where she was on the front steps. "I can't anymore."

He stepped through his door and put one hand around the back of her neck, and another on the curve of her bottom. He pulled her roughly toward him and kissed her, hard, on the mouth. She tasted beer and desire, and pulled away, but he did not let go.

"You know you liked it," he said.

She nodded. "I did like it," she said. "It's true. But it's not going to make me feel better about what I lost. My grief deserves more respect than I've been giving it. If we lived in another time and place, I guess I'd be wearing black so everyone would know."

Jack let his hands fall to his sides. "That's the girl I remember from high school," he said. "The good girl. The rule follower."

She smiled a mirthless smile. "I'm afraid so," she said, and turned and walked away.

•45•

Lily

At the end of June, Lily moved into the shed on the burned-out lot. There was nothing to throw out this time, nothing to assess. All her possessions could fit into four cardboard boxes. Eleanor brought home a set of eight-hundred-thread-count white sheets for the new bed, and Luke insisted on going to Target and buying towels for the little bathroom. "I'm all over Target now," he said. "I've got that place wired."

Gordon put the boxes in the back of Luke's truck, and they all drove together up the hill. The closer they got to the lot, the quieter they got, until they weren't speaking at all. When Luke pulled into the driveway, Eleanor turned around to look at Lily in the backseat. "Are you sure about this?" she asked. "Gordon and I are happy to have you stay with us for as long as you'd like."

Lily nodded, and gasped for air, because she was crying so hard and it was hard to breathe. "Tom and I moved to this

316

piece of land because we wanted to be together. We didn't want to get complacent about our love or our lives. We didn't want to take any of it for granted." She gulped more air. "I still feel all that here. I feel him."

"He would be glad that you're going to keep the ranch, Mom," Luke said.

"I don't know how I'll do managing the trees and all, but I'm going to try. And I want to be with Luna," Lily said. "I know it sounds strange, but I feel safe with her."

"It doesn't sound strange," Eleanor said. "It doesn't sound strange at all." She remembered when Lily and Tom first moved to Burlington, to a terrible little apartment with windows that barely kept out the cold. She kept wanting to give them money for a better house, better furniture, better window coverings, and they kept refusing. Eleanor was certain their marriage would crumble under the strain of those conditions, but it never did. She had been so wrong about them.

They all got out of the truck and carried the boxes past the burned-out house, down through the dappled shade of the avocado trees, and into the shed. There was a small box on the doorstep, wrapped in the comics from the newspaper and tied with twine. The card was from Nadine, and it said simply, *Welcome home.* Lily tore off the paper to reveal a pair of goat-skin leather gardening gloves, women's size small.

Lily stepped into the shed, set the gloves on the work-bench, and then placed her lumpy little ceramic bowl beside it. She dug into one of the boxes and got out a new stainless steel dog bowl, a red webbed leash, and a rubber bone, and set them on the floor.

"That's it," she said to her mother and her younger son. "That's everything."

THE next morning, Nadine arrived at eight o'clock, and from the shed, Lily could hear her truck stop, her door slam, and then Luna yelping. The noise grew closer and closer until the dog was at her door. Luna threw her body at Lily, her paws clawing her legs, her tongue wagging. Lily sat down on the floor and wrestled with Luna, and rubbed her belly and her ears, and Luna lapped at her face.

"This is one crazy dog," Lily said when Nadine appeared. She was carrying a chain saw in one hand, and a length of rope in the other.

"You're telling *me*?" Nadine asked. Luna lunged from one woman to the other and back again. "I'm just glad she's your problem now."

"Thanks for taking such good care of her," Lily said.

Nadine shrugged. "My pleasure."

"What's the saw for?" Lily asked.

"To remove the damaged branches from those trees," Nadine said. "We'll have to paint them with a calcium-lime mix to prevent bugs and decay."

Lily nodded. "Let me get my gloves," she said.

The three of them walked through the shade of the trees toward the part of the orchard that had burned.

"Tom was planning on going organic," Nadine said, "but I don't know if you want to make the switch right away. It will take a few months to complete the transition, and we'll lose some yield along the way."

"I want to make the switch," Lily said.

Nadine stopped and set down her saw. "He would have been a very good farmer," she said.

Lily's eyes teared up. She was so tired of being surprised, time and again, that Tom was really gone. Sometimes she was mad at him, and other times she just desperately missed him, and she wanted to yell at him, and to take him in her arms, and to tell him she was sorry, and to ask him to forgive her. Her relationship to Tom was still so complex, and yet he was no longer here for all the ordinary things—the chores and the meals, the discussions about what was going on that day. That was the part she missed the most.

She turned toward Nadine. "He was a very good husband," she said.

READERS GUIDE

1. *The Threadbare Heart* explores the intersection of marriage and love, and the same question seems to lurk in each of the character's minds: What makes marriage work? Which character has the answer you most agree with?

2. Throughout *The Threadbare Heart*, Lily and Tom alternate between cherishing their knowledge of each other and wondering if they are capable of knowing each other at all. What does it mean to truly know someone?

3. Eleanor and Lily both see the avocado farm as the answer to their familial problems, but for different reasons. Eleanor has money to burn and wants her loved ones near, whereas Lily sees the opportunity as a fresh start that could reinvigorate her marriage. Are their expectations met?

4. Lily is emotionally attached to the fabric she has collected throughout her life. She observes that Eleanor never holds on to things—or people—because holding on leaves a person

vulnerable to pain. Lily says that for Eleanor "fabric is just a means to an end." What does she mean?

5. Were you surprised at Gordon's feelings for Eleanor? Why or why not?

6. Lily's friend Marilyn and her mother seem to share the belief that you should put yourself first in marriage and in life. Lily feels differently; she credits her willingness to compromise as one of the keys to her long marriage. Whose beliefs serve them better?

7. The theme of love in marriage is at the core of *The Threadbare Heart*. According to Eleanor, love is an illusion and you're better off keeping it at a safe distance. On the opposite end of the spectrum is Gordon, who believes that love is a choice. Where does Lily fall on the spectrum? What effect does losing Tom have on her perception of love?

8. Ryan constantly compares his marriage with Olivia to that of his parents, and constantly comes up short. Can Ryan and Olivia's marriage be saved? Where do you think they might be five years from now?

9. At one point Eleanor refers to her first husband's sudden death as an "elegant solution" to the dilemma of her unhappy marriage. Is her brutal honesty refreshing, cold, or somewhere in between?

10. Do you agree with Lily's decision to send Tom's remains back to Vermont to be buried in a cemetery instead of cremated?

11. Discuss the physical relationship between Jack and Lily. What do you think of Jack? Is he an opportunist taking advantage of a vulnerable person, or is there legitimacy to this informal sort of therapy known as sexual healing?

12. Why do you think Lily decides to incinerate her wedding ring? How is the process therapeutic for her?

13. Grandma Hattie's lace becomes a significant metaphor for untapped potential. As Lily puts it, "The life of the lace had been one of longing, of waiting, of stories not told." How do you think Lily would describe the story she ultimately tells with the lace?

BEHIND-THE-SCENES MOMENT #1
THE GREAT DATE

This story was inspired, in part, by a real-life romance. My parents met on a blind date on their first weekend of college in 1956—and just like the characters in this story, they drove off in an old Studebaker, the girls sitting on the boys' laps. My mom had just started at Wellesley College and my dad at Harvard. There were four other couples on that same date, and two of the couples were married right after their college graduations—including my mom and dad. That was June 1960. Although my parents are both great individuals, they didn't have a great marriage—or at least not a long-lasting one. They were divorced when I was thirteen years old.

One of the other men on the original date was my dad's roommate, Doug. He married a lovely woman named Lesley and stayed happily married to her for thirty-eight years until her death from lung cancer. Six years ago, in 2003—which was forty-seven years after the weekend they met—Doug and my mother were married at a church by the sea in Santa Barbara. They make a wonderful couple, and I'm very happy that Doug is now part of our family.

BEHIND-THE-SCENES MOMENT #2
SANTA BARBARA'S WILDFIRE SEASON

I grew up in Santa Barbara, and have carried an image of the terrible beauty of wildfires in my head my whole life. I vividly remember standing outside our house in the dark, looking at the angry flames, the burning hills, the billowing smoke, and I remember hearing the adults talk about plans for escape, and plans for what to save. No one talked about moving away from the tinder-dry hills; it was considered well worth the risk to live in that beautiful red-roofed town.

When I was in the middle of writing this book, and after I had written the fire scenes, Santa Barbara was struck by two devastating wildfires. I live two hours to the south of the city, so I watched on TV, filled with the special horror of knowing that the devastation I made up on the page was actually happening to real people in real time. There was something very strange about that reality—as if my writing—my act of imagination—had somehow contributed to the fact of the fire in the real world. It's hard to explain what I mean, but it was a disturbing few days, where I questioned whether or not I should keep the fire in my book. I could choose whether or not my house stood or my character lived, whereas there were hundreds of people who could not.

And then my mother called to tell me that she had half an hour to evacuate from her home in Santa Barbara, and that she was packing her car and would be at my house by dinner. Suddenly, the lists I had made up of things my character remembered from her destroyed home were instructive. "Don't just take what you need," I told my mom. "Take some things you want, too." Along with clothes and some paperwork, she took the seal coat she's had since she was eighteen years old.

Her house was fine, in the end—at least this time. And I was left with the awesome knowledge of exactly how life mirrors story, and story informs life.